The Hawk and the Hare

THE
HAWK
AND THE
HARE

Based on a true story

JANET LOVE MORRISON

TIDEWATER
PRESS

Published by Tidewater Press
New Westminster, BC, Canada
tidewaterpress.ca

ISBN 978-1-7770101-2-6 (paperback)
ISBN 978-1-7770101-3-3 (html)

LIBRARY AND ARCHIVES CANADA CATALOGUING IN PUBLICATION
Title: The hawk and the hare : based on a true story / Janet Love Morrison.
Names: Morrison, Janet Love, 1962- author.
Identifiers: Canadiana (print) 20200194542 | Canadiana (ebook) 20200194569 | ISBN 9781777010126
 (softcover) | ISBN 9781777010133 (HTML)
Subjects: LCGFT: Novels. | LCGFT: War fiction. | LCGFT: Historical fiction.
Classification: LCC PS8626.O7596 H39 2020 | DDC C813/.6—dc23

Cover photos:
RHLI hat badge – Stan Overy
Red-tailed hawk – ©Can Stock Photo Inc. / pix2go
Troops of the Royal Winnipeg Rifles near Ifs, France, 25 July 1944.
 Source – Library and Archives Canada/Department of National Defence fonds/PA-116528

Maps:
Courtesy of the RHLI Historical Association

Printed and bound by Pulsio SARL

To my parents,
Janet Agnes Love and Ewen Morrison,
this is for you.

And to Master Dhyan Vimal, Founder, Friends to Mankind,
thank you.
That which I am is given to me by the gift of being with you,
for in this meeting I meet me too

NOTE

The Hawk and the Hare is inspired by a true story—my father's—and is grounded in historical fact and the original war diaries of the Royal Hamilton Light Infantry. However, the names and characters of the men he served with are my own invention; the personal stories of the real soldiers of 17 Platoon D-Coy are their own.

At the time this narrative is placed (and beyond), First Nations Indigenous Canadians were commonly referred to as Indians or even Red Indians. For historical accuracy, I have used these terms, with no disrespect intended to the First Nations soldiers who served in Canada's military during the First and Second World Wars.

Due to the varied settings and characters, some events are not in strict historical chronology, and some of the locations have been altered for narrative purposes.

WAR DIARY ABBREVIATIONS

Adjt: Adjunct
Adm: admin/administration
Amn: ammunition
Arty: artillery
AWL: absent without leave
Bde: brigade
Br: bridge
Bn: battalion
Civs: civilians
CO: Commanding Officer
Col: column
Coy: company
Ech: echelon
ENSA: Entertainments National Service Association
Fmn: formation
FMR: Fusiliers de Mont Royal
FUP: forming up position
H-Hour: time a combat attack or operation is to begin
Hr: hour
IO: Intelligence Officer
LAD: Light Aid Detachment
NCO: Non-commissioned officer
Offrs: officers
O Grp: Operations Group
OR: other ranks
Posn: position
PIAT: Projector, Infantry, Anti Tk Mk, a British man-portable anti-tank weapon
Pl: platoon
PW: prisoner(s) of war
RAP: Regimental Aid Post
SA: small arms
SL: start line
Tks: tanks
Tps: troops
Trg: training

PREFACE

When I was eleven years old, I knew how to run. I knew this to be true, because Miss McLaren, my Grade 6 PE teacher at Mary Hill Elementary, had picked me for our school's cross-country team. I didn't excel at sports, but couldn't wait to get outside and run through the park near our house in Port Coquitlam. Making the team was a significant achievement for me and I took it seriously, determined to do well.

So, on one dry fall Sunday in October, I was running steadily around and around our quarter-acre backyard, training for the next district meet. In the centre of the lawn, my father was raking leaves. When I stopped running, I breathed in air acrid with the smoke from neighbourhood leaf fires and noticed that my father had stopped too. He was leaning on the rake, watching me stretch.

Dad had a unique way of standing: always with his weight on his left leg, his hip slightly flexed, and his right leg extended to the side.

He put his rake down, walked over. "The meet's next Friday, isn't it? How are you feeling about it?" he asked me.

"Pretty good," I said.

"I'd like to show you something. Would that be okay?"

"Sure," I said, interested.

He lifted his right foot off the ground and then rocked it on the grass, whispering as he demonstrated, "Heel toe, heel toe . . . "

He looked down at me, serious. "If you want to run quickly and quietly, then you need to be aware . . . heel, toe, heel toe. Now, you try it. Walk first and then build up your speed."

I had to really think. I closed my eyes, imagining the sensation before trying it. Then, I slowly walked . . . heel, toe, heel, toe . . .

"Practise. In time you won't have to think as much and it will become natural."

I asked, "Where did you learn this?"

"From a friend."

"Which friend?"

"A friend from the war."

This was unusual. My father didn't talk about the war.

"What was his name?"

"Reggie."

"Was he from Saskatchewan too?" My parents had grown up on the Prairies and I knew they met after the war, then moved to BC. That's all I really knew—I'd never asked about their past.

"No, he was from Ontario, from a reserve. He was an Indian."

I thought about Ben, my Indian friend at school. He was nice.

I returned my focus to this new running technique. I knew my dad had lost a couple of his toes in the war, although I wasn't sure how. I tried to connect his running in the war to losing his toes, but it didn't make much sense.

"Why did you go to war?" I asked.

He looked at the ground. Then he looked me straight in the eye and said, "We went to help people."

"Did you kill people?"

"It was shoot or get shot."

In that moment I saw something flicker in my father's eyes, which looked beyond me and into a past I knew nothing about.

It would be many years before my father shared a few of his war memories. He told me that, whenever he was having a bad day, he remembered a moment on a road in Normandy. When a sniper had chosen another soldier and not him.

When I was older, my curiosity about those experiences grew. Once, instead of answering my questions, he handed me a copy of *The Canadian Army at War – Canada's Battle in Normandy*. In the margins were notes in the sloping, printed capital letters he always used. It was a way for him to pass on this part of his history without having to tell me directly. I grew to understand how difficult it could be for men like my father to speak of what had happened to them. "There's no glory in war—just insanity," he said on one occasion, after a Remembrance Day service. My parents, or someone in the neighbourhood, always hosted a party and, while Mrs. Atkins played the piano, the men would sing their favourite wartime songs and drink a little whisky.

As an adult, I wondered at both the horror and the arbitrariness of war. What twists of birth and destiny made one boy an enemy, the other a comrade? Why did one soldier, like my father, survive, while the man who stood next to him did not? Was it fate or was it chance?

One of the stories my father did tell my mother was of how fate had sent him a friend. And how that friend had given him a chance. This is my version of that story.

PART ONE

ENGLAND
APRIL – JULY 1944

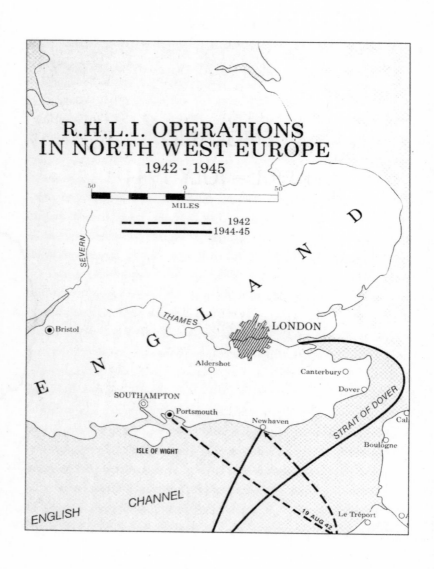

R.H.L.I. OPERATIONS
IN NORTH WEST EUROPE
1942 - 1945

Private Ewen Morrison stared out at the dark waters of the English Channel, pulling up his collar and rubbing his hands together as the convoy started up again and headed inland into the Sussex countryside. The twilight reflected a ghostly glow over the cliffs of Dover.

Southern England palpitated. Convoys of military vehicles rumbled through towns day and night as tens of thousands of Allied troops moved along the English roads. Traffic accidents were common. While ammunition factories worked around the clock, ships massed along the coast.

The invasion could be anytime. No one knew exactly when or where but the locals knew one morning they'd wake up and the troops would have vanished across the channel.

Ewen was relieved to be out of the hospital and rejoining the ranks, but he was anxious. Although his foot had healed well, his injury had taken a toll. Instead of returning to the Argyll and Sutherland Highlanders, he'd been sent to join the Rileys, the Royal Hamilton Light Infantry. He had a new group of guys to get to know.

His carrier jolted to a stop and someone shouted the order to get out. Ewen got down from the truck, swung his kit bag over his shoulder and followed directions to hand in his papers.

"You're assigned to D-Coy, Morrison. Ask for 17 Platoon. We're on a forty-eight-hour rest. We just got back from a long and nasty training exercise. Your timing is perfect."

Gravel crunched beneath his boots as he strode down the unfamiliar path. At the entrance to his barrack, he found most of the men of D-Coy heading for the pubs. A few nodded on their way out as Ewen walked in. He looked around for an empty bed.

"That bunk's free," said a friendly voice.

Ewen turned around and looked into the dark eyes of a solidly built soldier with straight dark hair and deep-set brown eyes. A hand reached out, joining the voice. "Reggie Johnson."

"Ewen Morrison." The men shook hands.

"Where you coming from?" Reggie asked.

"The hospital. A little run-in with a truck when I was on a motorcycle. I'm good now."

"Yeah, it's easy to get banged up. Driving on the wrong side of the road, the blackouts. Next Jerry's going to suggest giving all of us Canadians a motorcycle so we'll all end up in the hospital."

Ewen laughed.

"Who'd you come over with?" Reggie asked.

"The Argyll and Sutherland Highlanders. July '43. You?"

"I came over as a Riley in 1940."

"Dieppe?"

"No, I missed that. I was in the hospital myself. Cracked rib. The transport vehicle I was riding in had a disagreement with a tractor. Farmers! No respect for hunters, no respect for soldiers. Where you from?"

"Saskatchewan. You?"

"Ontario. Six Nations Reserve."

"Oh, yeah, I know the area a little. After I joined, I was sent to Brantford for training before we shipped out. Looked like nice fishing country. Not that I got the chance to fish."

"It is. Well, you've timed it right here. We've got two days off. Been training hard. The old man has had us practising assault crossings at the tidal estuaries and river crossings."

The only other man in the barracks was a dark-haired soldier, sitting on his bunk writing a letter. Finishing it up, he folded it into an envelope and placed it in his back pocket. Must be hard to write home, Ewen thought, when nothing was private. The orders had been read out four days ago—censorship was in effect, so no more sending mail through the civilian post. Every letter had to be in an unsealed envelope, handed in for unit officers to read before it was franked with the unit's censorship stamp; then it would be sent through the army's post office. Soldiers were only allowed to put their service number, rank and name on the back of the envelope.

He walked over to Reggie and extended his hand to Ewen. "Les Archer. You guys coming out?"

"Yeah, we are," said Reggie. "Drop your stuff, Ewen. Let's go."

The Friar's Oak was full of fellow Canadians and Les went to join an already crowded table. Noticing Ewen's hesitation, Reggie suggested they take their pints to a corner table. He made a point of taking the seat against the wall. "I always like to sit where I can see everything in front of me," he said. "And I always know my way out."

"Makes sense," Ewen answered. He hadn't thought of that before, but now his eyes travelled around the room, locating the doors.

"Cheers," Reggie said, raising his glass to the new guy. Ewen looked awkward. "What's the problem?"

Ewen hesitated. "Well, it's just a bit strange. Sorry—I know in Canada you guys can't drink, but you can here?"

Reggie laughed. "Yeah. That's the law at home. There's not much I like about being in the army, but I do like this." He took a long sip. "I can drink here and nobody gives me a look."

Ewen saluted Reggie with his glass. "Is that why you signed up? For the beer?"

"Sure. That, and King and Country." He grinned. "Can't vote, but I can serve."

"That's crazy," Ewen said. "But you still signed up?"

"There's history there, for sure. Back during the American

Revolution, we fought with the British. They promised us land, and then took most of it back. In the last war, many men on my reserve signed up. Women too. They volunteered because they believed it was the right thing to do. They were the first generation to leave the land and go to Europe.

"A lot of guys I know signed up because their fathers had done the same thing. Others were just bored on the reserve. Besides, it's a job—regular salary, food, clothes."

"Yeah, I know exactly what you mean," said Ewen. "The first pair of brand new boots I got was when I joined up. And a dollar-fifty a day is more than you get as a farmhand on the Prairies."

"For me it's also a bit of a family tradition. My father and my uncle served in the last war."

"I had an uncle there too. Killed at Passchendaele," Ewen said.

"Poor bastard," Reggie said. "My uncle made it back. He was a sniper, but the mustard gas destroyed him. When he'd come around for supper, my mom used to put a box of baking soda on the table. He'd have a couple of spoonfuls to coat his stomach before he ate. He'd generally end up throwing up in the outhouse out back anyway. My father, he was okay I think, but he was quiet. Didn't talk much."

"Bloody hell."

They both took another drink.

"So what's this nasty exercise you've just been on?" asked Ewen.

"It's not just this last one. We've spent all winter training around the countryside, wading rivers, embarking, disembarking, scaling obstacles, clearing minefields. Boat loading drills, compass marches, night marches. All we do is train, train, train." Then Reggie laughed again. "This time, the worst was the wood ticks, just outside of Alfriston. Really bad for C-Coy. 'Just some discomfort,' the officers said. Didn't bother me, though. I know how to keep those biters away—a medicine my grandmother taught me to make. Sounds trivial, but not having to scratch may save your life."

"Driving here today, I noticed a hell of a lot of material—looked like food, medical supplies, ammunition and equipment—camouflaged in orchards and woodland," Ewen said. "What's that all about?"

"Everyone is wondering when the call will come. It's got to be soon, with the way they're grinding us into the ground," Reggie answered. "A notice went up today—they need more volunteers for scout training. The lieutenant said I should apply. Guess he assumed that because I'm native I'm going to be good in the woods. 'Injun' skills' and all that garbage. You interested? We'll be trained for recce duty, going in advance to locate Jerry and find out all we can before we attack. We observe the number of troops, the activity, their location, identify the unit, the time and what type of weapons."

"Sure, why not?" Ewen figured the more skills he had, the better his chance to survive what was sure to come.

In the noisy pub, the two soldiers sat, smoked and drank, new friends brought together by this war far from both their homes.

April 9, 1944
2000 — The forty-eight hr rest period following Exercise "Step" is completed today. A movie was shown by the YMCA in the Offrs' Mess which was enjoyed by a goodly crowd of offrs and their friends.

Eisenhower's entourage drove off and the men dispersed back to their barracks.

"Home by Christmas. I don't fucking think so," said Connor Woods, barging through the door in front of Reggie. "Goddam brass are no better than the bosses. Think we're idiots."

"Shut up, Woods," said Phillips, returning to his bunk and picking up his book. Twenty men living in such close quarters, never getting a break from military protocol, made for some testy moments. Ewen had fit in by keeping his head down.

"Well excuse me, Professor. Why do you always have your nose in a book?"

"Most are better company than you assholes."

"I hope it won't be too inconvenient for you to take a shot at Jerry when the time comes. What's so fascinating anyway?"

"As if you care." Phillips' annoyance was plain. "It's called *The Great Gatsby*. Actually, Woods, you might like it. It's about a guy who swaggers around a lot pretending to be someone he's not so he can get laid."

Woods' fists clenched as he took a step toward Phillips' bunk.

Reggie moved between the men, his stance deliberately casual. "Really, Phillips? I would have said it was about how we can overcome the circumstances of our birth to achieve financial success."

Phillips' eyes widened. After a pause, he turned back to his book, muttering, "Doesn't seem to be working out too well for him so far."

Archer changed the subject. "Anyway, I hope Ike's right. I'd like to be home for my baby girl's first Christmas." Archer tapped his left breast pocket with his right hand. "They're both right here, and one day soon I'll be going home to them."

"What's your daughter's name?" Ewen asked.

"Dorothy. Nicole and me, we call her Dottie for short. She was born with a crop of black hair, just like her handsome old man." He picked up a deck of cards and sat at the table in the middle of the room. "Now, which of you gentlemen would like to contribute to the Dorothy Archer Education Fund?"

"Not so fast," said their corporal, Henri Paquette, taking the seat opposite Archer. "I've got two boys at home myself. Wouldn't mind winning a bit of money for their Christmas presents, whether I'm home or not."

"Only two, Frenchie?" Woods pulled up a chair. "I thought you guys bred like rabbits."

Paquette's jaw tightened. "Give me time, Woods. Can't do much about that from over here."

Again, Archer intervened. "Who else is in? I like a good-sized pot. What about you Epstein. Want to try your luck?"

"Why you asking me, Archer?"

"You got a problem, Jewboy?" Connor jumped in. "How did you even get into the army anyway?"

"Same as you. I walked up and down the room a couple of times, hopped across the room on one foot, then the other. Why? Don't think I can fight?"

"Come on, guys," said Reggie. "In case you've forgotten, Jerry's the enemy, not us. Lots of time for fighting once we finally get over there."

"Whatever you say, Chief," said Woods sarcastically. But he sat down.

"Hey, Epstein," said Peter O'Malley. "Why don't you and me take a walk? Go see what's going in with C-Coy. What about you, Burton? Wanna come?"

Rusty Burton, so-named for his red hair, looked up from the letter he was writing. "You guys go ahead. I want to finish this letter to Irene. Not sure how many more opportunities we're gonna get."

As Epstein and O'Malley left, Angus MacLeod, a cook from Halifax, joined the group at the table. "I'll tell you right fucking now, this waiting is making the lot of you right squirrely. Just deal the goddam cards."

As the game got underway, Reggie came over and sat on his bunk across from Ewen. "What about you, Ewen? You got any special girl pining for you?"

"No. Wish I did, but I don't. There was this one gal I saw at a dance back in Saltcoats. Beautiful dark hair. Believe it or not, her last name was Love. I wanted to ask her to dance, but I was too shy. But, hey, we could be in France any day now, pushing Jerry back to Germany. Maybe it's for the best, not having a sweetheart."

"Me, I've got my Rose," said Reggie. "She's a nurse. English. I hope I get to see her one more time before we ship out."

"How'd you meet?"

"At a dance. You know, that's one thing that really surprised me over here. At home, we'd didn't often go to dances where there were white girls. If we did, they'd act like we were part of the furniture. And those were the polite ones. No way they'd dance with us, even if one of us was stupid enough to ask. When I asked Rose to dance, she smiled this big smile and practically dragged me onto the dance floor. I guess she just saw a good-looking guy in uniform. Anyway, we write regularly, and see each other when we can."

1900 — The offrs played "A" Coy in volleyball and were soundly trounced in two straight games.

```
Royal Hamilton Light Infantry War Diary
May 30, 1944
Wootton Park North
0800 — The entire bn commenced hardening trg
today, all coys undergoing speed marches. A
shipment of the latest British and German mines
was secured for trg purposes.
```

Over the next week, the regiment speed marched—fifteen miles in three hours. When the Rileys weren't marching, they rehearsed and rehearsed battle approaches, had gas and camouflage training, and lined up for inoculations. They practised river crossings and waterproofed their vehicles. They studied German and British mines, were introduced to German booby traps and killing at close quarters. Then battlefield first aid was hammered into them—how to try not to die from the consequences of the practical war skills they, and their enemies, were being drilled in.

"Most of you already have some basic knowledge of first aid and have already been trained to use what you have on you," began their regimental medical officer, giving them a grisly refresher course. "But the only equipment you will carry is a first field dressing. If you need anything else, you'll have to improvise.

"Under most circumstances, you will have to look after yourself because your comrades must keep on fighting. I remind you—the fight is more important than any of us. It comes first. You *never* stop to fix up a comrade. And, if you're the one hit, do not expect anyone to stop. I repeat—do not expect anyone to stop. Your job is to fight, so you'll need to fix yourself up. A slight wound isn't a casualty; only a soldier out of action is a casualty. With most injuries, you can keep on fighting.

"If a situation presents itself where you do have time to help, remember, you're fixing up an injured man, not just an injury. And if you fall, then the only people near enough to help you in that moment will be your comrades.

"Okay, let's practise." The medical officer pointed to the floor. The platoon members sat down awkwardly inside the hut.

"Each of you has been hit by a machine-gun bullet just below the right knee. Your leg is certainly broken. Take your rifle with the bayonet and scabbard attached. Unload, take out the bolt and put it in your pocket. Take off the sling and use it to tie your leg to the rifle . . . " The instructor ended with, "Now roll over and crawl to shelter, or to where you can get help, or to a road where you will be picked up."

They were trained to control bleeding and wounds that needed special care; splint broken bones, treat burns and provide artificial respiration; how to carry a wounded soldier, what to do if under a chemical warfare attack and more.

"In conclusion, every soldier must know first aid. Your actions on the battlefield are as important as anything the medical officer can do after you or a wounded comrade arrives at the hospital. Remember, it's a little knowledge and a lot of common sense. Dismissed."

The medical officer's comments hit them all in the gut. The men of D-Coy looked at one another, each thinking, Are you going to be the one running past me when I'm hit? Am I going to have to patch a hole in your chest with a field dressing?

Archer raised his arms. "Well, men, if I get injured out there you all know what to do— stop everything and put me back together."

"Sure," Woods said. "We'll just ask Jerry nicely to stop shooting while we all gather round and, with our medical expertise, decide what to do."

Laughter lightened up the mood, but Ewen's anxiety didn't subside. He hoped that, when the moment demanded, he could remember what he had to do. Despite all the drills and training, he wasn't sure he was not going to end up letting the boys down.

That sick feeling seemed even worse after one of their speed marches. His damaged foot had been bothering him somewhat and he had struggled to keep up.

While the company lunched on field rations, he and Reggie sat on the grass, slightly apart from the platoon but close enough to hear Woods complaining about the food.

"These rations suck."

MacLeod stopped digging into his tin and said, "You know, Woods, I offered to bake bread and peel potatoes and the like for your meals, but the brass turned me down. 'magine!" He gestured with his spoon. "Said the North Atlantic convoy had more impor- tant things to protect than dainties for you. So stop being such a sook and just scoff it down."

"Asshole," Woods said.

"Ah, Connor," said Archer. "Let me put a smile on your face. As a favour, just for today, I'll give you my ration of cigarettes. That'll save you seven cents."

"You're going to start smoking eventually, Les. And then you'll want your fag ration more than a few extra pennies. Guys, who wants to bet on how long it takes before Archer starts to smoke like the rest of us?"

He got out his little black notebook. "Who's in?"

"Me," MacLeod said. Woods wrote down the names and bets as men shouted out their wagers.

Reggie shifted over to sit exactly opposite Ewen. "Ewen, what do you see over my shoulder?"

Ewen held a forkful of cold Irish stew in mid-air. First he looked at the lush English countryside and blue sky, the stuff calendars were made of. Then his gaze focused closer. "16 Platoon, on the grass, like us. Eating."

"Good. What else do you see? How many are there? Who appears to be in charge? What's their mood? If we're going to be scouting together, out there, we need to do this. Whenever we stop, position yourself to keep an eye for what's behind my back and I'll keep an eye on what's behind yours. We all have to watch each other's backs."

Ewen nodded, now observing 16 Platoon closely.

"There are two kinds of scouts, the quick and the dead," Reggie said. "That's what my grandpa told me. We have to be the quick ones. You know what they've been telling us in training, yeah? Scouts don't engage with the enemy, they gather intel, blah, blah. But I'm telling you the most important things—stay quick, stay quiet, stay invisible. Your life, and mine, will depend on it."

Ewen was struck by the intensity in Reggie's voice. He nodded wordlessly.

Reggie smiled. "Now, you need to give me a cigarette."

"Why? Are you out?"

"When an elder or teacher shares their knowledge with you, it's tradition to offer a gift of tobacco. I'm not an elder, but I could be a teacher in this case," Reggie said with a laugh, holding out his hand.

At the end of the long day, when everyone else was heading for the bath parade, Ewen sat on his bunk and took off his socks. He rubbed the two red, swollen stubs on his right foot.

"They look sore. You okay?" Reggie asked. "What exactly happened in that motorcycle accident?"

"It was last September, September 9. Not a date I'll forget. I'd only been here a couple of weeks and was on driver authority training for the signals corps. I turned a corner and met a half-ton truck coming the other way. I didn't have room to pass and my right foot clipped its running board. Both these toes were partially amputated and they had to graft another. Had surgery on my right hand and my back is buggered up too. I spent several weeks in bed rest, then they moved me to a wheelchair. Spent six months in a convalescent depot until they decided I was okay for route marches."

"That's tough," said Reggie.

Ewen shrugged. "They had an enquiry. 'Normal driving hazard,' they called it."

"Maybe that's one of the reasons you make so much noise when you run. If you make a racket like that on recce, neither of us is going to make it."

He pulled a pair of large socks out of his kit bag and handed them to Ewen. "Here, pull these on over your boots. You'll move quieter on the land." Reggie then pulled out a pair of moccasins. He winked as he removed his boots and put them on. "It's not standard issue, but don't tell the brass. What they don't know . . . "

"Might save us?" said Ewen.

They went outside. "Okay, now watch." Reggie began to run steadily, silently, around the yard by the barracks, his arms slightly extended. "See? Heel, toe, heel, toe." Even when he exaggerated the movement for Ewen's benefit, he made almost no sound. Ewen noticed his fluid stride and still torso.

"Now, man," he said as he ran around Ewen, "I know you're missing a couple of toes, but pretend like you've got them, okay?" He grinned. "You've got to *feel* your feet. Heel, toe, heel, no toe. Now you try."

Reggie watched silently as Ewen ran around him, eventually stopping to catch his breath. "I'm thirsty."

Reggie reached in his pocket. "Here, take some chewing gum. It'll be summer and hot and there's no way they'll have enough water for us, so keep a supply in your pocket. It creates saliva and will give some relief."

Ewen nodded as he chewed.

"Now, stop panting. Concentrate. When we're scouting, we can't even hear each other breathe. Ewen, it's that crucial. We have to watch and communicate in total silence. I can see you have a natural instinct for the land but you have to learn how to freeze and control your breathing, no matter how much you're panicking inside. If you feed the fear, even for a moment, it's all over."

"Where did you learn all this?" Ewen asked.

"A lot of us kids on the rez grew up hunting. I didn't do as much as some of my friends, but my father and my cousins and my uncles, they taught me to be patient and to watch, listen and learn. I learned to use weapons and to go a long time without food when I was really young."

Reggie turned to join the line for hot water. "Come on, enough for today. And you owe me another cigarette."

May 31, 1944
0800 — Coys will resume night trg this evening.

Royal Hamilton Light Infantry War Diary
June 6, 1944
Wootton Park North
1000 — Code word "ADORATION" received, signifying
that the Second Front had been opened as of 0200
hrs 6 June 44.

Ewen woke in the night, cold and semi-conscious. For the past two nights, the rumble of transport trucks and tanks driving to the final embarkation sites hadn't allowed anyone to sleep well. Curling himself into a fetal position, he pulled his blanket over his head. The groundsheet beneath him offered little insulation against the chill. I really have to piss, he thought, but I don't want to get up. Fatigue won and he went back to sleep with the wind and rain hammering against the platoon's tent. By dawn, the wind lost some of its strength and the rain stopped. Although heavy clouds sat in the northwest, for a short time the sun shone over the Straits of Dover.

Strict security measures had sealed them off from the rest of the country for days. The Rileys waited. The men knew the invasion was imminent; not knowing any details made the waiting harder.

At 0800 D-Coy ate breakfast and participated in another speed march. Then, along with the other hundred men in their company, they lined up for blood tests. As he was sticking Ewen with a painfully large needle, a medic said, "They're gone. I got to wonder how many ships and men there are out there now."

"Do we know anything?" Ewen asked. "Where exactly or which division?"

"Normandy," the medic said. "The 3rd Infantry Division." Later they and the other Canadians would learn that the pre-dawn destination had been a five-mile front, code-named Juno Beach.

Rusty, in line behind Ewen, said, "I just want to get over that bloody channel and get behind them. They're fighting and we're standing here getting jabbed for blood. When's our turn coming?"

"Shut up," said the medic. "There's news coming in now." He turned up the dial on the radio that sat on a table behind him.

Ewen glanced at his watch: 1200.

Dum-dum-dum-DUMM . . . Dum-dum-dum-DUMM. The well-known prelude to BBC news echoed the opening bars of Beethoven's Fifth Symphony. But the soldiers heard dot-dot-dot-dash— Morse Code for the letter "V." V for victory. Silence fell over the men lined up in the medical tent.

This is the BBC Home Service. Here is a special bulletin, read by John Snagge.

D-Day has come. Early this morning the Allies began the assault on the north-western face of Hitler's European fortress. The first official news came just after half past nine when Supreme Headquarters of the Allied Expeditionary Forces —usually called SHAEF from its initials—issued Communique No 1. This said:

'Under the command of General Eisenhower, Allied Naval Forces, supported by strong Air Forces, began landing Allied Armies this morning on the Northern coast of France.'

It was announced a little later that General Montgomery is in command of the Army Group carrying out the assault. This Army Group includes British, Canadian and United States forces.

The Allied Commander-in-Chief General Eisenhower has issued an Order of the Day addressed to each individual of the Allied Expeditionary Force. In it he said: "Your task will not be an easy one. Your enemy is well trained, well equipped and battle-hardened. He will fight savagely. But this is the year 1944. The tide has turned. The free men of the world are marching together for victory.

I have full confidence in your courage, devotion to duty and skill in battle. We will accept nothing less than full victory. Good luck, and let us all beseech the Blessing of the Almighty God upon this great and noble undertaking.

The following day Major-General Foulkes addressed the troops from the top of a Jeep. He said, "At ease, men. I'm sorry General Montgomery can't be here, lads. But he sends his best regards. As I'm sure you're aware he's busy with details for opening the Second Front."

Cheers erupted.

"This Division will be sent into action within a very short time. Your physical fitness is paramount at this time. Let's get the job done so we can all go home." And then he was gone.

Ewen held his foot over a puddle and gently tapped the water with his boot, watching the tiny waves ripple to the edge. He thought back to September 9, 1939, the day Canada declared war on Germany. He had been threshing at Theodore Leslie's, shovelling grain. The old farmers had talked about the last war, the Great War, reminiscing about the local men who had joined up in 1914. They wondered how many local boys would go off and how many wouldn't come home this time. Ewen had only been sixteen. Just over two years later, he became one of those Saskatchewan volunteers. Would he be one of the ones who made it back?

Phillips' voice brought him back to the present. "They actually went. Must have been when the weather broke," he said, looking up at the clouds. "It's our turn now. We'll throw everything we've got at them. That's what we've been training for."

Archer put his hand on his left breast pocket. Epstein rocked on the balls of his feet as if he could literally spring into combat.

Woods punched his fist into his palm. "This waiting has been eating me up. I just want to join the boys on the beach and chase Jerry back to where he belongs. I'm going to make them pay for Dieppe. Blood for blood. I didn't sign up to be a spectator. They'd better leave me enough Jerrys to kill."

Ewen looked at Woods, disturbed by his intensity but relieved they were on the same side.

All of the companies remaining at Wootten Park North were on high alert. Listening posts were placed around the camp and sentries, armed with Bren light machine guns, watched the skies, scanning for enemy paratroops.

On June 10, a battalion muster parade was called. Commanding Officer Lieutenant-Colonel Whitaker stood sternly before the regiment. He read out a statement—they must all be prepared for embarkation. "Any man going absent without leave, having heard this warning read, will become liable to be tried as a deserter and punished accordingly."

At 1400, the regiment received the code word "Cornelius," placing them under orders to be ready to move on six hours' notice.

Two days later, Lieutenant Coulson addressed the twenty-five men of 17 Platoon. "A new exercise order has been issued." Some eyeballs rolled, but the men listened. "It's called 'Pack,' and that's what we're going to do. If the battalion has to be ready to move out within six hours, we're going to practise now, so we can do it in four. We're going to run drills on the complete loading of operation vehicles. Quick and efficient.

"Packing has to be uniform throughout the unit. All ranks can now have only one small pack and one large pack. Pack them quickly and efficiently. The drill will begin with marching personnel moving on a short march with full kit from the company area in one hour. Paquette, take over." The lieutenant left them to it.

Corporal Paquette stood in front of them. "You all know the drill. It's extremely important that we know exactly where every item of equipment goes and where it should be. Make sure you roll up your gas cape and tie it to your belt, keep your respirator slung. Your T-handle shovel will be your best friend. Put your first blanket in your large pack and carry the second one in your haversack. Everyone check to make sure you've got everything.

"For all the stuff you can't pack, like care parcels and soap, leave them piled—neatly—at the foot of your bunk. The Rear Party

Officer will organize it. So, get packing. You are going to be ready to march when we're called."

When Ewen heaved his pack onto his back, he calculated that, along with his Lee Enfield rifle, he was carrying about 80 pounds. Weighing 140 pounds himself, it was enough.

Archer left his most recent parcel from Nicole at the foot of his bed, but kept his precious photo tucked in his pocket. Woods spread his kit across his blanket, tossing items he couldn't pack onto the floor between the beds. Reggie, turning from his haversack, tripped over a wooden box. "Hey, Woods! Neatly, okay?"

Woods turned and took a step toward Reggie. They stood nose-to-nose; Reggie showed no reaction. It was Woods who broke the silence. "You got a problem, Chief? Take it up with Frenchie. Don't slow me down and don't try to give me orders." He turned away and resumed packing.

Ewen was the only one to notice the altercation; everyone else was busy with their own kit. "Why do you keep putting up with that shit?" he asked Reggie.

"My father taught me a long time ago that if you lose control of your emotions, you let 'them' win. It's a lesson most Indians learn early."

Another week passed, yet they remained where they were. Bad weather in the channel damaged the Mulberry harbours being assembled in Normandy, delaying the daily shipment of 6,000 tons of supplies needed to support the invasion.

"Church parades, baseball games, volleyball games, ENSA shows. What do they think we're here for? The entertainment? Let's just get on with the real show," O'Malley grumbled.

"We're all edgy," Rusty said. "But Mother Nature's in charge right now."

Ewen heard Reggie call from the front of their tent. "Okay, guys. Listen up. Paquette asked me to read this to you. Daily orders."

Woods snorted. "Jesus. So now we have an Indian in charge?"

Typical Woods. "Don't be a jerk, Connor," Ewen said.

"First item, censorship, we know all that . . . Second item, here we go. Prisoners of war. 'Units are responsible for the return of PWs from fighting areas to Division PW Cage. Escorts should be approximately ten percent of the number of prisoners plus one officer per party of 200 PWs.'"

"Can you do the math?" Epstein shouted from behind Ewen.

Reggie continued to read. "'The treatment of PWs is governed by the Geneva Convention of 1929, under which PWs must be allowed to retain all personal effects and articles in personal use including metal helmets and gas masks. Sums of money in possession of prisoners may only be taken from them on orders from an officer and the amount must be properly recorded and a receipt given.'"

"Right, I'll be sure to have that receipt book handy," Woods said.

"Can't you just listen, Woods?" Ewen said. "Let him finish."

"'Identity tokens, badges of rank, decorations and articles of value may not be taken from prisoners. PWs in possession of personal rations will be allowed to retain them as this will simplify the problem of feeding.' Everyone got that?"

There was a general murmur of assent. Then 17 Platoon headed out to play baseball against the Essex Scots.

June 30, 1944
```
1600 — Capt. R.G. Hunter arrived in camp with
movement order. Veh party leaves at 0600 hrs, 1
July 44. Marching party leaves at 1445 hrs, 1
July 44.
```

PART TWO

FRANCE
JULY – SEPTEMBER 1944

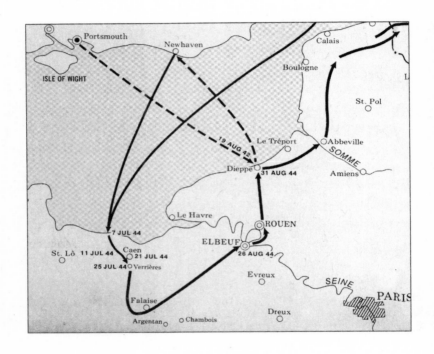

Royal Hamilton Light Infantry War Diary
July 6, 1944
Graye-sur-Mere, Normandy
0630 — Passage of the Straits of DOVER was made
without incident. At this time several flying
bombs passed over head quite close to the ships
and could be observed to excellent advantage
in the clear morning sky as they travelled at
terrific speed towards the English coast.

Canada's 4th Brigade, including the Royal Hamilton Light Infantry, the Essex Scottish Regiment and the Royal Regiment of Canada, had moved out on its seventy-seventh birthday. The men transferred from their transport ships to assault landing craft to get to the beach. Ewen braced himself, adjusting to the roll of the swells beneath. Waves sloshed against the metal. Behind him dozens of waiting ships stood off the beachhead; before him a long line of men waded through shallow waters and across the sand, their helmets like a shoal of pebbles. The magnitude of the operation overwhelmed him. Ewen Morrison, from the Tupper school district northeast of Saltcoats, Saskatchewan. In France. In Normandy. Rifle, rations, kit and two hundred francs in his pocket.

A brief slog through water and he was on the beach, imagining the landing exactly one month ago, how the guys had dodged for their lives. Now the entire area was signposted. The tide was out and the firm sand absorbed his weight. A tiny shell caught his eye and he bent down quickly to pick it up. A souvenir to add to the feather he'd found at Newhaven just before they embarked. A British sergeant shouted at his company, directing them to an assembly area. Rivers of soldiers flowed inland even as their comrades lay on stretchers on the beach, waiting to be evacuated. The Rileys marched inland about a mile to their position, where they handed in their Mae Wests. D-Coy deepened the existing slit trenches, dug latrines, and parked and de-waterproofed all the vehicles.

In the afternoon, they formed up with the rest of the massed ranks of the 2nd Canadian Infantry Division and the 4th Canadian Infantry Brigade. Lieutenant-General Simmonds had addressed them, telling them that they would be going into action soon and regaling them with how the 3rd Canadian Infantry Division had been engaging the enemy. Just as Simmonds finished, they'd seen a German plane shot down, the white of a parachute and the dark body suspended beneath floating gently towards the ground.

"Why doesn't someone shoot? He's an easy target," Rusty said.

"He's just one guy. He's done for. Plus, he might have some good intelligence for our side," Phillips replied.

"Bullshit to that. Kill the bastard." Woods glared, challenging anyone to disagree with him.

Later that evening, the air was filled with the roar of RAF engines passing over the camp.

"More bombers. Ours," Reggie had said, looking up from their slit trench. "Clearing the way for us."

In the distance was Caen, which, despite the firm hold the Allies had on the Normandy coast, they still hadn't taken. Ewen knew it was nine miles inland from their position, and the darkness was soon lit with a shower of incendiary bombs raining down on the city. The glow of huge fires filled the horizon. Streaking across the sky was heavy flak from the German guns defending their position. After a second wave of bombers, the flak was gone.

That night, their first in France, Ewen hunkered down with Reggie in a two-man slit trench, feeling like a mole. *This is it. Now it's real. I've been taught to kill and now I'm going to have to do it.*

"Do you think it'll be soon? Our first battle?" Ewen said, not really expecting an answer. It would be daring fate to talk about their future. The two men silently adjusted their positions, anticipating the stiffness that was sure to come.

Ewen thought back to the twelve-hour trip from England. On board they'd been lectured about the French people, how to cook compo and emergency rations and to purify water. They'd even had quizzes and prizes to keep them occupied. Archer had added to his nest egg playing cards.

Ewen laughed.

"What's so funny?" Reggie asked.

"Woods trying out his pickup lines in French. *'Bonjour, petite fleur. Je suis Canadien.'*"

Now Reggie laughed too.

Then, suddenly, a snake slithered down into their trench. Ewen screamed, his panic sending him scrambling against the trench wall.

"I got it." Reggie grabbed the slithering reptile and threw it up and over the ledge. Howls bellowed from a neighbouring slit trench. His other hand was on Ewen's shoulder, pulling him back into the trench.

"Damn it!" Ewen gasped. "I hate snakes."

"Breathe, Morrison."

Ewen pulled out a smoke and took a moment to light it, the flame missing the tip at first. Inhaling deeply, he looked at Reggie, who'd settled back down, his forearms resting on his knees.

Ewen thought, He's a good guy. Then, We're the good guys, aren't we? Isn't that what this is all about? Good versus evil, and we're on the side of what's right. Somewhere across the fields that spread out around them, in a village not far away, perhaps a Jerry was thinking the same.

Reggie looked up and closed his eyes. The wind found them below the edge of their trench, and he shivered. "The wind is from the west," he said, talking more to himself than Ewen.

Minutes passed. "What are you thinking about?" Ewen asked.

"I'm thinking that I'd like to be out of this trench. And up there." Reggie pointed to the dark sky above them.

"When I went to the recruiting office to sign up, I told them I wanted to join the air force. The man there, he told me I didn't have enough education. It was the army for me. That's what his mouth said. His face said, 'Dumb Indian.' That made my mother mad when I told her. She's a teacher, and she taught me and my brother. Where we lived on the reserve, we had our own school. And there were always lots of books around."

"I got to Grade 7," Ewen said. "Quit school after that. Most of us did. We got work on local farms when we could. Your mother was a teacher? Guess that explains a lot."

"My mother, every day she smudges sage and sweetgrass and says prayers for me."

"What's that? What's smudging?"

"Sage and sweetgrass are sacred medicines for us. They clean the mind, the body and the spirit. Sage takes away negative thoughts, sweetgrass helps to be positive and gives strength. My mother burns them together and asks the Creator to protect me."

"In your next letter, can you ask her to burn a little for me, too?"

"I already did, Morrison. Already did."

"What about your dad?" Ewen asked.

"Died when I was fourteen. I kind of became the father in the family after he passed. Frank, my younger brother, he liked to hunt and spent most of his time outdoors after. So I had to help my mother with all the chores and everything."

"That must have been tough. My mom died when I was eleven and I know how hard it is."

"Yeah, it was hard, and sometimes I resented it, but on the whole we had it okay. Me and my brother, we joined up at the same time. Frank lied about his age. Didn't want to be left behind. And he wanted a job too."

Reggie looked at Ewen, "What's your home like? Tell me about it."

"My family originally came from Scotland, Presbyterians, so it was church every week—hellfire and damnation sermons that seemed to go on forever. Guess that's why I can put up with the compulsory church parades on Sundays. We were poor as church mice, and so were our neighbours, but we had horses, different breeds. In spring, before fieldwork started, we'd clip their heavy winter coats, trim their tails and manes. My brothers and me sold the tail and mane hair for a few pennies for people to make horse collars."

He told Reggie he was the sixth of eleven kids, the latest in the family line of Ewens.

"Remember I told you about my uncle who died at Passchendaele in 1917? He was Ewen too. It was his first battle; he just came out of the trench and that was it for him. Probably didn't have time to even fire a bullet. We don't really know. He had a sweetheart in Canada—they were going to get married when he returned. She's never married."

"Really?" Reggie said. "That's damn sad." He shifted in the trench, trying to get more comfortable.

"Yeah, well, we'll be going into our first battle any time now."

"That's not going to happen to you, Ewen," Reggie said.

Ewen talked through the night, his stories taking them both away from a sodden trench in Normandy to the Canadian Prairie while overhead, the night sky was split by the lights and thunder of anti-aircraft fire, a constant barrage against the German planes flying over the camp.

July 8
```
0900 — Although all personnel had been previously
warned not to sleep in buildings or to drink
untested water, one pl of "C" Coy took shelter
from the rain under a lean-to and were found to
have fleas.
```

Royal Hamilton Light Infantry War Diary
July 11, 1944
Bretteville L'Orguilleuse
0130 — A 1 Ech arrived at their assembly area
and took up their posns. The area had not been
cleaned up.

Two days ago they'd been playing baseball against the Royal Regiment. "Come on, boys. Bets here." Woods had worked the men and raked in a tidy bundle of cash when the Rileys won 14–11.

Now Ewen marched with his platoon through the dark, anxiety keeping fatigue at bay. The regiment had been ordered to move up to an assembly area to prepare for going into the line—their first battle. About an hour after midnight they arrived at their position, an area littered with discarded German equipment, vehicles, guns and more. Wearily, D-Coy halted.

The damp air carried a gagging, cloying smell. "Reggie, are those bodies out there?" Ewen asked, not quite able to believe that the twisted shapes on the ground had once been men.

"Yeah, I think they are. That's what we're smelling." The dead, abandoned along with the metal when the enemy retreated.

They rose at dawn. Some of the men ate their biscuits and chocolate while they waited for the Tommy cookers and compo rations to show up, but Ewen had no appetite. They were ordered to begin burying the dead.

Most of them were wearing the uniform of the Waffen SS. Ewen, already wilting in the muggy heat of the morning, put down his pack and unbuckled his shovel—"your best friend" Paquette had called it. *My first burial duty. Graves for the enemy*. He walked over to the nearest body and looked into the face of a dead German. *The guy looks the same age as me—younger even*. He didn't know what to think, so he didn't; he dragged the body off the road and began to dig.

After a day of burial duty and clearing the area, the men

gathered at their slit trenches, waiting for orders. Archer read aloud from the RHLI News Bulletin. "Listen to this: they're offering a prize of 500 cigarettes for the best name for the news sheet. Entries in by 1200 on the 11th. I'm going to win boys. What would be a good name? If I keep selling Connor my daily ration and another twenty cigarettes a day to the rest of you bastards, then in—how many weeks?—I'll have a nice bundle of cash to send back to Nicole and Dottie."

"Don't count your money yet, Les," said Woods. "The bet's still on that you'll be smoking soon."

Paquette appeared. "Listen up. At 2330 we're moving out. We're marching to Bretteville sur Odon to relieve the 7th Seaforths. We're taking one route and the vehicles another; we'll meet and consolidate in the village."

"Night marching, again," grumbled Woods.

Everyone ignored him.

At midnight, just south of their objective, they came under heavy fire and took cover behind the hedges. Ewen made out some stone houses silhouetted against the night sky to the east. He thought it must be their objective. He recognized the smell—bodies, both German and Allied, left exposed to the sun. And with Jerry just over the ridge, there would be no burial duty any time soon. The dead would remain where they fell.

Artillery fire created so many flashes he was almost blinded. Their platoon huddled behind the hedges and dug in as best they could to wait for the rest of the regiment. Ewen was next to Woods when they saw a Jeep with two men—he couldn't tell if they were Rileys or from the Seaforths—take a direct hit.

Ewen turned to Woods in shock. The man's jaw was clenched, like a drawbridge, holding back his anger. Ewen worried he might do something stupid and put them all in jeopardy. I hope he figures out we're all on the same side, he thought. Then, *Poor bastards*.

A squadron of Sherman tanks took position, giving them some

relief. Before dawn the battalion consolidated in a wheatfield and an orchard on a hillside. The relief action had cost the Canadians two lives, with five men wounded. The companies dug their slit trenches deeper and waited. On the facing slope, the Germans also waited. The shellfire stopped briefly, mercifully, then recommenced.

"Johnson. Morrison." It was Paquette. The grey-faced men looked up. "The lieutenant wants you."

They were briefed—the battalion desperately needed to know who, what, and how many were on the other slope. They avoided the paths on the slope, and moved quickly, using the trees and grain as cover. "Stay close, Ewen," Reggie said softly before they set off. "And remember, no noise. This isn't England."

"You think Jerry can hear me coming over all this shellfire?" Ewen was frightened. "I sure hope the lieutenant knows what he's doing."

The lieutenant led them to the crest of the hill but, before they could descend, gunfire exploded around them. They fell to the ground, unable to tell where it was coming from, or how many enemy soldiers were shooting at them. "Withdraw," signalled the lieutenant. Together, they crawled back through sheaves of wheat to their side of the hill. Their first scouting mission was a failure.

Days passed, shells fell, no advances were made. The wet July sky was grey with low-lying clouds, perfect cover for the Luftwaffe planes that came out in force to attack the entrenched Canadians. Rendezvous points were moved from village to village. The regiment struggled to get rations to the troops as mortar fire disabled the soft-skinned supply vehicles. A water trailer fell through a temporary bridge near Verson.

Rumours, orders and countermands rode invisible telegraph lines between the companies and the platoons. *We're going to attack the village of Louvigny. No, not the Rileys; it was going to be the Royal*

Regiment instead—closer to the position. It's Athis—we've been ordered to clear the village. B-Coy: provide flank support for the Royals in Louvigny.

Defeated Jerrys from the surrendered garrison filled the PW cage.

July 21, 1944
0900 — Mobile baths visited the BN posn and the tps marched in pouring rain to obtain much needed baths. The rain continued without interruption throughout the day and the men, standing around in the mud, did not succeed in obtaining much rest.
1830 — Casualties since arrival of the bn in Normandy have been as follows: - Killed in Action – Offrs NIL, ORs 8; Wounded – Offrs 3 (of whom one has returned to duty) ORs 30; Medical Causes (incl battle exhaustions) – Offrs NIL, ORs 21.

Royal Hamilton Light Infantry War Diary
July 24, 1944
Vaucelles
0730 "A" Ech moved to a new posn across the
river ORNE in the suburb of VAUCELLES. On the
move all personnel were amazed at the terrific
damage to the city of Caen caused by the recent
heavy Allied air raids and the arty shelling.
On arrival in VAUCELLES it was found that very
little accommodation for vehicles was available,
and it was necessary to put the RHLI vehicles and
personnel into a cemetery.

"This is one hell of a place to sleep," Archer said. "You guys really know how to find French five-star accommodation. *Chez* Cemetery. I hope this isn't some kind of an omen."

They'd been in Normandy for only eighteen days and already the Rileys had lost fifty-two men—killed in action, wounded, invalided out with battle exhaustion. Ewen watched a couple of men settle into empty graves, too tired to dig a slit trench.

He set off to find some grass to insulate his own slit trench. Wandering amongst the headstones, Ewen noticed several of the graves had fresh flowers. It seemed odd to him that, even in this time of war and danger, someone was still tending to the resting places of the dead.

He saw a group of older women enter the cemetery carrying weathered wicker baskets. They wore oversized coats, which seemed peculiar in the heat, with faded kerchiefs on their heads. Each walked with purpose to a different grave, ignoring the troops who were setting up camp in their cemetery, took flowers out of their baskets and placed them at the base of the headstones. Then several of them pulled out small trowels and began to dig. Throughout the afternoon, more small groups of women came and went, leaving flowers at the graves, and digging.

"I don't get it, what are they up to?" Ewen asked.

"Maybe it's a French thing?" said Reggie. "Their way to honour the dead."

Intrigued, Ewen finally approached one of the grave-tenders. Trying out his invasion-training French, he said politely, *"Bonjour, Madame."*

She looked up, alarmed, then smiled when she saw his uniform. *"Bonjour. Comment allez-vous? Vous êtes Canadien?"*

Looking over her shoulder, Ewen could see the small hole she'd been digging. Grinning, she brushed away the dirt and pulled out a bottle.

"Avez-vous soif? Voulez-vous du Calvados?" she said. She pulled out a rag and wiped the soil from the bottle before handing it to Ewen.

"Merci," he said, smiling back. Ewen had heard of Calvados and knew the boys would welcome it after the attack on Louvigny. Besides, it had been a few days since the brigade commander had authorized a rum ration.

Shoving the bottle in his pocket, he thanked Madame again and returned to the corner of the cemetery where 17 Platoon was resting. Reggie and Rusty were writing letters, Woods was playing "We'll Meet Again" on the harmonica and Phillips was reading. Archer, MacLeod and the others sat or lay on the ground, staring up at a sky that was clear for once of planes and smoke.

"Fellas," he announced. "I've got a present for you." Ewen pulled the bottle from his pocket and raised it high. Then he pulled the cork and tossed back a shot. He gasped, choked and bent over, his hand to his throat. One swig and he was almost on his knees.

Rusty recognized a rookie's response to drinking the local brew. "If that's Calvados, handle with care. Officers aren't allowed to drink it."

"Well, it's a good thing there aren't any officers around then," said Archer. "Pass it to me."

"What the hell is in this stuff?" Ewen asked. He handed the bottle to Archer.

"It's made from apples," said MacLeod. "It's supposed to be about seventy percent alcohol. Before the war, they aged it for several years and it tasted like cognac. Guess now they make it in a few weeks. They should give it to Jerry—it will knock them out faster than us. Give me a hit." He held out his mug.

Archer poured and passed the bottle to Reggie.

"Better be careful with that firewater, Chief," Woods said. "You know what that stuff does to you people." Ignoring him, Reggie took another swig and passed the bottle to him.

"This is gut rot," Woods went on. "We're the guts and no one gives a rat's ass if we're maimed, dead or wounded. We're just the disposable bastards that the brass order around. March here, take that, kill them."

"So what did you think it was going to be like over here? A day out in Toronto?" Reggie said quietly.

"Shut up. The first time I saw those dead Jerrys, I knew why I was here. Payback. That's what we've been trained for. Killing the guys who kill us. I don't need an order to do that. I've heard that Jerry is killing our guys if they surrender. Forget the Geneva Convention. All that stuff about PW rights they told us? Forget that—any poor bastard unlucky enough to be taken gets a shot to the back of the head instead of a cell."

Reggie looked at Ewen, who knew what his friend was thinking. Woods' indiscriminate rage made them all vulnerable. At least they didn't have to take him on a recce, scouting for the enemy. They'd never make it back alive.

"We're not here for revenge, Woods," said Reggie. "I hope you figure that out soon. Before you get us killed."

Silence.

Sullen, Woods said, "All I know is that I'm going to kill as many of those bastards as I can. What goes around, comes around."

Archer, on cue, tried to lighten the mood. "Let's make a toast . . . here's to hoping we get canned peaches in tonight's rations! I've got to wonder who's been getting ours—it's been over a week since we had any."

The Calvados was finished. Woods stood up. "Okay, enough of you bastards. I'm going over to A-Coy. They've got some new guys there from Quebec and I'm going to practise my French. I don't want those boys getting all the mademoiselles. Need to dazzle those lovely French maidens with my handsome mug and my re-par-tee."

"I just hope you're a little more careful on this side of the Channel." Archer turned to Ewen. "Did I ever tell you how Connor here got his crooked nose? Bust-up with a Limey in a pub."

"Shut up. You're just jealous because I'm so popular with the ladies."

"Some of them might be fooled by your movie-star looks, but then the dance halls are some dark. My lovely wife waiting at home prefers my Irish charm to a poster boy like you."

"Yeah, well not all of us are lucky enough to have someone waiting at home." He walked off.

"Wouldn't have picked him as the type for learning a new language," Phillips observed.

"I know he sometimes sounds like a jerk," Archer replied, "but he's mostly just frustrated he didn't get dealt a better hand in life."

"He doesn't just sound like a jerk," Epstein weighed in. "And I don't care what his story is. He's an asshole."

"He's an asshole, all right, but he's not completely wrong about the brass," Reggie said to Ewen. "I heard six new recruits arrived yesterday. Supposed to be mechanics for the carriers, replacing those guys that got killed. Turns out none of them has been near a vehicle in years. Now they're being trained up fast." Shaking his head, he returned to his letter.

"Writing your mom?" Ewen asked

"No, Rose. She's here—they came over on a hospital ship about a week after us. She's at Bayeux now. I told her I'd take her for a dance in Paris when this is all over."

Happy for his friend, Ewen smiled. He didn't write letters—what was there to say? He knew that life was hard for his brothers and sisters still at home, and he didn't have a mother or a gal to write to. Allan, his younger brother, wrote from time to time, but the last had been when Ewen was still in England. He pulled out his western novel and wondered if he'd live to finish reading it.

```
1700 — CO's O Gp held at tac HQ. The intention of
the RHLI is to destroy the enemy in the village
of VERRIÈRES and to capture and hold the
position. The general plan was to attack with
three companies up and one back. H hr is 0300 hrs
25 Jul 44.
```

Royal Hamilton Light Infantry War Diary
July 25, 1944
Vaucelles
0300 — Infm received that SL had not been cleared
of enemy so the attack was delayed.
0430 — SL still not cleared by FMR but attack
commenced anyway.

For an hour, they'd waited, battle-ready and alert. Ewen vacillated between numb blankness and imagined, terrifying combat.

"Boys, let's see who can get a Nazi flag first. Who's in?" Woods whispered. The helmeted heads of 17 Platoon nodded as he got out his notebook to record the bets.

Thirty minutes. "Check your gear, men," Corporal Paquette told them. "We're moving to the SL—Troteval Farm. Now!"

Four hundred Rileys arrived at the farm, which had repeatedly switched from friendly to unfriendly. This was going to be their new HQ, but they weren't staying. They had to move on. They needed to take Verrières and clear it of the enemy.

Paquette pointed to a ridge, some thousand yards away, south of the village. "That's ours. We need to take it and dig in. Be prepared for anything. No one controls the battle once it begins."

Bloody hell, thought Ewen. We're attacking uphill. Against an entrenched enemy who knows the land. The shadowy wheatfields would give excellent cover for the enemy's machine guns and snipers. Ewen looked up to find the Big Dipper. *Will I see the stars tomorrow night?*

Then, the moment arrived. Zero hour. The Blue Patch boys, faces blackened with shoe polish, launched their attack.

As soon as they crossed the start line they were met by intense machine-gun fire, straight on and from both flanks. B-Coy got to the hedges and managed to quiet the machine guns after some fierce hand-to-hand fighting. From there, they headed towards the village. Shells and mortar fire rained down on them, deafening

them as the ground shook beneath their feet. In the point position, D-Coy moved forward to root out the enemy, attacking them
while their artillery bombarded the Jerrys. The men automatically
fell into their much-practised battle maneuvers as they moved up
through the wet grain: drop to the ground, crawl to a position
offering cover, observe where the enemy was firing from, return fire.
Not a drill this time; frenzy and confusion, with a desperate enemy
fighting to push them back into the sea.

Everyone moved forward. Soldiers dropped dead while the living
fought on. Through the hours they attacked from hedge to hedge
and field to field. On the other flank, what they thought had been
machine guns turned out to be tanks. The platoon's PIAT special-
ists, once in range, stood up and let fly. Two direct hits took out two
tanks. The CO ordered artillery that destroyed the remaining tanks.

The Rileys, fewer now, moved into the village. Ewen and
Paquette, working as a team, shoved open doors and scanned
rooms, guns raised. "Clear." Next door, kicked open. Systematically
they searched and cleared stone cottage after stone cottage.

Ewen paused behind the stone wall of a cowshed as the July sun
began to rise and drew a breath; the musk of decomposing bodies
and rotting cows hit his nostrils. He adjusted his stance to make
room for Paquette. Neither man spoke.

Nodding his head to the road, Paquette moved away from the
pock-scarred wall. Ewen followed. Side by side, they walked.

The first shot propelled Paquette backwards, and Ewen reached
out instinctively to break his fall. A second shot knocked Paquette
flat, pinning Ewen to the ground beneath him.

Ewen froze, his eyes tightly shut and his hands clutching the earth
as he heard the final death moan leave the body covering him.

Heart thudding, he tried to assess his situation. Concealed inside
the bombed-out remains of a stone cottage somewhere up ahead, a
German sniper stood poised to fire. His job was to delay the enemy
while his unit retreated. He would know that he had fired two bullets

52

but might not be sure he had hit both soldiers. If he moved, he would be next. Then he remembered something Reggie had told him back in England. Old hunters move on, inexperienced ones hang around. If this sniper was young, he would stay; a veteran would catch up with his unit. Ewen knew he had to move. Either the sniper was there or he wasn't. I have a fifty-fifty chance, he thought as he slid out from underneath the corpse. Move on, keep moving. It had been drilled into him. He had to find the rest of the platoon.

The morning air was filled with a mist that mingled with smoke to create an apocalyptic, eerie light. Verrières was theirs, but for how long? Could they hold it until reinforcements arrived? From the crest of the ridge, those who had made it looked through the clearing haze at the destruction spread before them.

Ewen was numb, grateful to be one of them. His mind kept returning to the village, replaying the scene over and over again. He imagined the German sniper thinking, as he and Paquette walking up the road: *They are making it easy for me... Now, which one should I shoot first? The one on the left or the right? Which one goes first?* It was all so arbitrary. *Why Paquette? Why not me?*

They needed to dig in. The shelling didn't stop, and Ewen's T-shovel vibrated in his hands as it plunged it into the Normandy ground. He shovelled his slit trench like a madman, determined to live another day.

The Germans sprayed the area with machine-gun fire, pinning the men down in their partly dug slit trenches. They were beaten off by infantry with PIAT grenades but their assault didn't let up. They continued to counterattack, firing mortars and shells throughout the day.

Lieutenant Coulson consolidated their position and took stock of casualties and ammunition. Ewen reported, "Paquette. We were clearing houses. A sniper got him." He tried not to think about Paquette's boys growing up without a father.

"Phillips! O'Malley! Get those men down." The lieutenant surveyed his surviving platoon. Pointing to a hand-drawn map, Coulson indicated the ammunition dump, Tac HQ in the centre of town, the PW point, the regimental aid post.

From his slit trench, Ewen willed himself to look back over the ground they'd won. The rear battalion HQ was now at the Troteval farm. Only a thousand yards away, but a distance they had covered with their lives. The corporal hadn't made it. Neither had MacLeod or Rusty. He saw their regimental pastor leaning over someone who wasn't moving. Ewen didn't know who it was. In England, the priests and reverends had managed the Sunday church parades; here they went unarmed out on the battlefield. Their pastor had been hit in the head by some shrapnel shortly after they'd landed, but had returned to duty the next day, giving solace to the injured and dignity to the dead.

At 1700, the counterattacks became even more intense. Finally, British tanks arrived. The 7th Armoured Division, the Desert Rats, took up positions behind the Rileys. A British commander, appearing quite oblivious to the shelling and wearing corduroy pants with suede shoes, called out, "What would you like us to shoot at?" The Rileys pointed out several targets. The Desert Rats hammered them until the Germans withdrew.

Their situation improved, as did their morale, but the battle wasn't over. Their positions were still threatened. Enemy intel was critical. That night, Reggie and Ewen were sent on patrol.

Ewen practised controlling his breathing as he prepared: face and hands blackened, hand grenade and knife ready in case of capture, nothing that could rattle or gleam, gum in his pocket.

A long list of unnecessary reminders belied Reggie's outwardly calm demeanour. "Remember Ewen, this isn't England anymore."

"No talking, hand gestures only."

"Be quick, be silent, be invisible."

"Stay close to me."

They crept toward the enemy position, hugging the hedgerows whenever possible, taking advantage of whatever cover was available when it was not, running silently when necessary. *Heel, toe, heel, toe.*

Ewen was frightened. *I can't see shit.* He feared ending up in an enemy minefield. He feared tripping a flare. He feared getting lost. He feared being taken prisoner. Most of all, he feared letting Reggie down. To combat the fear, he concentrated on using all his senses, alert for anomalies that might indicate enemy activity, using his training to recognize German ranks, weapons and vehicles. He and Reggie were the regiment's eyes and ears. Tomorrow's command decisions would be made based on the information they brought back tonight.

They spotted a group of enemy soldiers, moving towards their position. Reggie gave the signal to withdraw. Moving cautiously, they returned to their own lines and reported to the lieutenant. He ordered the men to let the Germans get nearer before giving the command to fire. Their platoon wiped out all but two of the Jerrys, who were taken to the PW point.

The next night, Reggie was ordered to go out on a scout patrol with the sergeant from another platoon. As he was putting his moccasins back into his pack, Reggie told Ewen what had happened. "We were spread out, and I heard machine-gun fire. I ran to where the sergeant was. He'd killed a lot of them. We went after the rest, but they got away. I think there were about twenty of them."

July 27, 194
0800 — Work commenced on completing lists of our casualties. This was found to be an extremely difficult job as a great many of the wounded had been evacuated from the battlefield immediately without passing through the normal unit RAP channels and had been dispatched to any available medical installations without any record being taken of names, regt numbers, etc. It has not yet been found possible to recover and bury many

of the killed owing to the battle still raging
around our posns at VERRIÈRES. Pending more
thorough investigation, RHLI casualties in the
battle of VERRIÈRES and the subsequent counter
attacks on the village, are estimated as follows:
Officers killed – 3, Officers wounded 8, Other
ranks killed or died of wounds – 42, Other ranks
wounded – 146. Not one of our men is in enemy
hands and none are known to be missing.

Royal Hamilton Light Infantry War Diary
August 5, 1944
Louvigny Woods
1300 — The bn spent the day in adm, giving
the men a chance to rest, wash their clothes
and clean their weapons. Secs and pls were
reorganized so that the bn could once again go
into action at full strength.

Archer opened his tin of sausage and read the label aloud, "Listen up: 'May be eaten hot or cold. To heat, place unopened tins in boiling water for the minimum period as indicated. Sausage and pudding cut into half-inch slices may be fried, using margarine, if preferred . . . ' Who's got marg?"

"For extra protein stir in a few flies," Woods said, without looking up from writing a letter. "Everything is so disgusting, no wonder we're all suffering from the shits."

"That's something to write home about. See if you can get that past the censors," Ewen said.

"They can't send medicine for our guts, but they can drop bales of wool so we can make earplugs. So we won't go deaf from the bombs and can sure as hell hear orders." Phillips' tone was acid.

"I've lost count of how many slit trenches I've dug," Woods said. "We live in holes in the ground in our own shit and piss. It's damn hot and you can't eat for all the flies and wasps. Les, you stink worse than the food."

"Well, I haven't lost count of how many baths I've had in France," Archer said. "By my calculation, it's been eighteen days since the last bath, which has been the only one since we landed on that beach. So, that's one bath in thirty-three days. That delightful perfume you smell must be the delousing parade . . . Ahh, the lovely aroma of anti-flea powder, nicely blown inside my collar and pants by a tube."

"How do you keep track? I don't even know what day of the week it is anymore," Epstein said.

The regiment had been relieved from their positions at Verrières, each company in turn replaced by men from the South Saskatchewan Regiment. The handover had been difficult, with the enemy dropping flares over the area and sending in fighter planes to strafe the departing troops. The noise from the anti-personnel bombs had been horrific. Once again they'd marched through the night, arriving in the woods around Louvigny at 0330.

"What's in the paper?" Ewen asked Archer. He liked Archer, who always seemed to be in a good mood, and who was a fountain of information, both trivial and useful. "Have they picked a winner yet?"

"No. It's still just the RHLI News Bulletin. Guess everybody was too busy staying alive to come up with clever names. Says here that Hitler fired some of his generals—maybe he's looking for someone to blame for how badly we're beating them."

Reggie joined the platoon but, instead of sitting down with the others, walked over to his trench and sat cross-legged on the ground. He did not look happy. Worried, Ewen went over to him.

"What's wrong, Reggie?"

"It's the lieutenant. Coulson ordered me to report to the battalion HQ."

"Why? Are you in trouble?"

"Yeah, I think I am." Reggie reached into his pocket and held something out to Ewen—two stripes.

"What? Corporal? You've been promoted? That's great, Reggie!"

"No, it's not. I told the lieutenant I didn't want it. I'm a private, a scout. Don't want any more than that. He told me there'd been an NCO selection board last night. And I'd been selected. Told me to get on with it. That it wasn't a request, it was an order."

"You'll make a great corporal, Reggie. I trust you, and so do the others. Besides, it means some extra cash, doesn't it? That's got to be good."

"You think I care about a few extra nickels, Ewen?" he said

angrily. "You think guys like Woods are going to like me being their platoon NCO? Not on your life."

Before Ewen could reply, they heard a holler. "You guys D-Coy?"

"Yeah, we are," Reggie called back. He uncrossed himself and he and Ewen walked over to greet the reinforcement.

"I'm Cowboy. I'm with you guys." Built like a bull, his nickname suited him—he looked like he'd been born on the range with a lasso in his hand. The newcomer put his kit down, wiped his brow and scanned his surroundings.

Reggie put out his hand. "I'm Reggie Johnson and this is Ewen Morrison."

Archer, Woods and the rest of 17 Platoon checked off their names, some with a casual wave, some shaking Cowboy's hand.

"Where are you from, Cowboy?" asked Ewen, introductions over.

"Southern Alberta, around the foothills. My old man is American, my mom Canadian. She's from Alberta and they ended up settling down on a ranch."

Ewen's eyes rested on the new guy for a moment: the less you knew about a new guy, the less the pain you'd have when he was killed. He thought about Paquette, MacLeod, Rusty and the others. He hadn't been in France for a month and already he was exhausted, mentally as well as physically. Ewen figured if he didn't say much, then he wouldn't bring anyone else down with him. *What did it matter anyway? Our little platoon in this fucking confused mess, why bother?*

"Who's our sergeant?" asked Cowboy.

"We haven't got one," said Archer. "Had a corporal. He got hit taking the ridge at Verrières. Didn't make it, and we haven't had one since."

Ewen looked at Reggie, who looked uncomfortable. *You'd better get used to it, fella. You're the man now.*

"We've got one now, Archer," said Reggie.

Heads raised, eyes surprised and curious. "Who?"

"Me."

A few of the men congratulated Reggie, most said nothing.

Woods glared, took a swig from his canteen and spit it out. "This water tastes like bleach. It's disgusting."

"I hear they're taking it from the Orne," Archer said, breaking the silence. "With all the dead animals and bodies floating in that river, is it any surprise we've all got the shits? Welcome to 17 Platoon, Cowboy."

"It's coming from the flies," Reggie said. "They land and eat the dead animals, everything dead, and then they land on our food. There's millions of the bastards . . . there's tons of our shit, tons of Jerrys' shit . . . thousands of open latrines. Not much we can do."

Woods stared at Reggie. He wasn't going to let it go.

"On the prairie, if we had a real dry summer and the sloughs had dried up," Ewen said, "Out would come the old witching willow to find a new spot and we'd dig a new well."

"That's fucking marvellous." Woods had wandered back. He glared at Ewen and refused to look in Reggie's direction. "We'll be sure to do that if we ever stay somewhere long enough and find a willow."

"Hell," said Cowboy. "We're on the same side as the brass, and any old jackass can be a pessimist. I don't believe in making mountains out of molehills. And I prefer my mountains molehill-sized."

"See if you feel the same way when you've got the shits like us," scoffed Woods.

Ewen, hoping to get Woods off his rant, asked, "Cowboy, what's your real name?"

"Ellison Crowell Rowdon."

"Well, Ellison Crowell Rowdon, just so you know, we've got a couple of bets going on," said Woods.

"What's that?" said Cowboy.

"The first one to get a Nazi flag wins the pool. And the other is how long until Archer starts to smoke. You in?"

"Of course," said Cowboy.

Woods got out his notebook.

Reggie spoke for the first time since announcing his promotion. "Morrison, we're on recce patrol tonight. Archer, we need one more man, and that's going to be you. I know you haven't been trained, but I'll brief you and keep an eye on you. We need Jerry's location, strength and firepower. A bonus would be capturing one for questioning. The CO wants our patrolling to get aggressive. We've been ordered not only to gain information and prevent the enemy getting information about us but to harass him as well. We go out at 2300. There won't be any artillery fire until 0330."

Taking out a map, Reggie showed them where they were headed, the boundaries between their two sister regiments and themselves. He said, "Significant activity was observed here today; we're going to find out anything we can."

Ewen nodded even as his nerves tightened. With each night's patrol, he was becoming more comfortable in the darkness, and with the danger. He and Reggie had trained in unarmed combat, concealment and camouflage, compass and map reading. Reggie had taught him to run quietly, and he had become practised at using all the dips in the land to maximum advantage. But Archer was new to all of this. How would he manage?

That night, under the stars, the three Rileys finished covering their faces and hands with black shoe polish. Reggie turned to Archer. "Remember, Jerry has the advantage. They've had over four years to get to know this countryside. Hand signals only."

Archer and Ewen both nodded.

Reggie looked at his watch and said, "2250. Ten minutes." He tightened up the laces of his moccasins; Archer and Ewen slipped thick socks over their army issued plimsolls.

The three scouts moved like ghosts, Reggie in the lead, sliding on his belly. Whatever the hell there was out there, he was going to find it. Behind him, Ewen crawled on hands and knees. Archer, in the rear, copied their moves. Only experience would get them used to the Norman terrain and sounds of the French night.

Soaked with sweat, covered in dust and mud, they paused in a ditch at a crossroad to look, listen and learn. Reggie lifted his right arm just a few inches off the ground. The signal to stop. The moon slipped out from behind the clouds, revealing the silhouette of a bunker—they had found the enemy. From the ditch, they observed and memorized.

Then another signal from Reggie: time to start back. They had one hour before the artillery barrage resumed. It was crucial to get back on time and to remember the exact password.

Finally, they got back to their side and found the sentry.

"King . . . " Reggie whispered.

" . . . Pin," the sentry answered. The three scouts passed.

They reported in to their command post and returned to their slit trenches: not even the mosquitos and the stench kept them awake.

RHLI News Bulletin, Vol.1, No. 31
Say fellas, how about a few contributions to the sheet once in a while. Anything of interest is always appreciated, even the odd bit of corn: And then there was the rearline soldier who thought "discussion was the better part of valour."

Royal Hamilton Light Infantry War Diary
August 6, 1944 — War Diary
Louvigny Woods
0900-1200 — All coys trained in area near camp.
Loading of vehs was practiced and the fmn in
which they would travel. All vehs and weapons in
the bn were checked by LAD.

They hadn't been told much—just that another operation was imminent, any day. D-Coy had a new major, and 17 Platoon spent the morning training in loading and unloading the armoured vehicles that had arrived the night before. Whatever the next operation was, they would be riding, not marching.

"Up, in, onwards," said Fraser, one of the new mechanics who'd joined the regiment a couple of weeks earlier. "Thanks to the Sherbrookes, you're going into your next mission in these here kangaroos. Hold twenty-two men each and they're bulletproof. Ya see, they've taken a tank chassis and . . . "

"Shut it, Fraser," said Woods. "Just show us the best way to get comfortable in these crates. I'm not sure I can drag myself and my kit up there. My guts are still killing me."

Cowboy looked pale in the morning sunlight. "You guys sure know how to welcome a fella. I've got the shits now too."

Even Archer was complaining.

"We're all tired. And we're all sick," said Reggie, "but at least we're not going to have to hike. The faster we get this loading and unloading done, and get through the formation drills, the sooner we can have a break."

"Whatever you say, Corporal Chief," said Woods.

"Yeah, I say. Now do."

Ewen could see how pissed off Reggie was. He could also see that he wasn't going to let the resentment of some of the platoon get to him. He continued to keep his emotions strictly under control. *Sure glad it's not me.*

Epstein looked at Archer, who was leaning against the kangaroo, and asked, "How do you share a slit trench with Mr. Cheerful day after day?"

"Woods and me, we go way back to school days. He had it kind of tough with his old man so he used to spend a lot of time at my place. Kind of got in the habit of looking out for me. Got a job at Stelco and ended up being the shop steward. Hates any kind of bully: in the schoolyard, in the factory, now the Nazis."

Epstein wasn't convinced. "Be better for everyone if he focused on them and gave the rest of us a break."

For the rest of the morning they rehearsed for a play without knowing the plot: columns of vehicles, four abreast with only two feet between them; practice runs through make-believe minefields towards an imaginary objective.

Twenty hours later, Lieutenant-General Simmonds issued the detailed op order for Operation Totalize. D-Coy's new major shared it with Lieutenant Coulson, who shared it with the men. They were headed through German lines south of Caen to secure a firm base on a ridge in the Caillouet area.

"Point 46, Square 0655. It's about five miles from the SL. On a Sunday drive it might take fifteen minutes," he said, handing the rough map over to Reggie, who scanned it carefully.

"I have a suspicion it will take us a little longer," O'Malley muttered. A gesture from Reggie silenced him.

"H-hour is tonight. 2330."

The Rileys eyeballed each other in disbelief.

Reggie unfolded the map and pointed out their route step-by-step. "These route maps don't show a lot of detail. Here's the Verrières line we're going to break through. There's Rocquancourt. There's our target. We're going to be in the column formation we practised. Jerry's not going to make it easy for us."

At 1700, a hot meal arrived. "Ah, the last supper," joked Archer.

"Johnson, you've been out there, you've seen the territory. Do you think we'll be able to do it? Bust our way through?" asked Cowboy.

"Yes," Reggie said. "Look at what they've sent us. We're not walking in like at Verrières. We're going to be safe in a kangaroo's pouch."

"It sounds like more bullshit from the brass." Woods glared at the corporal. "Dead in the dirt. That's all of us. Only a matter of time."

"Shut up, Woods."

Ewen was startled. He'd never heard Reggie speak that way to anyone. Those within earshot stopped eating.

"No plan is perfect. No one knows how it will play out. We've got our skills and our training. We've got good men around us. Stop thinking about your guts and start thinking about them." He pointed to the rest of the platoon.

"Asshole," said Woods.

"Corporal Asshole," said Reggie.

Archer laughed. And then the steak and kidney pudding was interesting again.

"A most daring plan" the captain would write later. The RAF Lancasters laid down heavy bombing over the target area thirty minutes before H-Hour. Their column set off, following the tapes and coloured lights dropped by the advance tanks. Small arms fire was easily ignored. But when a couple of the kangaroos ran into bomb craters, forty-four men had to scramble to find places in other vehicles. "Fuck, fuck, fuck," shouted Fraser.

A single 88mm gun, terrifyingly close, began to fire on the advancing column. Confusion, casualties, panic. From there, things got worse.

As Reggie had observed, no plan was perfect. Sometime around 0500, they found their target, Point 46—abandoned. The CO gave the order to move down and take up a position some two hundred yards away. The entire area was covered in smoke—courtesy of Jerry—and the men were thankful for the cover it provided.

Dawn broke and with it came a fresh assault, but the Rileys held their ground. One dead, thirteen wounded. The fatality was the officer in charge of 17 Platoon, D-Coy. Lieutenant Coulson wasn't going home.

```
MR 071563 SHEET 7F/3 1/5000
1700: About thirty-five prisoners were taken.
The Adjt Captain went forward to find out
requirements of amn, water, food, etc
```

Royal Hamilton Light Infantry War Diary
August 11, 1944 — War Diary
Etavaux
1800 — A search party consisting of five Jeeps and
twenty men swept the area between VERRIERES and
ROCQUANCOURT in search of equipment for the Bde.
2100 — Battalion O Group held. The Bde plan was
to prevent the enemy from withdrawing. The RHLI
objective was to be the village of CLAIR TIZON.

"Take cover!"

"Hold the line!"

"Incoming!"

"More ammo!"

"Keep firing!"

Pandemonium. No one knew what was happening, and each man fought for himself, in a self-contained bubble of instinct: move, duck, don't get hit. The German Panther tanks were throwing everything at them and winning. The barrage of mortars blasted up. Machine-gun fire came from all directions; mortars created fountains of stone and mud and blood.

"Stay down!"

"Medic!"

"I'm hit!"

"Medic!"

The wounded, those capable of walking on their own, attempted to find help. Medics triaged, stopping bleeding, treating shock and alleviating pain as best they could before stretcher-bearers heaved men back to the nearest casualty station.

"Do something!" Ewen recognized Woods' voice, but not the shrill note of panic. He ran over to find Connor kneeling on the ground, one bloody hand grabbing at the medic, the other pressed against Les Archer's abdomen.

Ewen grabbed Woods, pulling him up and back. "Let him do his job!" he shouted into Woods' face.

The medic ripped apart bandages, applied dry plasma, injected morphine. "I'm trying to get a pulse!"

Two stretcher-bearers ran towards them, crouching low.

"Okay, let's go, let's go . . . get him out." The medic stood, scanned the area and ran to the next man down, while the two stretcher-bearers loaded Archer onto the canvas and retreated towards the casualty point.

Woods, his usual swagger gone, leaned over and vomited. Ewen's mind was reeling. What could he say? He reached out to put his hand on Woods' shoulder when he felt one on his own. It was Reggie, his face black with boot polish and splatters of mud. Their eyes met. "Let him be." Reggie's hand, still on his shoulder, seemed weighted with small comfort.

"Woods. We gotta go. Up." Reggie helped him get to his feet. Ewen half expected Woods to shake him off, but he rose, silent and numb, and began moving forward over ground pockmarked with blasted holes and shattered trees. Destroyed and abandoned tanks littered the landscape.

The trio moved on through the carnage, regrouping with their platoon—those who'd made it—at their new position. Epstein was dead. No one knew what had happened to Phillips. The survivors dug in.

Now it was almost silent, except for some distant mortar fire. The lull allowed Ewen time to think, something he did his best to avoid. Always having something to do kept his fears at bay and helped him repress dangerous emotions.

All around them was death—the human remains of both armies and dead cows and horses. Other horses moved slowly, their heads swaying back and forth.

Reggie saw the look on his friend's face. "The Germans used those horses to bring supplies. I think all the bombing has made them deaf. They're shell-shocked."

Ewen heard a horse, neighing in distress. Medics were taking care of the injured men, but no one was tending to the innocent beasts caught up in the battle. He spoke for the first time since Archer had been hit. "I can't stand it, Reggie. I can't take this." He grabbed his rifle and began striding towards the injured horse.

"Wait," said Reggie. He caught up with Ewen. Together, the two men stepped through the destruction to dispense mercy in the only way they could.

August 13, 1944 – War Diary
1400 — A burial party from "A" ech swept the area covered by our trps in the last 24 hours and buried 20 men . . . CO went to Bde O gp. He returned with information that the battalion was to attack orchard at MR 0544, sheet 7F/3.

Royal Hamilton Light Infantry War Diary
August 14, 1944
Tourneau
0800 — IO from Bde arrived with orders for the
bn to move north to Gouvix . . . for twenty-four
hours rest as our men were exhausted.

They had marched from point to points on maps they hadn't ever seen: Le Bequet, Le Mesnil, beyond and back. Always with the enemy laying down heavy fire as they advanced. Then onto their next target, Tourneau. Was the town still in enemy hands? Was it clear? They had arrived to find only a handful of Germans, none offering any resistance. But barely twelve hours later, the Rileys were on the move again.

They'd taken up positions in Gouvix a short time before they heard the rumble of RAF bombers approaching.

Looking up, Cowboy said, "Now there's a sight, good thing they're on our side."

"Yeah," Woods said, "Hope they blast those German bastards back to hell."

Shading his eyes against the sun, Ewen looked up and nodded. The aircraft were flying low. Then the bomb doors opened. He could see the bombs, like eggs, in the bomb-bays. They began to cascade down towards them.

"Shit!" O'Malley yelled. "Run! Head for the German slits!" Marching in, they had come across perfectly dug German slit trenches, approximately six feet long, two feet wide and thirty feet apart. It was as though a machine had gone down the road punching holes.

Ewen leaped into an empty German slit trench as the first bombs landed. More came. One after another, one after another . . . bomb after bomb. The whistle from the time they were launched to when they hit the ground terrified Ewen.

Then it stopped. Ewen crawled out of the slit trench. *Bloody hell, now our own side is trying to kill us. I volunteered for this?* His head pounded. He couldn't see clearly through the smoke and dust. One by one the men emerged. Miraculously, all were accounted for. Many of the vehicles weren't so lucky; mangled wrecks surrounded them.

"What a shitty mess," Ewen said.

"Getting bombed by our own side. How much more can a man take?" Woods said.

"I gotta wonder who relayed those coordinates," Cowboy said.

"We're just numbers," Woods said. For once, no one argued with him. Then, surprisingly, he started to laugh. "You know what Archer would say?"

"No," said Reggie. "What would he say?"

"No idea. But it would have been a great joke." Woods stopped laughing and shook his head. "I hope he made it. And that he's making the nurses in Bayeux laugh."

Fountaine-Le-Pin. Villiers-Canivet. The road to Falaise. The platoon marched through the dark, then halted. "Where's the damned track?" asked Lieutenant Wilkinson, shining a flashlight on the map. Coulson's replacement, Hanson, had only made it a couple days of before he'd been wounded and sent back behind the lines. Wilkinson was their third lieutenant in six weeks.

"Johnson, come over here."

"Sir."

"Look at this map. We're supposed to follow this marked track to our next position, but I can't see a damned thing. Can you see a path?"

Reggie looked into the blackness in front of them, the only flashes of light coming from the enemy's mortars. "No, sir."

"Some damned Indian scout you are."

March. Consolidate. Dig in. March again.

Ewen and Reggie were ordered to recce ahead. "There's a bridge

marked here at 121357. Find out if it's still there," said the lieutenant. What they found was not what the brass wanted to hear. The
bridge was no longer there and that the banks on either side of the
river were too steep for any of their vehicles, tracked or wheeled.

August 16, 1944
MR 127363 Sheet 7F/6 1/50000
0300 — A RAF pilot came through our lines. He had
been shot down four days previously while flying
a Typhoon in a dive bomb attack. He had slept by
day and travelled by night until he made contact
with our troops.

Royal Hamilton Light Infantry War Diary
August 19, 1944
Damblainville
The bn cleaned up and rested, and maintenance of
vehicles was stressed.
1100 — RC communion was held in the village
church.
1400 — Protestant communion was held.

Bivouacking in a pear orchard, the men were grateful for the respite. Most chose to rinse out their clothes to try to get rid of the dust and the fleas.

Ewen stood in his army issue underwear and boots. His damp wool uniform was draped over a branch, drying.

The late afternoon sun felt good on his back but the quietness disturbed him. He felt jittery, restless. He stretched up, back and then forward. He twisted his torso from left to right a few times, encouraging his muscles to relax. He rubbed his puffy eyes.

When he opened them, he noticed a bundle of fur hiding in the grass. A rabbit. One of its ears, normally upright, hung down. The animal appeared dazed, shell-shocked. Ewen knelt down to see if the creature would allow him to get close.

Ewen said, "Hey there, lil' fella. I know how you feel." With two fingers, he gently stroked the rabbit's head.

He thought of the rabbits at home. How they used to go bounding over the prairie at a pretty good speed. He thought about the winter months when they would travel from grain bin to grain bin to oat stack. When there was a crust on the snow and the moon was bright, he and his brothers would gather around the feed stack and play what they called rabbit games, hiding in the stack and watching the rabbits at close range. Then they'd whistle to see the rabbits perk up, their ears vertical—for Ewen, it was a magical sight in the moonlight. The next day, he'd race across the snow, following their tracks to find their secret home. He never did.

73

Cowboy was rummaging through his gear. "Don't suppose you've got another bottle of Calvados hidden, Morrison?" he said. "Sure could do with a bottle of anything right now. Guess it will have to be coffee. You want some, Woods?"

"Yeah. That would be good."

"All that training, at home and in England," said Cowboy. "It doesn't set you up for getting bombed by your own side."

Woods lit a cigarette and passed it to Cowboy.

"Listen, Cowboy. We just have to look out for each other. Fuck the generals. Let's just get the bloody job done and go home and forget we ever lived in this shit. I live every day fuckin' afraid of tomorrow, but hey, we go on."

"You don't strike me as the frightened kind, Woods," said Cowboy.

"Hell, of course I am. I'm not an idiot. But I go on. Have to. One of us has to get that Nazi flag sooner or later. Come on you bastard, get that coffee made."

Reggie, who'd finished washing up and was writing a letter, looked over at the rest of 17 Platoon, talking, unwinding, dozing. Then a flash of white in the woods caught his eye.

"Quiet. All of you."

The men stopped what they were doing and looked at their corporal, who was looking at the edge of the forest. Their eyes followed his and then they saw it.

"Jeez. Is that Jerrys?" said Ewen.

Out of the trees came seven exhausted, battle-worn Germans in blue-grey uniforms. Hands behind their helmetless heads, they walked single file towards the Canadians. The one in front held what appeared to be a filthy, formerly white, pillowcase.

"They got guts, just walking out like that. Holy shit. I haven't seen a live German yet," said O'Malley.

Woods reached for his notebook. "Before they get here, I'm willing to bet one of them is named Helmut. Anyone in?"

The Germans neared the Rileys, foe meeting foe. In his other hand, the German in front held what Ewen could see was one of the Safe Conduct leaflets dropped by the Allies, guaranteeing German soldiers they'd be taken care of if they surrendered.

Yards apart, they looked into each other's eyes.

Woods went for his rifle. "Bloody bastards."

"Stand down!" Reggie yelled. "Morrison, Cowboy, grab him. This isn't a battle, Woods."

Woods yelled at Reggie. "I don't give a shit. Remember Les, all shot up?"

"Woods, when you get angry, you get stupid. Shut the fuck up." Reggie turned to the approaching Germans and held out his hands, palms facing down.

The leader looked directly at Reggie and, in lightly accented English, said, "We are from a Panzer division. We wish to surrender."

"Nazi bastards," shouted Woods.

"I am German. I am not a Nazi," said the soldier, not taking his eyes from Reggie.

"We accept your surrender," said Reggie. "You will be taken to HQ for interrogation."

The Germans stopped moving forward but kept their hands raised behind their heads. They looked shattered, filthy and very hungry.

Reggie said, "Cowboy, Morrison . . . search them."

Ewen and Cowboy searched them one by one. No weapons. Just apples. They each had apples in their pockets. Reggie gestured for them to get on their knees and keep their hands behind their head.

"I'll be right back, need to find the IO. Woods, behave."

Woods approached the kneeling men.

"So, what are your names?" When one answered "Helmut," Woods turned to the platoon and grinned.

"Nice watch," he said, pointing to the leader's wrist. "You got any francs on you, Jerry?" he asked another.

The Germans didn't move, but their eyes sought each other anxiously.

Ewen said, "What are you doing, Woods?" The big man had grabbed the watch off the German's wrist and was reaching into the pocket of another.

"Shut up."

"You can't steal from them," Cowboy said.

Woods ignored both of them and moved among the rigid Germans.

"Woods, what the hell are you doing?" Ewen yelled. "Leave it."

"This isn't stealing, this is collecting souvenirs. They can keep their photos."

"Stop. Now. Or you're going to be written up." Reggie was back. "Woods, give them back their stuff. Now."

Ewen was relieved. They look so scared. I would be too if the Jerrys had me prisoner. Please don't let it happen to me.

Reggie looked down at the leader. "Where did you learn to speak English?"

"In Canada," the German said.

"Canada?" Reggie repeated, surprised. The other men looked at each other and then back at the enemy soldier.

"Yes, I was born in Germany, but my family immigrated to Canada in 1927. We lived on a farm in Manitoba. Listening to Hitler's speeches, I was called back to the homeland. I wanted to help rebuild our country. Then all this started. I had no choice, I had to enter the Wehrmacht. I had to fight." He paused. "And now we have lost and I am here."

"Well, that's ironic," Ewen said. "You'll be going to a PW camp in Canada. That's where all of us would like to be right now. But we're heading for Germany, where you'd all like to go."

The German translated for the other six.

"If you walk into those trees," he said, talking only to Reggie, "You will find more Germans soldiers. But they are dead, German bullets in their backs. When we were retreating, some men wanted to surrender. The SS said you Canadians don't take prisoners, and they shot those who refused to press on. We got away. We took a chance on you."

"You can get up now," Reggie said. "O'Malley, Morrison. There's a Holy Roller three hundred yards east, with three more PWs there. Get these guys over there. Charters' platoon is taking them back for questioning."

Hours later, Reggie and Ewen smoked in their slit trench.

"He was just an ordinary farm boy, like me, Reggie. If only we got them all to surrender, we could all go home," Ewen said.

"Yeah, he thought he was fighting for his people," said Reggie. "And look what his country has done."

Well used to each other's company, they didn't need to speak anymore. They sat in their trench, blowing smoke up into a sky that was soon, once again, filled with enemy bombers. The planes dropped flares and then bombs on the regiment, but no casualties were suffered.

When it was over, O'Malley shouted from his slit trench, "At least it wasn't the RAF bombing their own side again."

RHLI News Bulletin, Vol.1, No.33
Odds 'n Ends
Up to last night the tactical air force had destroyed more than five thousand enemy vehicles and over two hundred tanks in forty-eight hours. It looks like Jerry isn't going to have a wheel to stand on pretty soon.

```
Royal Hamilton Light Infantry War Diary
August 21, 1944
Damblainville
1030-1100 — A bn O gp was held. The CO informed
us that the FALAISE gap was almost closed and the
enemy was on the run . . . Bde intention was to
reach the Seine and if it had not been crossed,
to cross it and form a br head for following tps.
45 reinforcements came up to A ech and 26 were
allotted to A Coy and the balance to other coys
in order to bring all up to 80 per cent strength.
```

"Tell the men, Johnson," Lieutenant Wilkinson ordered. He'd just returned from the operations group meeting. There was good news to share with 17 Platoon—they were winning and were going to be going east with new reinforcements.

There was also bad.

"Les Archer is dead," Reggie said. There was nothing he could add, and his face showed no emotion. Ewen felt for his friends, the living one who'd had to break the news, the dead one who wouldn't be going home to his wife and baby girl.

Ewen looked at Woods, whose face was frozen with disbelief and pain. *He really thought Archer was going to make it.* Woods and Archer. What an unlikely pair. He remembered when he'd first met them back in England. Woods' ego and aggression. Archer's generous, good-humoured spirit and his jokes. His belief in why they were here, always diffusing negativity and complaints. And now his daughter would grow up without a father, just like Paquette's sons. *How many more children, on all sides, civilians and soldiers, will grow up fatherless because of this war?*

Reggie spoke. "The battle for Normandy is almost over. Jerry is on the run and we're going after him. We're heading to cross the Seine River at Elbeuf. We move out in an hour."

News of the dead had become common. No one talked about it. The survivors were just damn glad they made it another day.

Reggie walked over to Woods. "I'm sorry, Woods," he said.

"Sorry! What's it to you? What do you care? You weren't his friend. Why him and not you? Fucking Indian."

"Hey, Woods, that's not okay!" Ewen raised both his hands, palms facing the angry soldier.

"You're upset, Woods, we all are," said Cowboy, "but we have to look out for each other."

"Fuck you guys." Woods stormed off.

"Let it go," Reggie said. "He just lost his best friend. Leave him alone."

Reggie's face was still, betraying no resentment. Ewen knew what that must have cost him. Since they'd arrived in Normandy, it seemed that racial, religious or social differences hadn't mattered. Even Woods mostly kept quiet. They were all just Canadian soldiers doing their job and fighting together to defeat Jerry. Trying to stay alive. *Guess not. Guess sometimes we take a break from hating the enemy to hating anyone who's not "one of us."* Ewen was sad. Sad for Archer. Sad for Woods. And sad for his friend who had to hide his emotions to do a job he hadn't asked for, with responsibilities he hadn't wanted.

Early evening and the sound of a harmonica sounded a melancholy tone among the gathered men. Connor Woods sat on the ground, playing a eulogy for his friend. The words that accompanied the notes filled Ewen's mind:

> *Oh Danny boy, the pipes, the pipes are calling*
> *From glen to glen and down the mountain side*
> *The Summer's gone and all the roses dying*
> *'Tis you, 'tis you must go and I must bide*

He remembered. A year ago—he'd not been in England long and was still with the Argyll and Sutherland Highlanders—he'd been on furlough and staying with the White family in Edinburgh. Like many of the locals throughout Britain, the Whites welcomed servicemen into their homes, giving them a break from military life. Ewen remembered standing beside the piano, listing to Nan, the mom, playing "Danny Boy" and several other favourites. He had left a few personal things with the Whites, as a lot of soldiers did, to be sent back to Canada if he was killed. Would he get to hear Nan play "Danny Boy" again? Or would she be packing his things and mailing them back to Saskatchewan?

The music stopped and Woods tucked his harmonica in his left breast pocket. From his kit he pulled out paper and pen and began to write.

When he'd finished, he called Ewen over. "Morrison, sorry about before. I was out of line." Ewen was grateful and surprised. He could only guess at how much it was costing Woods to apologize.

"Can you read this?" Woods handed him a thin sheet of paper. "It's a letter to Nicole, Archer's wife."

Ewen nodded and sat down to read.

> *Dear Nicole,*
>
> *I'm sure by now you've received the telegram. I know there is nothing I can say to make you feel better. But I want you to know how much Les cheered up me and the boys. Although I thought he wore rose-coloured glasses all the time, the fact that he chose to see the good in everything was special. He was always the life of the party and cared about his mates.*
>
> *When she gets older, tell little Dottie that her father fought hard to make the world a better place for her to grow up in.*
>
> *I'll miss him too.*
>
> *Be seeing you,*
>
> *Connor Woods*

"It's perfect, Woods," Ewen said. He handed the letter back.

The regiment was marching eastward, passing burned-out tanks and vehicles, and the dead soldiers, dead horses, dead cows that lay everywhere. Bulldozers were clearing through mechanical, human and animal remains to allow the Royal Hamilton, the Essex Scottish and all the others in the Brigade to move forward. They weren't defending positions anymore – they were advancing, pursuing a retreating enemy.

The sun—if it had been shining—would have been on their backs as 17 Platoon walked along a county road. A shout from the rear—"Heads up!"—was followed by the sound of a deep rumbling engine. Startled, the men moved off the road and drew their weapons. Ewen and the others fired without effect at the German amphibious tank that rumbled past them, going at its top speed, heading east towards home. Two hours later, four more enemy tanks rolled through their lines, oblivious to their small arms fire, on the road back to Germany. "Bloody hell," said O'Malley. "We need eyes in the back of our heads!"

The Germans had fallen back to the Seine River, near Rouen, but the bridges over the river were blown. Reggie and Ewen, on forward night patrol, saw them cutting trees to make rafts and strapping barrels together—anything to cross the river and escape the advancing Allied armies.

As well as destroying bridges to slow down their enemies, the Germans left other deadly traps. Fraser, the mechanic, reported that a C-Coy troop carrier had run over a mine. "Twelve guys on board, all injured. They're lucky no one copped it."

"The CO ordered pioneers forward, to clear the road and verges. Lieutenant says it's done, and in record time too. We're good to go," Reggie explained to the platoon. They went, but the going did not go as planned. Arriving at a junction, and consulting a map, the major ordered the column to turn left. They'd only gone a half-mile down the road when they came up against roadblocks—felled trees and deep trenches—that made the route impassable for the vehicles. "Another fucking screw-up," grumbled Woods, as they were ordered to withdraw back to Elbeuf. Reggie, Cowboy and Ewen were sent out to find troops who'd got lost, struggling with the inaccurate maps they'd been given to work their way back.

The next day orders came down that they were to attack enemy positions in the Fôret de la Londe. At dawn. D-Coy, untrained in forest fighting, walked into a firestorm: heavy machine-gun fire and mortars. In the dense woods, tree branches fell like deadly javelins, causing horrific danger to the already vulnerable soldiers on the ground.

"Fall back, fall back" Lieutenant Wilkinson shouted. Smoke swirled through the trees, covering their retreat.

Later, Reggie told them what he'd learned. "After the CO ordered the attack, battalion HQ told him that the area was full of Jerrys. They tried to warn us, to call us back, the lieutenant said."

"Didn't try very hard, did they?" said Woods.

"Oh, they tried. But with our radio broken, the message didn't get through."

"Snafu."

Officers and men were dead. More officers and men were missing. Ewen was part of a patrol sent out to find them.

August 29, 1944
Elbeuf
1400 — During the day the men had no food and heavy rain caused considerable inconvenience.

Gazing out from the back of the canvas-covered troop truck, a welcome respite from marching, Ewen, unshaven and with red-rimmed eyes, was utterly exhausted. He saw green fields. Live cows. Crops ready to be harvested. And some villages virtually untouched by bombing. The sight of an intact apple orchard took him back to the last orchard they bivouacked in. He wondered how that rabbit was managing.

A breeze blew through the back of the truck. Ewen closed his eyes and breathed in the clean air that smelled of earth, a smell like home. He opened his eyes and looked up to see a hawk circling slowly, looking for prey. *He can see the whole picture from up there. It's as though he's reminding me how to observe.*

If not for the fleas and lice, Ewen might actually have relaxed.

The truck came to a halt and he came back to the present. The regiment was entering Rouen, on the north side of the River Seine. The entire population seemed to be burning with liberation fever and the convoy could only inch its way through the crowd.

The reception was astonishing. Church bells rang and people lined the road, mile after mile. The Rileys rode past grateful people and bombed-out buildings. Locals climbed aboard their vehicles, kissing and embracing their liberators. They cheered. They wept. They danced. They laughed as they hadn't laughed for five years.

The battle-shabby and exhausted soldiers loved every moment. Every kiss was impossible to resist. Over and over again, glasses of amber-coloured Calvados were shoved in their hands as the convoy crawled through town.

"This is the good stuff!" Cowboy yelled.

Flowers and more flowers were thrown at their vehicles. French tricoloured flags flew from balconies. Elderly hands and children's hands reached out to touch and thank them.

Ewen thought: this is why we're here, to help people. Over the past two months, just trying to stay alive, it was something he'd forgotten.

The column, once through town, picked up speed, leaving behind the calls of *"Merci, Canadiens!"*

Cowboy said, "We're just freewheeling now, boys!"

Ben Wilson, 17 Platoon's latest new recruit, sat across from Reggie playing the spoons.

"How long have you been here, Corporal Johnson?" Ben asked.

"You mean France?"

"Yes."

"Since July 6. D-day plus thirty."

Ben's round, smooth face glowed. Our new Blue Patch boy, thought Ewen. *Everything about him is so young.*

His head resting against the canvas, Ewen calculated. *That's fifty-seven days. I've made it fifty-seven days.* What frightened him was how good he was getting at his job. How the carnage, the explosions, the smells, death . . . how it was all becoming routine. Not so long ago, on the farm, he'd been running around barefoot with his brothers. He could barely remember the boy he'd been. Reggie's voice brought him back to France.

"Where'd you learn to play the spoons?" Reggie asked Ben.

"Oh, my ol' man loves Bluegrass. I couldn't bring my banjo, so I brought my spoons."

Ben had joined them the day before. Reggie eyed the new arrival closely. He came right out and asked, "Are you underage?"

"Yes, but I'll be eighteen in a couple of weeks, September 17." Ewen thought of Reggie's brother, Frank. He'd enlisted underage too. Ewen's older brother, Finlay, was in the navy and, last he'd heard, was somewhere in the Atlantic. His younger brother, Allan, was training to be a paratrooper. Ewen hoped the war would be over before he was sent over.

Cowboy asked, "How'd you pull that off?"

"I had a brother, born a year before me. He died when he was four months old, but he was christened, so I took his birth certificate to enlist."

"So, Ben isn't your real name?" Woods asked.

"No, it's Cam, but I'm used to Ben now."

"What about your parents? Didn't they figure it out?" asked Reggie.

"No. Well, maybe. But they didn't really notice me much anyway. They had more important things to deal with," Ben said.

Cowboy asked, "Why'd you join up?"

"I didn't want to miss my chance to get over here and do my bit. I figured you old guys needed a little help."

Reggie leaned forward, "Would you like some advice?"

"Sure."

"You got to put down those spoons and start looking. You need to see. You need to watch. All the time. Observe, that's your word of the day. What did the last signpost read?"

"No idea."

"And always listen. When you hear a weapon cocking, how many clicks? That will tell you if it's a Jerry weapon or a friendly," Reggie said.

Woods chimed in. "In hand-to-hand combat, forget fair play. Gouge his eyes, slam him in the balls, head butt, forget the rules. Do what you have to do to stay alive . . . aim to kill."

Ben nodded, his eyes wide.

"Infantrymen are always on the ground," Reggie continued. "It's good being connected to the land. You have to learn to be at home on the land. If you're at home in it, you can fight in it.

"You did basic training, didn't you? Well, out here you have to know your weapons even better than they told you. Know your knife is sharp. Know your rifle's clean. They're parts of you. There's no separation. You can't get lazy—ever. I don't rest until I've cleaned and checked my weapons, whatever situation I'm in."

Ewen could see that Ben was eager, taking it all in. It reminded him of four months ago—was that all it'd been?—when he'd been the new guy, grateful for Reggie's experience. He passed Ben a cigarette. "Here, give this to the Corporal."

Ben looked confused but passed it over. "Thanks," said Reggie, pocketing it.

"What else?" Ben asked, not wanting the lesson to stop.

"Learn to recognize the sounds of the different incoming shells, so you know what to expect on impact," Reggie said. "And always keep your eyes open. Keep an eye out for the next hole in the ground for cover. And if you're in a position where you see a group of Jerrys together, watch carefully. Look at their uniforms, look for their insignia. If you can't see it or they've removed them, look for the one who's gesturing or pointing, he'll be the senior man there, the officer. He's who you take out first.

"Your instinct to survive will decide if you're going to live or you're going to die. You have to make decisions in a split second that could determine your fate or the life of the guy next to you. You have to learn to drop hesitation and go with your gut."

Ewen said, "We've all had to learn how to survive. In the chaos, you'll have to make decisions in the moment. Just do, there's no time to think."

Ben nodded. "Thank you, sir."

"I'm not 'sir.' I'm corporal. You know that, don't you?" said Reggie.

"Yes, sir." They all laughed.

The truck travelled, gears grinding, through the French countryside.

At 1730 the convoy stopped for the night. They didn't have any rations left so the cookers got called up to churn out an evening meal for 587 battle-weary Rileys.

After dinner, when they were having a smoke, Ben asked Ewen, "The corporal—he's a Red Indian, isn't he?"

"Yeah, he is."

"Guess that it explains it, then."

It works both ways, Ewen realized. Assumptions could be positive or negative. Ben was like Lieutenant Wilkinson, who seemed to think that Reggie had mysterious tracking skills. Like the officer back in England who set Reggie up for scout training.

Cowboy came over, took out his cigarettes and offered one to Ben. The boy hesitated, then took one. Cowboy lit it for him.

In seconds he was coughing his guts out.

"I don't really smoke," Ben confessed. "Don't drink either."

"You will, you will," said Woods. "Bets anyone?"

September 1, 1944
Biville
1200 — We reached our objective. The bn deployed forming a bn fortress. A meal was prepared well supplemented by fresh eggs and butter which had been hidden from the Germans by the local civilians in eager expectation of our coming.

Royal Hamilton Light Infantry War Diary
September 1, 1944
Bouteilles
1330 — The coln left BIVILLE and proceeded
without a break to a small town outside DIEPPE,
BOUTEILLES. Here we caught the first glimpse of
the English channel and occasional glimpses of
the outskirts of DIEPPE.

Wooden stakes, about fifteen feet high, stood like stripped tree trunks in the fields on either side of the road to Dieppe. "What are those poles?" Ben asked Reggie.

"Rommel's asparagus. Jerry's way of trying to stop our paratroopers," Reggie explained as they rumbled along.

Suddenly, their carrier stopped, and Reggie jumped down onto the dusty road. The column of vehicles in front was at a standstill.

"What's going on?"

"Big ditches—two of them across the road," a man shouted back.

The Canadians didn't have to wait long; a group of Maquis arrived and boarded them over. The column rolled forward.

Dieppe was still out of bounds—the recce patrols had reported mines and booby traps, so D-Coy set up camp in an orchard. Ewen pounded in a tent stake, careful not to hit his fingers.

"I'm dreaming of a shave and some dry socks," Ewen said.

"Yes, I'd prefer a bath instead of washing my feet in my helmet," Reggie said. "Set up that tent faster, Morrison. You're going to be a lance corporal."

"What? I'm getting a promotion? Does that mean I get a bath and clean clothes?" Ewen said, scratching his back. "I can't take the lice or the fleas anymore . . . I don't know if I have any skin left." A medic had given him some calamine lotion, which helped some. "Let's hope there's a nearby stream and enough gasoline to run a water heater, so the mobile bath can get set up."

Woods sat on the grass, unpacking his kit. He asked, "Hasn't anyone ever thought of a summer uniform? You'd think someone could have come up with something cooler. This wool is damned horrible in the heat and it's itchy, then it takes forever to dry when it gets wet. Even with a handsome face like mine, it's going to be tough to impress the ladies with my French looking like this."

"Hey, guys! Come look at this," Ben shouted. He waved the rest of the platoon over to a flat bit of land beyond the edge of the orchard. He was crouched next to a concrete pillbox, with his hand on something hidden in the grass.

"It looks like an old cannon," said Cowboy. "Hasn't been in action for a long time. Look, it's been spiked." He pointed to what looked like a bolt head.

Reggie stood next to a deep, round pit. "This is one of Jerry's mortar pits. There's more. There. And there." The ground around them was dotted with abandoned sites for the enemy's heavy artillery. "This is where they would have fired on our guys trying to take Dieppe." Reggie shook his head and looked to the sea.

The men stood silently. Morgan, who'd transferred in from B-Coy, said, "That was a fucking disaster, that was. Too many good men died."

"Where you there, Corporal Johnson?" asked Ben.

"No. I was in hospital with a cracked rib. But I knew men who were, and who died here."

It was Morgan who told Ben the story of August 1942. How six thousand men—almost all Canadians—had sailed across the English Channel on the night of the 18th on a mission to destroy the enemy infrastructure around and in Dieppe. "We were a test run for future invasions. We were supposed to strike the fear of God in Jerry and boost morale for the Allies. Instead, the Germans found out we were coming and were waiting for us."

They landed on the beach at 0500 and were mowed down in their hundreds by mortars, artillery and machine-gun fire. Six hours later, the commanders called the retreat, leaving behind more than nine hundred dead and almost two thousand taken prisoner.

"And now we're back." He stubbed out his cigarette in the grass.

Ewen got his bath. When the water hit his back, he winced in pain, but the feeling of being clean, at last, provided some relief.

"How are you doing, Ewen?" Reggie asked as the two men shared a smoke after one of the best meals they'd had in weeks.

"Okay, I guess. You?"

"I'm just remembering. If it hadn't been for the accident, I would have been here. It could have been me killed by a shell from that pillbox over there. Instead it was Joseph."

"Joseph?"

"A friend of mine. He was Haudenosaunee too. That's People of the Long House. We didn't know each other before, but we met when he joined the Rileys. He volunteered, like me."

"He was here—at Dieppe?"

"Yeah. He's still here. Or maybe he isn't."

"What do you mean?"

"I've heard there's a cemetery not far from here. Where the people who died in '42 are buried. I think I'm going to go take a look."

Ewen hesitated, unsure. "Would you like me to come with you?"

"Yeah, Morrison. That would be good."

The glow of the September sun, sinking towards the horizon, cast a warm light over the rows and rows of numbered crosses. The grass between them was short and well-tended, the markings on the crosses neat and legible—someone had been caring for this place. The dead had been honoured, the fallen Canadians respected.

Reggie and Ewen were not alone. Other officers and men were walking along the narrow grass paths that separated the rows of markers, talking quietly or standing silently in front of a cross. An officer, smoking a pipe, approached them. "If they wrote a book about this place, it would be one of the greatest in the world. It is a monument to the spirit of French resistance. It is a monument to us." And then he strolled away.

"I was sad, Ewen," Reggie said, looking around the cemetery. "But when I look at this sacred place, if Joseph is here somewhere, he's being honoured." He put his hand on Ewen's shoulder. "Let's go back now."

September 1, 1944
Dieppe
1830 — It was hard to discover the feelings and emotions of the men in the bn who had lived through that eight hours of hell on the beaches, but it was apparent from the looks and expressions on their faces that they were enjoying the fulfillment of a desire that could only be satisfied by the capture of DIEPPE and captured by their Regiment alone.

Royal Hamilton Light Infantry War Diary
September 2, 1944
Dieppe
1700 — Dieppe was placed in bounds. Parties were organized and were guided by personnel who had fought in Dieppe, down to the beaches where they eagerly swarmed over the German defences, which now lay charred and in ruins, smashed by their own demolitions and broken by Allied bombings.

Reggie and Ewen sat on green grass; a novelty they no longer took for granted. Their gear lay scattered on the ground in the afternoon sunshine, as they'd spent the day mending, cleaning and repacking their kit. Morrison, usually an organized man, was content to leave the clutter for the moment.

Nearby, Wilson and Woods were jamming, Connor on the harmonica and Ben on his spoons. They were attempting a rendition of "Roll Out the Barrel."

"I got a letter from Rose," Reggie said. He put the letter into his breast pocket and leaned against a tree.

"She's left Bayeux. She's at a field hospital now. Just a bunch of tents in an apple orchard. She said the first day Caen was taken, casualties went straight from the front line to the hospital instead of going through the Advanced Dressing and Casualty Clearing stations. When she saw the wounded arrive in their mud-caked bloody uniforms, she said it was merciful they were on morphine, especially if they've had emergency amputations."

"Those nurses and doctors have it tough in a different way, I guess," said Ewen.

"Yeah, they do. But she's still holding me to a dance in Paris," Reggie said.

Ewen said nothing.

"Sometimes I think I should break it off with her. I could die any day and I don't want her living in hope. She's worrying too much about me."

Ewen hated it when anyone, especially a friend, talked about what might happen to them. He wanted to change the mood—finally, they'd had a break. "Yes, but you might be giving her something to hope for. She's got that dance to look forward to."

"You get any mail, Ewen?"

"No." He picked up his battered novel.

Reggie took out a notebook, wrote something on a blank page, then ripped it out. He nudged Ewen.

"This is my mother's address. Don't argue, just take it."

Ewen knew not to argue with the corporal. He took the piece of paper, folded it and tucked it at the back of his novel.

"You never really told me much about your mom," Reggie said. "What happened?"

"It was February '34. Ten years ago now. After she gave birth to my little sister she died of hemorrhaging. We knew she was going to die that night. I tried to stay awake. All night long, I sat on the floor in her room, I told her I would stay with her. But I fell asleep and she was gone when I woke up. I let her down."

"You were eleven, Ewen. How could you let her down?"

"I wanted to be there for her, but I fell asleep."

"Well, with all the luck you've had since Juno, she's probably keeping an eye on you now."

"Maybe."

"If I don't make it, Ewen, I'd like you to visit my mother. She'd like you."

"I won't need to visit her, Reggie," Ewen said. "End of discussion. Besides, the Jerrys are retreating, so many are surrendering. Paris has been liberated and soon you'll be going for your dance with Rose. It's got to be over soon, don't you think?"

"Rumours are we'll be home for Christmas. I'd sure like to believe the worst is over."

Ben and Woods switched songs. This time they practised "It's a Long Way to Tipperary."

"Woods is a strange guy. He likes music and learning things French. Then he can go wild, almost seems like he enjoys killing. Especially after Archer got it. I don't get him. And I'm afraid he might do something crazy one day and get us all killed."

"Yeah. I know he resents the hell out of me. Never did like me. Not since the first day we met in England. Every time I have to give an order, I swear I can hear his teeth grind. But if he ever hated me as much as he hates Germans, I'd be a dead man."

"You remember that Jerry from Manitoba?" Ewen asked. "That made me think. There was a German family who had a farm near Saltcoats. When we call these Germans we're fighting the Hun or Jerrys, it's like they're not real people anymore. They're just the enemy, with no name. When I've had to look at their faces, when we do burial duty . . . They're someone's son, or father, or brother. Those people in Rouen? Celebrating their freedom, cheering us? That made me okay with being here. But I'm not going to hate, not the way Woods does."

"That's good, Ewen. Being like Woods is dangerous, especially out here. When he gets angry, he stops thinking, he stops looking. I wish I could make him see that, but I can't. I'm the last person he'd take advice from."

The night was one for celebrations and Reggie went to find some friends in the Royal Regiment. Ewen headed down to the beach with Morgan and some other men who'd been there in '42.

He noticed a soldier from the Queen's Own Cameron Highlanders standing alone, staring at the sea. They caught each other's eye. Ewen nodded.

"It was a hell of a day," the soldier said.

"You were here?" Ewen asked. The man looked like he wanted to talk. Ewen was ready to listen.

"Yes. We set sail from Newhaven late Monday afternoon. In the wee hours of the morning, the motor stalled on our landing craft. We had to transfer to a spare boat, which made us late for the party.

"When we got to the shore, we had forty yards to run to a stone-wall breaker. Why I wasn't hit, I'll never know. We went over the wall into the village of Pourville and proceeded up a country road. Moving inland, we passed by a few dead German soldiers. They were tied with a rope around their throat and with their thumbs behind their backs. They'd been shot in the back. They were supposed to be taken back to the boats as prisoners; some idiot on our side shot them. We got to a short embankment—there was a hedge on top—then we were pinned down by machine-gun fire for two, three hours.

"One of my friends was hit. I bandaged his arm while we were pinned down. Then the hand of another guy who had also been hit. One of our men was wounded severely and two of my good buddies were ordered to take him back to the beach. They used a house door as a stretcher. My buddies, they were killed, but the wounded guy, he got back to England.

"Seemed like hours later, we were ordered back to the beach for the trip home. Alas, no boats. Then we realized the situation we were in . . . " He stopped, staring out at the water, moonlight shimmering over the gentle waves.

Ewen put out his hand. "Ewen."

The Queen's Own Cameron Highlander shook it, "I'm Don." Without another word, he turned toward the town.

Ewen faced the English Channel. He looked out at the waves rolling in and out and in and out. He thought back to a couple of months ago when they'd departed from Newhaven—a hundred miles across the water—for Juno. He thought of the piece of paper with Reggie's mom's address. He picked up a stone and rolled it around in his hands.

Ewen stretched out on the rocks. The itch on his back felt a little better. The residual warmth in the stones pressing against his tired muscles actually felt good. He closed his eyes and listened to the seagulls and the wind. He dozed off and then woke suddenly, panicked. He reached instinctively for his rifle, but once again relaxed when he realized where he was.

After a while, he stood up and pocketed the stone. He'd add it to his collection: feathers from Aldershot and Newhaven; the shell from Juno.

The seagulls accompanied him along the cobbled street heading from the beach and into town. Ahead, he recognized a few soldiers from A-Coy.

"Hey, Morrison, come with us! Let's forget the war for an evening. I'm going to get drunk and then I'm going to drink some more."

"I'm in," Ewen said. They found a café; the owner, standing in the door, saw their shoulder patches and shouted in heavily-accented English, "Come in, come in!"

"Welcome, welcome. Behind the back of the Bosch, I said, 'The soldiers with *les pièces bleues*, they will be back.' And here you are at last!"

He brought out his best bottles of cognac, buried for the past five years, and bottle after bottle, glass after glass, he poured.

> 2000 — A dance was held in the town hall, the
> Maison de la Fete, for the officers of the 4th
> Bde . . . One could not help but notice the
> strange mixture on the faces of personnel who
> had visited the town previously. Some were gay,
> some were lost in reverie, but all enjoyed the
> hospitality of the French people. DIEPPE was
> avenged and this celebration was a fitting close
> to the agonized scenes of two years ago.

Royal Hamilton Light Infantry War Diary
September 3, 1944
Dieppe
1100 — A memorial service was held in honour of
the heroes of 1942 at the cemetery of the Canadian
soldiers. It was attended by personnel in the BDE
who had returned from the assault on DIEPPE. As
the evening before was celebrated with merriment,
this morning was spent in reverence and silence
for those who had fallen.

The rehearsal for the parade was held in the morning, all regiments drilled for the march-past through Dieppe planned for the afternoon. Ewen knew this was going to be very different from any other parade he and the Rileys had ever marched in.

At 1300, Ewen, placed on the outside left, stood listening for the "Forward, march" command. He looked straight ahead.

"This is nuts," he whispered to Cowboy. "We've got to be a mile from town and I can hear the crowd. I can't even hear the bagpipers."

"That's not a bad thing, Morrison," Cowboy whispered back. They laughed.

"Five years to the day that Great Britain declared war on Germany," said Ewen. "You were twelve years old, kid," he added, looking over at Ben.

"Yes, I guess I was. Can't believe I'm here now."

Fifteen thousand men, all the units of the 2nd Canadian Division, were lined up six abreast, ready to march past the town's mayor, officers, their Commander-in-Chief, Lieutenant-General Crerar, and thousands of French citizens.

As they entered the town, flowers cascaded over the troops from the balconies above. Men, women and children lined both sides of the route, cheering and waving. For the past five years, the citizens had been forced out of their homes to watch their occupiers march;

now they were free to celebrate their liberators. Euphoria rose from the crowds and enveloped the Canadians.

The soldiers' steady, rhythmic march came to a brief halt. A young boy broke away from his mother and darted onto the cobbled pavement. He tugged Ewen's pant leg. Ewen's blue eyes looked down into a pair of brown ones.

They boy held up a ripe pear in his hand and offered it up to Ewen. *"Pour vous, monsieur. Maman et moi, nous vous remercions. Je suis Guy!"*

Ewen was speechless. He broke ranks and got down on one knee. The lad threw his arms around his neck and hugged him tight. Ewen hugged back, his throat swollen. It took everything in him not to cry like a baby.

"Forward, march" came the command.

Ewen gave the lad one last hug, took the pear and stood up. This was a moment he wanted to remember, every detail—the boy's smile, his eyes, his worn but polished shoes. One green sock stopped just below his knee and the other had fallen down around his skinny ankle. A faded blue shirt was neatly tucked into a pair of homemade brown shorts.

Ewen wanted to hold on to the innocence. After all the killing, here was life.

The boy grabbed Ewen's hand and held it tightly, running to keep up to the marching men until a young woman, also with dark eyes, came out of the crowd to reclaim her son.

"Merci, merci," Guy shouted.

"Merci, merci," Ewen replied.

The following day the convoy left Dieppe with a great sense of both satisfaction and purpose. Loaded up, they headed out at noon. Their route went northeast, following the coastline before heading inland to Abbeville. Through the back of their carrier, Ewen saw the ruins of a castle beyond a stone wall that lined the road. They rolled past abandoned defence positions and battered signs with skull and crossbones that warned "*Achtung Minen!*"

When they reached the Canal de la Somme, Ewen thought of his Uncle Ewen, his namesake. Another soldier in another war. Pte Ewen Morrison, 255999 of the 12th Company Machine Gun Corps. Killed in action on November 13, 1917, at Passchendaele. Twenty-seven years ago in the Great War, the war to end all wars.

He thought of the official letter his grandmother had read to him: "Your son, having no known grave, is commemorated, by name, on the Menin Gate Memorial, Ypres, Belgium."

I wonder what he would think of this. Another world at war in just over twenty years.

From there they drove onto Forêt Domaniale de Crécy and to Bois de Verton. They travelled all night through drizzling rain, resulting in poor visibility which slowed the convoy down considerably. More abandoned German camps with empty pillboxes, mines, concrete placements and weapon slit trenches appeared through the mist.

"Look at that," said O'Malley, pointing to a tarnished tuba half buried in mud. "They left their marching band behind!"

The Blue Patch boys, along with the rest of Europe, thought that quite possibly the war would be over soon—Paris was liberated, the Allies were sweeping across France and into Belgium, the Germans were on the run.

"Do you really think we'll be home by Christmas, Corporal?" Ben asked.

"I don't like to predict the future. We'll see," Reggie answered.

"Even if Jerry is on the run, he's still a dangerous son of a bitch," Woods said. "Who really knows what to believe? Us guys out here are the last to know anything."

"I don't want to sound negative," added Cowboy, "But we're still a long way from Berlin."

"Who's in the pool that says we'll be home by Christmas?"

shouted Woods. He got out his notebook. "Come on, boys, ante up!"

"We always seem to be betting and giving you money, Woods. Is anyone ever going to win any of these pools and see some cash?" O'Malley asked.

"What do you think pays for all our drinks?" Woods replied.

RHLI News Bulletin, Vol. 1, No. 40
FRANCE
American patrols are in action along the MOSELLE RIVER and are approaching the town of METZ about eleven miles from the German frontier. Events are moving so quickly that correspondents are having a hard time keeping in the picture with the news but it is definitely known that the Belgium frontier has been crossed.

PART THREE

BELGIUM
SEPTEMBER – OCTOBER 1944

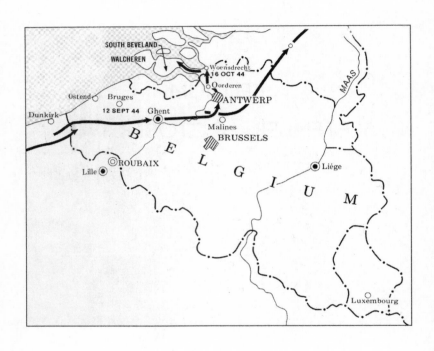

SOUTH BEVELAND
WALCHEREN

Woensdrecht
16 OCT 44

Oorderen

ANTWERP

Ostend   Bruges

12 SEPT 44   Ghent

Dunkirk

B E L   Malines

BRUSSELS

L   G   I

U   M

Lille   ROUBAIX

Liége

MAAS

Luxembourg

Royal Hamilton Light Infantry War Diary
September 11, 1944
Varssenaere
1530 — The bn moved off via OUDENBERG, 7097,
WESTKERKE, 7095, JABBEKE, 7597 sheet 30 1/50000,
to bn conc area. In every town and village along
the route the Belgian people gave us a tremendous
welcome. Every house displayed the Belgian flag and
flowers, fruit and kisses were thrown in abundance.

Every move forward on the road to the Belgian border seemed to take place at night, and always in rain—pouring, heavy, intermittent or drizzling. It was impossible to dry anything out, even when sheltering in old stone buildings along the route. The mechanics cursed as they worked to keep the vehicles operational. Only the fresh vegetables and eggs offered by the locals brightened the gloom; Ewen cooked up omelettes with mushrooms and onions for the platoon as more rain fell beyond the open barn doors. "Too bad MacLeod's not around. Not very pretty, Morrison," said O'Malley, shoving a forkful into his mouth. "But sure tastes good."

More reinforcements had arrived just when they reached Ostend, and MacDonald ("Don. No jokes, it's old") and Marks ("Jim. No, not a sniper") joined 17 Platoon. Ben was still the youngest, the kid. They'd all kept quiet about him being underage.

The rain let up long enough for them to clear the harbour. D-Coy was assigned the task of going through the beach area, which turned out to be a treasure trove of ammunition, food and discarded equipment. Most of the men pocketed items as souvenirs. "Still no Nazi flag, guys," said Woods. "Pool's still on."

"See that out there, Ben?" Reggie pointed to two half-sunken ships in the distance. "Those boats are filled with concrete. Jerry's way to block the harbour."

It was Reggie who discovered the entrance to a tunnel in the

103

dunes, which lead to an amazing network beneath the sand. He led Ben, Ewen and Cowboy on an exploration for more booty left behind by the Germans. In a concrete pillbox just off the promenade, Cowboy came across a file of papers, which he handed over to Reggie. "Do you think this might be important?"

"Yeah," the corporal said, scanning a couple of the documents. "It's all in German, but there's a lot of map coordinates and numbers. I'll get this to the IO ASAP." The lieutenant would tell Reggie later that Cowboy's find had been the complete records of the German defences of Ostend.

They'd moved out of the coastal city the next day and were now camped a mile and a half south of Bruges, where they'd been ordered to relieve the 4th Canadian Armoured Division. They'd been told the city was still in the hands of the Germans, a lot of them.

Lieutenant Wilkinson called the platoon together. "A civilian informant has just told HQ that the Germans have left. The major needs that confirmed. Johnson, Morrison and new guy— Wilson—you need to join 16 Platoon for a recce."

Ewen was worried. This was a day mission, and with men he didn't know. He looked at Reggie, who was looking at Ben. *Another untrained scout.* The corporal took the kid to one side and spoke to him quietly. Ewen knew that whatever Reggie was telling the boy, it would help keep him alive.

On patrol, they spread out and advanced cautiously, moving from cover to cover to avoid any Germans in the area. Their goal was intelligence, not clearing. By the time they'd reached their lookout point, a railway bridge about half a mile from the city, they'd encountered no enemy.

Ewen looked out at the beautiful old town. *It's like a castle city, surrounded by a moat.* Then Reggie was at his side—he hadn't heard him at all. Johnson said nothing, just pointed towards the rooftops.

Ewen looked again, and then he saw the black, yellow and red Belgian flag flying from a number of buildings. He nodded at Reggie. *Understood.* They reported back to the major, who radioed battalion HQ. The civilian's information had been correct. Bruges was clear. The German occupiers were gone.

Two companies were ordered in to set up positions on the bridges that crossed the canals to clear the mines and roadblocks the Germans had left at the entrances to Bruges. Jerry had also blown a number of the bridges, but a demolition platoon constructed a sturdy replacement from telegraph poles, secure enough to support the weight of troop carriers and jeeps. The Rileys stood at the ready as their CO had the honour of driving the first Allied vehicle into the liberated city of Bruges.

The greeting they received made Rouen seem like a sedate tea party. Thousands of people poured into the streets, thronging the troops, delirious with joy. Having survived so long, it was as if the people could not bear to let their liberators leave. Hands reached up to touch the Canadians, tears rolling down the faces of men and women alike. Ben's face glowed when a pretty blonde girl blew him a double-handed kiss. *He's seeing the best of it. The good part, the reason we're here. I hope he doesn't have to see the worst.*

"Why the fuck are we here?" demanded Woods. The battalion was dug into a defensive position, spread out across an exposed area, dots on a map around Rexpoëde. The Rileys were back in France.

"Jerry's right over there! He's got a great view, looking right at us. Johnson, I might as well strip and run around naked, shouting 'Shoot me now, Helmut!'" Another shell landed nearby and all the men ducked automatically.

"Shut up, Woods. That's Bergues. We know Jerry is there, but we don't know how many and where they're holed up. Morrison and I are going out tonight with Lieutenant Baker from C-Coy.

He's asked for us. Think you can shut up enough to come along?" Ewen looked at Reggie, alarmed. *What is he thinking!* "We need someone who's not a new guy, Woods. Try to put your experience to good use and not get us killed," Reggie said.

At 2200, Reggie had changed into his moccasins, Ewen into his plimsolls. They rubbed polish over their faces and Johnson handed Woods some woollen socks.

"Put them over your boots," Ewen explained to the confused man. "They'll help you to move quietly. Don't argue—it works."

Baker, the C-Coy scout patrol lieutenant joined them. A stranger, dressed in civilian clothes but with his face darkened with what looked like soot, was at his side.

"This is Théo. He knows the area and is coming with us as a guide," Baker said.

The men shook hands. "*Étes-vous Maquis?*" asked Woods in his best Québécois-accented French.

"*Non.* I am *Witte Brigade*—White Brigade. We are the Belgian resistance," said Théo.

The five men moved silently, sometimes walking, sometimes crawling. Even Woods managing to control his blundering. They noted roads and fields that had been flooded by the Germans, marked the position of barbed wire barricades, where mines would need to be cleared. They identified the best points to place charges in the twenty-foot-high stone wall that surrounded Bergues. They observed Germans moving around a church steeple.

"Bet that's where they've got guns positioned," whispered Woods. Reggie punched him in the shoulder, put his hand to his mouth and pointed angrily with two fingers at the man.

In the early morning hours, they reported to the battalion HQ, set up at Quaedpyre. At 1200, the Rileys were ordered to attack Bergues: H-Hour, 0430. A huge petrol-fuelled fire greeted them and, unable to move forward, they were ordered to return to their positions. Twenty-four hours later, the battalion moved off, back to Belgium.

September 17, 1944
Antwerp
1600 — The bn was met by recce party who led the
coln through ANTWERP to the bn area. The RHLI
took over from the ROYAL WELSH FUS, 53 Br Inf
Div. Our role was to guard the docks and port of
ANTWERP.

Royal Hamilton Light Infantry War Diary
September 17, 1944
Antwerp
1800 — D Coy and A Coy together were established
in the area 627027 and were known as the "Lock
Force". This was the most important part of the
bn area as the locks and br which Lock Force
guarded control the water level in the whole of
the ANTWERP harbour.

"This city, it's beautiful," said Reggie, as they rode through the streets of Antwerp, which seemed untouched by the war and by the Germans who had so recently departed, retreating from the advancing Allied forces and the White Brigade resistance. The tricolour flags of Belgium hung from windows and balconies on buildings un-pockmarked by bullets. Women holding toddlers by the hand and carrying shopping bags waved at the troops. Men dressed in suits walked purposefully as if heading to important meetings. Streetcars rumbled along, carrying ordinary people, going about their ordinary business.

"Look!" Ben pointed to a shopfront. "An ice-cream parlour! Can you believe it—I'd sure love some of that."

Ewen wondered if he even remembered what ice cream tasted like.

The column turned into a square, and the view shifted suddenly.

"Bloody hell," Cowboy said. "Look at that. What's going on?"

Ten naked women were being jeered at and spat upon as a crowd paraded them down the street. Their tormentors had shaved their heads and painted swastikas on their bottoms and foreheads. They were crying, hunched over as the mob pushed and dragged them past the cafés and shops.

"We gotta do something!" Cowboy went to leap off the carrier. Reggie stood up and grabbed him. "No! You know we can't do anything. Our orders are not to interfere with the people."

Outside the centre of the city, the regiment arrived at their new position at the port—cranes, canals, wharves, locks, but no supply ships. The river, which ran north towards the North Sea, was empty of vessels. At the docks, however, the evidence of the war was everywhere: soldiers patrolled, on full alert, sheds and marine buildings showed signs of mortar attack, and walls were decorated with bullet holes.

17 Platoon was ordered to the ops centre, set up in a large shed. The major briefed them using a detailed sand table model of the harbour set up in the centre of the room. "We've got control of the port and dock area, but it's not secure. Jerry is everywhere. They've given up the city, but they are determined to prevent us from opening the port to our supply ships. You saw the river—that's the Scheldt. German forces are well established on both sides, gun batteries along the fifty-mile stretch to the sea." The major pointed to the key areas on the model.

"We're under attack here, and we must, at all costs, prevent the enemy from demolishing the locks. There's a lot of fog here, which allows them to get too close to our position. All of you men, you cannot let your guard down once. Be armed at all times, be vigilant. Any stranger could be the enemy. We need intelligence, so the CO has ordered that each platoon do recce patrols beyond our position here. Capture any German you can and bring him back for interrogation. The more we learn, the sooner we can clear them out. We need this port open. We need ammo, supplies, equipment.

"Lieutenant, get your men to their billets and report back here at 0730."

The men lined up by the streetcar tracks at the edge of the dock area and boarded a yellow trolley. "Welcome to your new troop carrier, gentlemen," said Lieutenant Wilkinson. "Don't worry about correct change—I don't think the Belgians are going to make us pay the fare." The middle-aged motorman smiled and saluted his passengers. Then he pulled the lever to shut the door and the trolley rumbled along the tracks heading back towards town.

Platoon HQ was a large, comfortable house only a few stops along the line, still some distance from the city centre. The men revelled in forgotten luxuries: beds, running hot water, electric lights, and fresh, hot food. Reggie and ten of the men, including Ewen, were stationed here. The rest of 17 Platoon was in a similar house next door.

"I've heard this is the diamond capital of the world. Maybe you'll have time to pick up a nice stone for Rose, Reggie," Ewen teased. "Stay on the trolley tomorrow and go shopping for a ring."

His friend didn't smile back. "Don't talk like that, Ewen. Don't talk about the future. Not yet."

After dinner, the men relaxed and smoked in the parlour. Ben held a cigarette to his mouth and puffed without sputtering. He had improved since his first try. He parked the smoke on the edge of an ashtray and pulled out his spoons. *Tap, rat-a-tat, tappety-tat.* He played confidently, his hand waving as the silver flashed against his thigh.

"Where'd you learn to play so well?" asked Marks, admiring the boy's skill.

"Oh, my dad played in a bluegrass band and almost every Sunday afternoon him and his work buddies from the steel foundry jammed in our basement. They played at the old hall every now and then, but mostly they just jammed for fun in our basement."

He stopped playing, and then said shyly, "It's my birthday next week. Maybe we'll get some passes and then I could get some of that ice cream. Maybe even a big slice of chocolate cake to go with it."

"Hell, kid, you'll be legal. Should we let the CO know? You want us to start calling you Cam then?" said Woods.

Everyone laughed. Ewen had noticed how Woods had taken the boy under his wing. Reggie had been supervising him, but it was Woods who spent time with him, going from jamming to drilling him in hand-to-hand combat, teasing him without mercy all the while.

"When we get that pass, I'm going to buy you your first drink,"

said Woods. "What do you all say to checking out the Grand Boule-
vard and getting this kid hammered?"

"Really, Woods, to be honest, I'd rather have chocolate cake,"
Ben said, his cheeks reddening. "Then maybe the cognac."

"We've corrupted the poor guy," Woods punched him in the
shoulder. "First smoking, now drinking. You're going to go back to
Hamilton with a bunch of bad habits, bud."

"Well, I'll risk it," said Ben. He put his head down and began
to play again. Woods pulled out his harmonica and together they
played "Pistol Packin' Mama."

Later, Tristan, their host, joined them. He sat next to Reggie and
Ewen.

"When they release you, you must come to my brother's restaurant, De Swaan. Leave your money here, everything will be, as you
say, on the house. I will give you directions."

"Thank you, sir," said Reggie. "We appreciate your hospitality."

After all they had seen that day—the lovely old buildings, the
women and children walking unafraid on the sidewalks, the damaged and dangerous harbour—Ewen was filled with questions, but
the first concerned the one sight that had disturbed him more than
any other.

"Sir, this is the first time that things around us have seemed
normal. Almost peaceful. But we saw some women today, in the
middle of town. It was like they were being paraded, but they were
naked. That seemed wrong. What was that all about?"

"Ah, yes. Since liberation, many people have been taking
revenge. The Germans who did not leave fast enough were caught
and beaten. They are prisoners now, in the zoo. It is fitting, don't
you think, that animals should be kept in cages? Collaborators,
those who welcomed the Germans and shared their beliefs, they
are in the cages now too. They betrayed their countrymen. Those
women you saw, that was their punishment for entertaining the

enemy—their shame for all to see. Many families had German soldiers and officers staying in their homes. They romanced the young girls." Tristan looked hard. "Before you came, I had five Germans living here. I had to feed and house them. I had no choice. They were not unkind to me, and I knew they just wanted to leave and go home, but it was not easy. I fought in the Great War, and to me Germans will always be the enemy. But now you are here! And I am glad of it." He shook their hands. "But, like those Germans who sat here just a few months ago, I think that you, too, just want to go home. Home to Canada and your loved ones."

That night, Ewen dreamed of the farm and moonlight and hares racing from the barns bounding across snow-covered fields. He didn't know what Reggie dreamed of.

September 18, 1944
2300 — Recce patrols were sent to OORDEREN and WILMARSDONCK and located no enemy but received reports from civs that enemy patrols had been entering both villages every day.
A recce patrol with one member of the Belgian White Bde was sent out. This patrol never returned and it is suspected that they were taken prisoner.

Royal Hamilton Light Infantry War Diary
September 20, 1944
Antwerp
2100 — The CO granted six hour passes on the basis of 7 1/2 per cent, permitting the tps to visit ANTWERP, which was apparently well stocked with ice cream, beautiful girls and beer.

Each day they crossed the border between life and death on a yellow trolley. From the comforts of their billet with Tristan, the streetcar carried them back to the war, where machine guns, mortars and snipers waited. D-Coy was badly overstretched, trying to cover more ground than they had manpower for, while the constant fog made it easy for German infiltrators to make deadly attacks on the Canadian riflemen.

"This is surreal," said Marks as they rode down towards the docks. "Don't you think it's crazy, Cowboy?"

"Cheer up. The COs giving us some passes to town. Tomorrow, I'm going to drink myself under the table, then get up and dance with any beautiful girl who'll have me."

"Okay, Morrison, Woods and me are in the lead. Cowboy, Ben and MacDonald after us. Tonight's password is 'Apple Sauce.'" Reggie pointed at the model, "We're headed for this area, over the railway tracks and past this house—it's B-Coy's HQ. We're going to ambush and capture any Germans we can find. This fog is going to make it difficult for us and easy for them. They know this area really well, we don't. Stay sharp and follow my lead."

Reggie stood quietly, watching the men prepare to move out. He went over to MacDonald and spoke quietly, pointing to his feet, then his ears. He crossed the room to a store of captured German weapons and selected a Mauser rifle. Reggie took it over to Ben, who was looking less confident than he had been recently. "Take this," he instructed the boy.

"A German weapon?" asked Ben. "Why?"

"Remember what I told you? If the Jerrys hear one of their own weapons, they won't know it's us right away. It may give you an extra few seconds. Listen for the gunfire, locate it and shoot. Don't doubt, just do it."

"Yeah, yeah, I get it," said Ben.

Woods put his hand on the kid's shoulder. "Stay close to me, Wilson. Remember what I've been teaching you about hand-to-hand combat. Fight dirty." He winked.

Woods said, "Let's get this job done boys, we got paid today. And tomorrow it's party time in Antwerp. Bet I make it there first—anybody in?"

At 2330, with blackened faces and black toques, they set out towards the railway tracks, moving through fog-shrouded streets flanked with warehouses.

As they crept forward, Ewen felt even more grateful for the skills Reggie had taught him. This was far more dangerous than what they'd experienced in France. He moved quietly, listening intently—which sounds belonged to the enemy, which were normal for the docks. At regular intervals they stopped to look, listen and learn . . . and to signal one another to creep further on.

Hours passed. The platoon had just passed the house where B-Coy was based when enemy fire exploded from the fog, followed by running grey uniforms. Shouts and machine-gun fire deafened them. Then screams. "Fall back!" Reggie yelled, "Get to the HQ."

Ewen turned and ran towards the big house. He heard another scream and more shouting—German voices rising with the English.

Looking back over his shoulder, he saw Rileys running towards him, and Reggie and Woods, dragging a slumped Ben between. "Morrison, Cowboy, keep moving, keep going!" Reggie shouted, waving them onwards with his rifle.

Ewen barged through the door, MacDonald at his side, and Cowboy right behind. Reggie and Woods cleared the threshold as other Rileys covered their retreat, firing into fog at the enemy infantrymen, moving around the building. On the other side of the wall, they could hear crashing, grunts and small arms fire—Germans and Canadians fighting hand-to-hand for their lives. Ewen stabbed a Jerry who'd crashed backwards through adjoining doors. Cowboy was wrestling with another and had managed to pin him to the floor. His knife flashed, and then he collapsed as a bullet hit him. Outside, the enemy still stalked, firing at the Canadians, pinned down in their own HQ.

In the corner, Woods was bent over Ben, who was slumped up against the wall. Sweat shone on his grey face, and blood dribbled from the side of his mouth. "The medics are coming, kid, you're going to be on your way, you little bastard. It's going to be okay."

"Did we win, Woods?" the boy choked.

"Yeah, we did. We did."

"I don't want to die."

"You won't, not on my watch."

Reggie was beside Cowboy who lay motionless on top of the dead German. He gently pulled the big man off and rolled him onto his back.

After what seemed like an eternity but was actually only minutes, they heard engines. Outside the walls, shells began to rain down on the enemy, who retreated back into the night. Smoke bombs followed, to cover the retreat of the men inside the house.

Woods slung Ben over his shoulder. Ewen went to help Reggie, who was staggering under Cowboy's weight. Somehow they made it back to their position.

Ben was dead by the time the medics arrived.

September 21, 1944
0600 — The enemy were successful in entering the pl HQ located in a large house, and bitter hand to hand fighting followed. Both sides suffered casualties.

Royal Hamilton Light Infantry War Diary
September 21, 1944
Antwerp
1400 — We received the support of a squadron of
Typhoon bombers, the target being a fort which
was strongly held by the enemy. Two direct bomb
hits were scored and the whole area thoroughly
strafed.

That night they went to town—Reggie, Ewen, Woods, MacDonald, Marks, O'Malley and the rest. Cowboy had taken a bullet in the side, lucky it missed his lung the medic said, and had been moved to the hospital.

At De Swaan, Tristan's brother made sure their glasses were never empty. They asked for chocolate cake with ice cream for their dessert.

The bars were bright, the dance music loud, the girls beautiful, the night long. Woods wouldn't make it back to Tristan's. The lieutenant wouldn't write him up.

In Tristan's parlour, Ewen sat alone—it must have been about three in the morning. He'd been the solitary passenger on the yellow trolley back to their billet. All he wanted was silence. Last night, he had killed a man. He may have killed many more, he couldn't be sure. But none were like this. He remembered the texture of Jerry's uniform in his fist, the feeling of the knife entering his body, the smell of his breath. Then he thought of all the bodies he had buried. He'd added one more.

There was a knock on the door, then Tristan entered the dim room. He was carrying a tray, with cognac and two glasses. "May I join you?" he asked. Ewen nodded.

As Tristan struggled to open the bottle, Ewen noticed for the first time the deformed fingers on his left hand. He made a move to help, but then stopped—he wanted the older man to keep his dignity.

116

He poured them each a glass, and Ewen tasted it, savouring the mellow flavour.

"At home, that's in Saskatchewan, not many people can afford booze. And certainly not stuff like this. Mostly it's homemade brew that costs twenty-five cents a bottle. At the country dances, the men hid it in the woodpile so they wouldn't be in possession in case the law dropped by. I remember the night I took my first swig. There was some huffing and spluttering, I will confess. The older guys said it would put hair on my chest. I'm still waiting."

Tristan laughed.

"Can I tell you a joke, Tristan? One from our news bulletin. They like to keep us smiling."

"Of course," the old man answered.

Will you try some of my angel cake? asked the young wife of her husband.

No thank you was the reply.

Are you afraid it isn't good enough? she asked.

No, I'm afraid I'm not good enough.

Good enough for what?

Good enough to become an angel.

"Who died last night?" asked Tristan.

"Ben Wilson, the kid. Today is his eighteenth birthday. His real name was Cam, he used his dead brother's name so he could enlist underage. Cowboy, he's in hospital. Shot in the chest."

"That is very sad, my son. Let us toast: to Ben's birthday and to Cowboy's recovery."

The two soldiers, one old, one young, smoked and drank in silence.

"This is hard," Ewen said. "This taste of normal life—it makes it so much harder to go back to that hell. I've dreamed of moments like this, just walking down a street, seeing people living ordinary lives. Sleeping in a bed again. Then I wake up and have to get on that damned trolley and do what we have to do. I've stopped counting how many of my friends have died . . . I quit. I don't want to know how many."

Ewen felt bleary-headed, and it wasn't all just drink. He looked around the tidy parlour—so homey, so comfortable. "I don't think some of the guys are going to make it back here tonight."

"Will they be in trouble?" Tristan asked.

"Oh, not much, slap on the wrist. How can they get charged with desertion for a couple of hours off when we've had three months of this hell? Besides, we're so short of men the brass needs every man jack of us."

Another sip of cognac.

"What was it like, Tristan, when the Germans were here?"

"*De Witte Brigade*, they kept our hope alive. When the Germans first came, the Resistance was small. Locals would give wrong directions to the Germans, or when they'd enter a restaurant, everyone would just get up and walk out."

"Really?"

"Yes, but the greatest difficulty was knowing who to trust. I told you about the collaborators, the ones now in the zoo? You had to be careful what you said and to whom. Best not to speak of politics. Then, the Resistance started to cut telephone wires to the airfield. Some members were caught and executed but, because Antwerp is a port, railway workers could travel freely around the country. They took great chances to pass on information—where the Germans stored gasoline and the names of the troops and where they were."

"Wow, that took guts."

"Yes, they were brave men and women, even children. There was a young woman who repaired damaged fishnets by the harbour. The Germans would bring her their life jackets to fix. She flirted with them and found out which units they served with, where they had been and where they were going. Her information made a difference. It was good for morale and it gave all of us hope.

"Under the Occupation, you know, at first, the Germans were polite and friendly. As the war continued and their rations became less and their homeland was getting bombed, they became anxious. The ordinary German soldier wants this war to be over and to go home too."

Tristan coughed and swirled the golden cognac around in his glass.

"Have you heard the word *Sippenhaft*?"

"No. What does it mean?" said Ewen.

"The Nazis put the fear into their own soldiers. If they don't follow orders the Gestapo will punish their relatives at home," explained Tristan.

"What kind of punishment?"

"They'll get sent to concentration camps or executed. One young German soldier who stayed with me, he had been a music student at university. He told me once that his commanding officer put a gun to his head and threatened to shoot him if he didn't keep fighting. If anyone of them surrenders, they'll be tried as traitors and shot . . . and so would their families back home. Their next of kin will be known as enemies to the Reich. They had to swear an oath of loyalty to Hitler so any form of defeat is a betrayal. That is how ordinary men become monsters."

"Do you think we're monsters, Tristan? I've killed. I've done things to other human beings I never imagined I could do. How can I do this? How can I feel it's okay to kill another human being?"

"I understand, and you will kill more before this war is over. But let me ask you, when you killed, what were you making a stand for?"

"To stay alive. To keep my mates alive. To help people. To free people."

"I say this to you, as one soldier to another. When you go home, and I believe you will go home, people will ask you about life here. Don't talk of the horror, don't keep that alive. Talk of the liberation and celebration. Of the times in the pub with your friends. Keep those memories, bury the rest. Don't fuel them, don't keep them alive in your heart."

"Tristan, we won't be home for Christmas, will we?"

"No. I do not think so."

September 22, 1944
1600 — The RHLI was ordered to extend its posns forward to the gen line of the canal which runs immediately SOUTH of the rlwy line, to prevent enemy infiltration into OORDEREN and WILMARSDONCK.

PART FOUR

THE NETHERLANDS
OCTOBER 1944 – FEBRUARY 1945

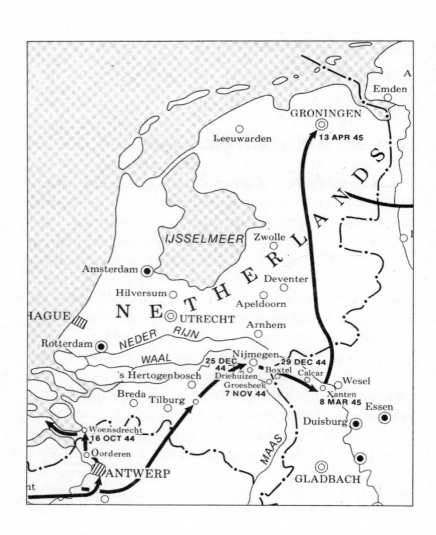

Royal Hamilton Light Infantry War Diary
October 15, 1944
MR 626186 Sheet 3 1/1000 (near Hoogerheide)
1230 — CO and party returned from air recce of
the Woensdrecht area. Coy comds brought in their
pl comds and NCOs to BnHQ to study tentative
plans for attacking, using a sand table model
constructed by the "I" sec.

Reggie and Ewen headed back to their position to brief what was left of 17 Platoon.

In the last two weeks, since leaving their position at the Antwerp docks, the battalion had moved into the Scheldt peninsula, routing out Germans and interrogating captured enemy soldiers. Civilians, with haggard faces and hungry eyes, provided information when they could. "The Germans, they have left Eeckeren. It is clear."

Mortar fire, shelling, machine guns, snipers, ambushes—Jerry was making the Canadians pay for every yard they gained and every town they took and cleared. Enemy planes flew overhead, dropping bombs and strafing the beleaguered troops. At each new position, the men dug in deep, pockets of the enemy always on their flanks, constantly counterattacking. And now the four companies of the Royal Hamilton Light Infantry had been ordered to capture the Woensdrecht heights.

"Did you see those Red Cross guys yesterday, Ewen?" Reggie said. "All the civilians have been ordered out. Old men and women pushing wheelbarrows with everything that is precious to them. Their homes destroyed. Everywhere you look there's dead horses, pigs, cows, goats. And men. I didn't think it could get worse, but it has."

"The colonel keeps asking for reinforcements, and what do they send us?" Ewen complained. "Untrained guys who breeze through Aldershot. I hear he even had to teach some of them to shoot a rifle."

"I hope he taught them how to load it, too," said Woods, who stood up as they arrived. "What's the word?"

Before either could answer, three new men turned up.

"You guys D-Coy, 17 Platoon?" asked one, in a French-Canadian accent.

"Yes, we are. I'm Johnson and this is Morrison, he's number two here. That's Woods there. Who are you?"

"Hi, I'm Claude Desroches."

"Frank Wozniak."

"Danny Castle."

Three freshly-shaved recruits stood in clean uniforms. Three grizzled veterans stood in mud-stained battle dress. All six lit up cigarettes.

"Where were you before?" asked Reggie.

"I was in the sanitary squad," said Danny.

"Me, I peeled potatoes," said Frank.

"I'm a driver, supply trucks. We're supposed to be temporary."

Ewen exchanged a look with Reggie, who said, "Okaaay. First things first. Get digging. Get your slit trench dug, over there. When you think it's deep enough, dig it another foot deeper, you'll need it. Then come join the rest of us for the briefing."

Woods opened a new pack of smokes, then pulled a face. "Bloody hell, half of them are mouldy. Everything is fucking waterlogged in this godforsaken place."

The three reinforcements looked at Woods as if he were a rabid dog about to bite, then followed Reggie's order and went to dig their slit trenches. "Do you know how to use a shovel?" Woods shouted at their departing backs.

"What the hell?" Ewen said. "They're not temporary! What is the brass thinking? Cooks and truck drivers! What's going on at home when even our sanitary squad guys are being put on the front line?"

"You know what's going on back home," snorted Woods.

"Seems like they've run out of men with the balls to do what needs to be done. So now they're conscripting guys and promising them they won't have to fight. Cowards! Guys like you and me, we can't get our leave. While pansies like that, those bloody Zombies, sit on their asses and kids with no training get thrown into combat. Whisky warriors in Ottawa—I'd like to see them out here without any training."

"Give it up, Woods. They're all we've got," said Reggie.

"Yeah, Corporal Chief?" Ewen hadn't heard Woods say that in a while. He suddenly realized how close Woods was to losing control. First Les, then Ben. Woods was hiding his fear in aggression. "The Black Watch was cut to pieces. All their company commanders are dead. It was a bloodbath. Most of their new guys were like Huey, Dewey and Louie over there. They barely made it beyond their start line. They were annihilated and we're up next."

He tried to light a cigarette, and Ewen saw a tremor in his hand. "Slogging through soggy beet fields, smoking fucking mouldy cigarettes . . . "

"Well, we've got about twelve hours to teach them what they need to know," said Ewen.

"You've got to be shittin' me. We're setting up a kindergarten," said Woods. "They'll be killed before they know it. They think they're just here temporarily? The shock of being out there will kill them before a bullet does."

Woods gave up on the cigarette and pulled out Ben's spoons, tapping them against his hand. The sky darkened. Raindrops began to fall. The wind picked up and brought Lieutenant Wilkinson with it.

"Gather round," he called. The new guys joined the rest of the platoon for the briefing. With the men surrounding him, Wilkinson proceeded to give details using maps and aerial photographs taken that afternoon. "This is our goal, Woensdrecht. It's a night attack, double axis, box formation. It's on slightly higher ground and Jerry's dug in. This is the artillery fire plan. Our support is going to lay on heavy shellfire on the enemy positions. Rate of advance will be one hundred yards every four minutes. We have to advance and hold position within twenty-five yards of where they're falling. And stay there until they stop."

"Jesus," said Morgan. "Are you telling us our bombs will be landing twenty-five yards in front of us—in the dark—and once they're finished, we charge?"

"Exactly. Then, before the Jerrys can recover, we'll be all over them. We have to get control of the railway and highway. The old man believes fire and movement and the element of surprise will determine the outcome. He says to lean in and get to our objective before Jerry has a chance to recover. Our success signal is 'Balmy Beach.' Morrison, if the wireless breaks down, you're our runner to Tac HQ to confirm we've done our job. Forming up at 0245, H-hour is 0330. Get ready."

Fucking hell, thought Ewen, when the lieutenant left.

"Don't worry Morrison, I'll have my eyes on you," said Reggie, "You just run like those jackrabbits you told me about."

The three recruits looked stunned.

Reggie said, "Listen, you rookies, in a night attack it's easy to lose your sense of direction, but just follow the fireworks, they'll go off every fifteen seconds and you'll have to grope in the dark. Now, never lose your shovel—digging in can save your life. As soon as you reach your objective, start digging in. You can bet the Jerrys will be getting ready to come back. Don't be a hero, just get this done so we can go home.

"And another thing: we're always watching and so is the enemy. Never salute out there, 'cause Jerry will see and will know which is the soldier and which is the officer. Might as well put a target on his back for the sniper." He continued to explain what he could with the time they had—which wasn't much. "You look nice now, but don't use your water to shave or keep clean, you'll be needing it to drink and fight on."

"We're going to get to see who has cast iron balls before this is over," said Woods. "I'm going to kick some ass." He left. The new guys were speechless.

October 15, 1944 – War Diary
2315 — SL reported clear and everything in order
2359 — Hot supper was served in all coys.

Royal Hamilton Light Infantry War Diary
October 16, 1944
MR 626186 Sheet 3 1/1000 (near Hoogerheide)
0330 — "H" hour. Terrific barrage opened up 200
yards forward of the startline. Over 104 guns
were used in the barrage.

Five hundred Rileys stood at the start line, five hundred yards southeast of Woensdrecht, looking towards the gentle hill. Ewen's guts twisted; he couldn't shake the feeling that he might not come back after this one. He willed his body to stop shaking. A week before it had been Thanksgiving. Reggie had told him that for his people every day was Thanksgiving, that each day they gave thanks for life and for the world around them. Ewen had started doing the same. Today he gave thanks for still being alive but couldn't help looking around. *Which of us will live to see tomorrow?*

Seconds later, explosions filled the night and Ewen's mind went blank. Artillery screeched through the sky. The glow of rising and falling tracers reflected on a generation of faces and their fixed bayonets. The assault began. The noise, deafening though it was, didn't block out the screams from down the line. Horrified, Ewen saw Allied shells exploding on their own men. They leaned in—as ordered—and followed the storm of firepower one dangerous step at a time.

The wireless worked: D-Coy reported "Balmy Beach" at 0500, and Ewen was spared a race back through the devastation to deliver the message. "Argos," "Rough Riders", "Tigers"—by 0550, all four companies reported they had taken their objectives, but they also reported that the enemy was still out there, making them feel the vulnerability of their position.

The ambush came at 1000. German paratroopers, with tanks and shells, executed a counterattack, descending on the Canadians. Chaos and madness followed. Ewen saw one platoon leader, clearly terrified, running back down the hill, his men following.

Below, he made out the colonel, who pointed his pistol at them. Ewen couldn't hear what he was shouting, but the CO's meaning was clear: *Go back! Defend your position!* They obeyed the pistol, not the man, and turned back.

In the hours that followed, desperation took over. The Germans had the upper hand. Every man brawled for his life, and savage hand-to-hand fighting ended the lives of sons, brothers, husbands and fathers.

Ewen jammed his bayonet into the gut of the German para-trooper. Their eyes met. The man's body buckled and his enemy died; a part of Ewen died with him.

Reggie yelled, "Victor Target!" and Ewen dove into a slit trench, where he huddled up and counted the seconds. Another massive concentration of shellfire, fired by their own side, plummeted down. The earth throbbed and shook; men screamed in response. Is this how I die? Our own guns blowing me up?

It stopped. Still alive, Ewen steadied himself.

He saw the Canadian tanks, now silent, pull back from the line. Overhead, wave after wave of Spitfires and Typhoons dropped tons of bombs on the enemy.

Ewen's vision blurred as he tried to read his watch. Ten o'clock, twelve hours since Jerry had hit back. *How am I still here?* He was waiting for water, food, ammunition, for someone to tell him it was safe to climb out of his slit trench. Ewen didn't know if they were winning or losing. The three new guys were dead: Huey, Dewey and Louie—he couldn't remember their names. He'd witnessed Woods get sliced in half by machine-gun fire, and Morgan blasted to smithereens by a shell—one of ours? Poor bastards. Lieutenant Wilkinson, he'd been hit too. Ewen had seen him fall, but defended his position, as he'd been trained to do. For hours he'd seen the RAP guys moving among the bodies, ducking and weaving, getting the wounded back to safety and leaving the dead where they lay.

Ewen didn't know where Reggie was, if he was still alive. Curled up in his mud hole like a rat, he wrapped his arms around himself. The relentless rain pounded down, cascading over the lip of his slit trench. *I just can't take it anymore.*

October 17, 1944

```
1740 — The battalion area was shelled and
mortared intermittently. All coys were on the
alert to prevent enemy infiltration. We did not
have enough bodies on the ground to completely
control the WOENSDRECHT feature and it was
possible for the enemy to infiltrate. The enemy
appeared to suffer very heavy casualties from
our arty fire which was used unsparingly, but he
continued to reinforce his posns.
```

Royal Hamilton Light Infantry War Diary
October 21, 1944
Woensdrecht
1315 — The RHLI were to be relieved by the
QUEENS OWN CAMERON HIGHLANDERS of 5 Bde and to
concentrate for an attack on the neck of the
SCHELDT after a twenty-four-hour rest.

Two battle-exhausted soldiers were once again sharing a slit trench, this time in a Dutch barnyard. The dead, human and animal, lay waterlogged in the killing ground around them. Reggie and Ewen had hours to wait before nightfall, when they were going to be relieved, company by company, under the cover of darkness. "It's going to be tough, Ewen," Reggie said. "All of D-Coy is going to have to move real quiet. Jerry is out there, waiting to cut us down."

Ewen started to shake again. He wasn't sure if it was cold or nerves. "The three new guys copped it, the lieutenant. Woods. He was a bastard, but he was brave—didn't get his Nazi flag, though."

"O'Malley took a bullet. I saw him dragged away on a stretcher. He might be okay," said Reggie. "MacDonald, Marks—they're gone too. 16 Platoon was overrun. They're all dead or wounded. Some might have been taken prisoner. I think we're down to about half our guys."

A stream of water broke over the top of their trench and Ewen shrieked. "It's a fucking snake, Reggie, it's a fucking snake!" He panicked and tried to crawl out. Reggie tackled him and dragged him down. A sniper's bullet glazed Ewen's helmet.

"It's just water, it's just water, there's no snake, Morrison!"

They collapsed in the mud.

Ewen heaved. Reggie put his hand on his friend's back. Reggie adjusted his legs, leaned back against the mud wall and looked up into the sky, the rain washing his face.

"If you were flying up there, Reggie, what do you think you'd see?" Ewen said, then spat.

"A whole lot of death."

Time passed. "We'd better eat," Reggie said and reached into his pack for rations.

"I can't eat this garbage anymore," said Ewen. He'd lost his appetite, and it seemed like he hadn't eaten in days. He couldn't control his shaking hands and struggled to open the tin.

"Jeez, Reggie, I can't see a damned thing."

"It's probably the flash from the artillery that's hurt your eyes. It will go away. Here, let me help you with that," said Reggie.

Ewen dropped the tin as he tried to hand it over. It disappeared into a puddle.

"Damnit," said Reggie. His hands splashed around in the water, feeling for the open tin in the dark. "Got it. But shit, Morrison, you can't eat this. Who knows what's in this water? We'll share mine."

They sat in the mud, sharing Reggie's cold stew. "The craziest thing happened yesterday," he said.

"What?"

"We were hunkered down east of the hill when two Jerrys approached us waving a Red Cross flag. A couple of teenagers, I doubt they even shave yet. They just walked into the village. They both spoke very good English, and one said, 'Hello, please don't shoot. We have four of your wounded, they're lying on the ground. Our company commander said we can't do anything for them, we don't have any transportation. Please, come and get them.'"

"That took guts. Did you trust them?" asked Ewen.

"Yes. We got an ambulance, took two medics and four stretchers. The two Jerrys showed us the way. While the medics were getting things organized, one Jerry said to me, 'Canadian, I would like to surrender, but if we don't fight to the death, our families will be killed.' He told me about his younger sister, Elsa. Ten years old. Said he was afraid for her and that he hoped we'd get to Berlin before the Russians. The poor kid. In another time we could have talked about something else. They helped us load up the wounded and we gave them cigarettes. They liked our cigarettes. Then, we shook hands, and drove off with them waving goodbye like we'd just had a Sunday visit."

Plain crazy, thought Ewen. Then, God, my feet feel bad. He hadn't taken his boots off for weeks. *I hope to hell I don't get trench foot.* He loosened his laces and rubbed his ankles. The stubs of his two left toes pulsed with pain. "What I wouldn't do to for a tub of hot water and a pair of dry socks," he said. "Yesterday, when you were hanging out with Jerry, I found a rabbit in a cage. Stuck in the cage was a note, written in English. It said, 'Please feed my rabbit. Thank you, Bart.'"

"Did you find something to feed it?" asked Reggie.

"Yeah, some of my rations. Poor thing. If it can survive our grub it will get through the war. I hope Bart and his rabbit see each other again. What are these people going to do when they return to what's left of their homes?"

"I don't know . . . how will anyone get on with their lives?" After a moment he said, "I'm breaking it off with Rose."

"Why?" asked Ewen.

"She worries about me. I worry about her. It's better to break it off now. Who knows, she might be thinking the same thing. I haven't seen her for months. She can't depend on me. Maybe when this is all over. If something happens to me, she'll get stuck mourning me and could miss out on meeting someone else."

"You're nuts! She must be quite a gal to be nursing over here, and she seems to like you a lot," said Ewen. He longed for a sweetheart, someone to write to. *After the killing I've done, who would want to be with me? I've done things I never thought I'd have to do.*

The shaking began again. "Hey, Morrison," said Reggie. "I've seen a lot of goats around here. You got any farm goat stories for me?" So Ewen told his friend about Mrs. Leslie and her trio of goats which she kept for their milk, and how those goats would get into the garden and eat the clothes off the line, climb on top of the barn and once in a while even go in the kitchen. And Mrs. Leslie would curse at them in Aberdeen Scotch and Mr. Leslie would puff on his pipe and say, 'Why don't you get rid of the buggers?' As Ewen talked, and Reggie listened and laughed, his hands lost their tremor.

At 2300 it was their turn to move. As Reggie had predicted, it took considerable time but by 0100 the takeover was complete. Behind the line, at their new battalion headquarters, they found out what this attack in the Scheldt had cost their regiment: 167 causalities, dead or wounded.

"We're the only two originals left since Juno, Morrison. Everyone else in our platoon has been killed or wounded."

Reinforcements arrived en masse, all from other divisions and none with infantry training. Jerry is fanatic, and we're throwing weak men at his guns, thought Ewen. It seemed to him that Ottawa, sending untrained troops to their death, was now the enemy too.

October 27, 1944
MR 53417 Sheet 3, 1/100000
0900 — The CO visited all coys and spoke to the men about basic principles of inf tactics, including two principles, (1) The object of inf was to close with the enemy (2) fire and movement. The reinforcement personnel were apparently ignorant of basic inf tactics. The CO explained the role of inf and how it must work to be successful.

Royal Hamilton Light Infantry War Diary
November 1, 1944
Malines, Belgium
1300 — The bn arrived at MALINES. There was some
confusion regarding the coy areas, due to the
late allocation by bde.

Ewen woke up with a massive hangover—he wasn't sure what day it was but he knew he was AWOL and he didn't care. He remembered the bath parade two days ago, and the miracle of being granted a twenty-four-hour pass to Bergen op Zoom. Was that where he was? He rolled over on his back and stretched from head to toe. A luxury. He had his battledress on, but he had taken his boots off. He looked at his watch: 0800. He was supposed to return to HQ by 2000—yesterday. Or was it the day before yesterday?

He remembered driving away from their latest position in a troop carrier with Reggie and others, guilders in their pockets and almighty relief in their hearts. He remembered arriving in the medieval town square, Dutch flags hanging from balconies, and admiring the swanky Hotel de Draak, where Canadians from many regiments were arriving for a party. They were hosting a Halloween party and it was one crazy time.

Every bar and restaurant seemed packed with Canadians. Tables were full, but chairs appeared from somewhere and everyone made room somehow for the newcomers. First, they drank beer, then they moved onto cognac. They ate a hot meal that tasted like real food. He and Reggie partied with some guys they met from the South Albertas and the Lincs, who'd just liberated the town, and none of them shared war stories. While his brain was still functioning, Ewen tried to process the transition from a muddy rathole to a sparkling clean restaurant. Then he stopped trying to process and had another drink.

Lovely ladies invited the soldiers up to the dance floor. Ewen, the Saskatchewan wallflower, danced and danced. There was one girl—he couldn't remember her face, but he did remember how good she smelled when he held her close. When the band struck up "In the Mood" he found dance steps he didn't know he had. He let it all go, pushing the fear and grief into a box and locked it shut.

At some point, he lost Reggie. He didn't care. He had new friends, lots of them, and boy, were they having a good time. He had a hazy memory of the moment when he decided he wasn't going back. Latrine duty, court martial? Or the front line? Some hard time would be just fine—anything was better than the hellhole that was the Scheldt.

But now, as hungover as he was, he knew he had to go back. But not yet. He put his head back on the pillow and fell asleep again. Fuck the war.

Ewen woke up a few hours later and made his way back to the battalion HQ near Goes. It wasn't there, and neither were the Rileys. He hitched a ride for the six-hour trip to Malines, back in Belgium, where the regiment had relocated earlier in the day.

"You're 48 hours and 59 minutes AWOL, Morrison," the D-Coy major berated him. "You're back to a private. You knew when you enlisted that the army has your ass. It decides where to send you, it owns every hour of your day and night."

Yes, thought Ewen. And I volunteered for this.

"I know you've been through hell, we all have, but it's procedure. I'll do what I can for you. The regulations say a court martial will have regard not only to the nature and degree of the offence, but also the previous character of the accused. I'll vouch for your character, but you're going to be under the very watchful eye of Sergeant Johnson. He'll decide what duty to assign you."

"Sergeant Johnson, sir? Reggie's been promoted?"

"You'll find a lot has changed since you took your little jaunt, Morrison. Dismissed."

When he located 17 Platoon's billet, not an easy task, Reggie welcomed him back ("*Private* Morrison") and gave him burial duty for three days. The new Sergeant Johnson read from the RHLI Daily Orders: *It should be remembered at all times that leave is a privilege and should be treated as such. Breaches of discipline on the part of the Canadian Military personnel on leave will be subject to severe disciplinary action.*

Ewen took his "best friend" and dug and dug. He'd heard that more than five thousand Canadian soldiers had died in the past few weeks in Belgium and the Netherlands. *I guess someone has to do the job. Might as well be me. I've done worse.* As he shovelled, he contemplated his own mortality. *Would it be so bad? Is it death I fear, or how I'll die? Maybe death isn't so bad. Am I getting used to the idea of dying? Life doesn't exist without death. The war goes on. These guys are dead, yet the war goes on. It will go on without me.*

Ewen stood, looking at the body of an unknown soldier. He looked around at the rows and rows of crosses. He thought that the dead deserved a grave, a place to rest. *Their families will never know how their loved ones spent their last moments. Or how they ended up in a hole in the ground a world away. Most likely, no one will ever visit this grave. Will someone end up digging a hole for me?*

He thought back to the family homestead, to the room where his mother lay dead on her bed when he was eleven years old. Would he let his platoon down too? He resumed shovelling and didn't stop, the work a buffer against the depression.

At the end of the third day's duty, he joined the platoon for coffee and a briefing. It was now Reggie's job to do the lecturing.

"We're rationed to seventy-five cigarettes a week and two tablets of soap per month." He snorted when he came to the instructions for preventing trench foot "A little late for us poor sods who just fought in the polders."

Ewen said, "Someone needs to let Jerry know that when I'm sitting there powdering my feet, I'm just taking care of them and am not a threat."

"And get a load of this," said Reggie. "Postal Regulations:

explosives. Experience has shown that these are being transmitted by mail, weapons which are loaded with live ammunition. Crazy, I can't believe guys are actually sending loaded weapons in the mail. It must Jerry weapons for souvenirs."

"Let's just send Jerry a bunch of bombs in the mail and get this over with," said one of the new guys. There were lots of new men in 17 Platoon, and Ewen wasn't sure he wanted to get to know their names.

November 4, 1944
2300 — A flying bomb landed in the vicinity of the railway station in MALINES and caused severe property damage. Ten civilians were known to be killed and it was estimated that several more would be found in the debris.

Royal Hamilton Light Infantry War Diary
November 5, 1944
Malines
1400 — A reinforcement draft arrived consisting
of one officer, who was recently returning from
hospital, and twenty-eight ORs, most of whom had
been wounded and were returning to the unit.

"Who are these smart-looking guys? Look at you, all dressed up. And you don't even smell. Am I in the right place?" Cowboy dumped his kit on the floor and took in the new accommodation for 17 Platoon. "Or did I die back in the hospital and this is heaven?"

"Cowboy! Welcome back! It's good to see you, fella." Ewen and Reggie jumped up and pounded the big man on the back. Reggie made the introductions to all the new platoon members, those who'd been drafted in since Cowboy'd been carried away from the Antwerp harbour on a stretcher.

"Yeah, I had to come back. They didn't think you sorry bastards could make it to Berlin without me," said Cowboy. "And here you are back in Belgium. Not making much progress, are you?"

"That's going to change. Hang on, Cowboy," said Reggie. "I've got to see these guys out."

A group of six new Rileys were heading to Brussels on a twenty-four-hour pass. Reggie read them riot act: look smart, behave politely, treat the locals with respect—pay your bar bills—and don't give your hat badge away as a souvenir to any girl you meet. After he'd shut the door behind them, the three friends caught up.

"The hospital was horrible. Guys without arms, legs, burns, way worse off than me," Cowboy told them. "The moaning and the groaning, it drove me crazy in the night. Made me think of the time the barn burned on the farm and I heard the livestock dying and couldn't do anything about it. I couldn't wait to get out of there. Had a lot of time to think, though." He looked the same, Ewen thought, but then not.

"Did I ever tell you about Kelly Yellow Eyes, Reggie? He's Indian, like you. Kelly, he was a ranch hand on our place for years. Soon as I was old enough, I rode the fall gathering with Kelly and he taught me a lot. When I was lying in that hospital, remembering the wind that blew down by the docks, thinking of that night we got ambushed, well, something he said came back to me. I'd been complaining about the wind on a high ridge we were riding along, and Kelly got mad at me. Made me dismount and look down into the ravine. Then he said, 'Let the wind wash over you, let it clean you . . . put your face into it and take a big drink of it, taste its fresh gifts. You need to make an agreement with the wind or it will push on you your whole life and beat you down.'

"Lying in that hospital bed, I thought maybe I made an agreement with the wind that night. That I wasn't going to let it beat me down."

"Wow," said Ewen. "Getting shot's turned you into a philosopher, Cowboy."

"Shut up, Morrison." Cowboy shoved him. "You know what else Kelly told me? 'That which does not kill you . . . at least didn't kill you.'" They didn't talk about the others who had died, the ones who had not made an agreement with the wind. They couldn't.

"Some guys in the hospital, not so badly banged up, like me, were real pissed at having to head straight back to the lines. They didn't give us much time to get stronger before they ordered us back here. We should have had a month's leave in England coming."

"Desperate times, Cowboy," said Reggie. "After all that's happened, we're real short of manpower. And these new guys are so green. We're glad you're here. We need you to have our backs, don't we, Ewen?"

"I've got something for you, Reggie," said Cowboy, reaching into his pocket. "You won't believe this. I was in Number Eight

Hospital in Antwerp and I just happened to meet a lovely nurse whose name is Rose."

"Rose?"

"Yes, and when she found out I was a Riley she pounded me with questions, wanting to know if I knew some guy named Reggie. I told her she was wasting her time with you, that I was a much better catch. But it seems, for some reason, she's true to you."

"Maybe she just got to know you. How is she?"

"Well, she made me promise to deliver this letter to you direct. She said to tell you that she's sorry it's so short—they don't give her much time to do anything but work—but she'll write again as soon as she can."

Later, Reggie handed the letter to Ewen to read.

"I shouldn't, Reggie, it's personal," he said, putting up his hands.

"It's okay, Ewen. Nothing in here I wouldn't want you to see. You don't get any mail, so here. So you don't forget how to read!"

Dearest Reggie –

I was so relieved to meet Ellison and hear you're doing okay. It was nice to get first-hand information and not the censored military version from the front.

Last week we were still in France. Then we received word that some of us were moving to hospitals in Brussels and Antwerp. I'm in Antwerp. After the tent hospitals in France, working in a building is so welcome.

We've got so many patients. The hospital is so crowded, everyone works day and night. Their injuries are so bad it breaks our hearts. I look into their eyes, and I can see their battle exhaustion. I can bandage and give medicine, but I can't heal the damage done to their minds.

Antwerp is getting bombed regularly with the V-1s and V-2s, but I guess it's silly for me to even mention that in comparison to your world.

I'm living in an apartment with ten other girls. Our landlady, and others on the block, are out every morning sweeping and scrubbing their front steps, even if their windows are blown out. I guess it takes their minds off things and I'm sure that it's better than living under the Occupation.

Take care, my love, and don't forget your promise: now that Paris is liberated, I expect my dance!

I miss you and pray for your safety.

Love, Rose

"That's really nice, Reggie," said Ewen, handing back the letter. He thought his friend looked sad as he folded it and put it back in his pocket.

Bn ROYAL HAMILTON LIGHT INFANTRY (OVERSEAS) Daily Orders
LETTERS OF CONDOLENCE
1. All ranks will under no circumstances pass on any infm regarding cas. This does not mean to imply that personnel are prohibited, when writing home, to mention, after infm that has officially gone fwd to next of kin, that a particular friend has become a cas.
2. The intention is that personnel will not under any circumstances, mention the unit's cas, by number or name, when there is no reason to warrant such infm going forward.
3. All ranks are cautioned that, unless cas are intimate friends or relatives, the discussion or mention of cas in correspondence should not be made.

Royal Hamilton Light Infantry War Diary
November 10, 1944
Groesbeek, the Netherlands
0630 — The I sec established an OP at MR 756533,
which commanded an excellent view of C and D Coy
areas and overlooked the extensive Reichswald
forest, where the German army had concentrated
the bulk of its war materials prior to its
assault on Holland in 1940.

In the pouring rain, the Rileys had loaded up and driven approximately 150 miles from Malines to Groesbeek, back in the Netherlands, to relieve a British Division in a sector in the Nijmegen area. For the next three months, or so they were told, while the brass planned for the final offensive into Germany to end the war, the First Canadian Army's job was to hold the line along the Maas River.

From an approximate two-mile distance, the Rileys saw German land for the first time, a forest of deciduous trees silhouetted against the winter sky. Littering the no-man's-land between their position and the Reichswald Forest lay evidence of September's Operation Market Garden—torn parachutes and shattered Waco gliders.

In October, the Red Cross had evacuated the local population and the German Army evacuated those who had been living in no-man's-land. After that, battalion intelligence assigned each house a number, logged on detailed maps; information on the enemy's comings and goings in each house was imperative. Regimental orders demanded aggressive patrols to gather intelligence and find out which German divisions they would be up against in the next operation.

Compared to the slit trenches of the past few months, "digging in" took on a new dimension. Winter had arrived and the Rileys knew they would be there for a while. The men dug and sandbagged actual dugouts as well as utilizing those previously built by the Brits.

Late in the afternoon, Ewen and Reggie heard the now familiar, "Are you guys D-Coy?"

"Yeah, we are. I'm Johnson, this is Morrison. The rest of the guys are in the bunker next door."

"I'm Cornelius Gibbs." A lean recruit, looking very composed and collected, offered his hand. Ewen accepted.

The second man introduced himself. "Stan Dabrowski." His cheerful voice and optimistic eyes reminded Ewen of Archer.

"And I'm Alexander Reiss. Call me Sandy," said the third.

"Reiss, that's German. Do you speak German?" asked Reggie.

"Some. My grandparents were Vistula—Polish—Germans, and they emigrated from Russia to Saskatchewan. And I'm Jewish." It was clear he felt the need to explain, and that he'd done it often.

"We can use your German on patrol. Excellent. Okay, fellas, you're just in time. Listen up," said Reggie. He shepherded them out of the rain and into his dugout. "The brass wants patrols to start up as soon as possible. We need to identify which regiment we're up against and what their strength is. Jerry has police dogs, so if you come across a dog on patrol, kill it."

Now I have to kill dogs. When did pets become the enemy?

"You've had basic training, haven't you?" Reggie asked the new guys. All three nodded. "Out here, now, things are a bit different. In the cold weather, Jerry will be the least alert at the end of his shift. And they'll change shifts more often in the cold weather." Ewen prayed that this time the new guys knew what Reggie was talking about.

"We'll be taking turns as forward companies. And when we do, the kitchen will send up two hot meals a day. One just after dark and breakfast just before dawn. Compo rations, but hot. Food and ammunition can only be brought up in the dark. We can't move around much in the daytime, because Jerry's got a bird's eye view of our positions. Right now, we're in the rear, but still make sure you stay close to a dugout. Stay alert. Questions?"

"Is it true you two are the only originals left in this platoon since Juno?" asked Stan. "That's what they told us when we checked in at HQ."

"Yes, it is."

"Can you give me . . . us . . . advice?"

"About staying alive? Don't deny your fear. Don't be ashamed because you're afraid. Accept it, use it to keep you alert," said Reggie. "Okay, get settled. Sandy, you'll be on standing patrol with Morrison and me tonight. Be back here at 2300."

A few short hours later, Reggie, Ewen and Sandy prepared for the patrol. Step by step, Reggie explained their orders. He wanted to make sure the rookie was clear on exactly what had to happen. Sandy watched the two seasoned soldiers carefully. *Guess he figures if we're still alive, then we must be doing something right.*

"The password is 'Potato Chip'. Repeat it, Sandy."

"Potato Chip."

"If we get separated, your life depends on remembering it. We get new passwords every night and I've got it mixed up myself, but you only do it once."

"In this fog, those gliders out there look kind of eerie." He shivered in the mist.

"Yes, and be careful around them. They're probably booby-trapped and there might be Jerry trenches around them," said Reggie.

Worming their way onto the ground in no-man's-land, a gust of wind came up and something snapped. Sandy jerked. Ewen pointed to a parachute hanging in the lower branches of a tree. Another gust and the silk snapped against a branch. Sandy nodded and continued forward.

Moments later, a glider groaned, metal on metal. Ewen saw the man's body jerk again. *Bloody hell, he's overreacting to every sound. Any moment now, he's going to run for it.*

Ewen saw Reggie signal Sandy, getting his attention. He pointed to himself, and then at Ewen, then moved his arm horizontally above the ground, his palm facing downwards. Sandy nodded. Message received.

They reached their first objective, one of the numbered buildings, and confirmed there was no sign of enemy activity. They expanded their search area and didn't come across any Jerrys or dogs, although they heard gunfire in the distance. Another patrol? They headed back to their side, with little to report for their eight-hour recce.

"Potato . . . "

" . . . Chip."

Night after night the regiment patrolled.

"Tonight, we ambush House 25 and we need to capture a Jerry," said Reggie. "We have to sort out our own route. The password is 'Vancouver Island.'"

They were fired upon as they passed through a forward section, but kept going until they were opposite House 25. Then, they were fired upon from a glider south of House 27. An MG 42 fired from the House 26 area. They also noted movement in the area south of Houses at 30 and 31. Again, at 0700 they reported back, without a Jerry. The major was frustrated.

The next night was "Greta Garbo."

"We need to survey this area for slit trenches," said Reggie, pointing to the map. And we have to find out which ones are occupied. We leave at 2359."

They found a lot of enemy slit trenches in the orchard, but none were occupied. The straw was quite dry, so they surmised they'd been dug recently. They still hadn't seen, heard or encountered any Germans.

Days passed as the Rileys struggled to capture a German or to identify the German regiment along their front. Division continued to press all regiments to secure a prisoner. They must get information. After twelve days, their CO upped the ante—the patrol who brought back a prisoner would get a week's leave. Still 17 Platoon couldn't capture a German.

One rainy dark night, Reggie and his platoon, stationed on the forward position, were alerted that a patrol was on its way up.

"Patrol on the way men, keep an eye," said Reggie.

Thirty minutes later the CO and four of his officers showed up. Reggie approached, didn't salute, and spoke briefly to the old man himself. Then they moved on.

"You won't believe it, Ewen," Reggie said. "I could smell the rum on them. I offered to go out on patrol for them, but the old man just said, 'We've got it covered, son. We're the All-Star Patrol!'"

"Jesus, they're nuts," said Ewen.

"Everyone cover their asses!" ordered Reggie. "If Jerry captures them, there will be hell to pay."

Someone forward stepped on a piece of slate, and the snap seemed frighteningly loud.

"Bloody hell, the whole front probably heard that," said Reggie.

The enemy opened fire from a darkened window of one of the houses. Reggie's platoon, and the rest of those in the forward position, let rip at the building. The Germans put their heads down and the All-Stars retreated safely.

"That's the nosiest patrol I've ever heard," said Ewen.

Patrol Report Night 19/20 Nov 44
RESULTS
House thought to have been cleared but NOT
entered by patrol. Established that the house was
held before the assault by one sec of the enemy
all but one of which succeeded in escaping along
comn trench to house before or during assault.
One enemy killed in comn trench which runs SE
side of house 57. Only papers on body was a
paybook which is now turned in to higher fmn.

Royal Hamilton Light Infantry War Diary
November 23, 1944
SW Gennep
1430 — Bn HQ group was formed up . . . and moved
off to the new area at CUIJK. The route was
across the MAAS RIVER via the pontoon br at MOOK.
At this time the stream was rising and both
approaches to the br were under water. We were
unable to take the direct route via the river
road as it was under observation by the enemy.

The Black Watch moved in and the Rileys moved eight miles southwest of Gennep to the reserve position for a rest. 17 Platoon was billeted in a barn equipped, for a change, with electric lights, although they only worked sporadically.

Once settled in, Reggie called them together. "The major figures we're here for about a week. Tomorrow we get a bath parade . . . " he was interrupted by a couple of cheers. "But all we get is a clean pair of socks."

"Seriously, no clean shirts or pants?" said Cowboy.

Reggie unrolled several mimeographed pages. "Now, for the fun stuff. This is our training schedule, and we're going to be busy. Back to school for some of us, new stuff for you new guys: mines, booby traps, first aid, flame throwing, gas training, weapon training, wood fighting, village fighting, night attacks, defence attacks, frontal attack, platoon in attack, battalion in attack." He paused and looked at the faces of the men, some bored, some alert, some nodding off. "There will be lectures on how to camouflage in the snow, more map reading and compass work. The Medical Officer will be briefing on VD, hygiene and first aid, and they'll be giving us typhoid boosters and typhus injections. As for hygiene, there'll be a delousing parade and, at some point, a clothing and blanket exchange. Oh, and for light entertainment, our regimental history for you rookies."

"Not much of a rest, is it?" said Gibbs.

Ewen wasn't sure what to make of the new guy—he seemed to be trying too hard to show that being at the front was nothing to him, but his confidence didn't ring true. Dabrowski, on the other hand, carried himself with a certain ease and, out on patrols, had proven himself reliable. Someone you wanted at your side and at your back.

"Why did you sign up, Stan?" Ewen had asked him shortly after he'd joined the platoon.

"Well, my parents are from Poland. They immigrated to Canada after the last war, in 1920, and started a printing company in Hamilton. When Hitler said the Poles had raided Germany, we all knew it was a lie, but that was his excuse to invade Poland and start the war. I have uncles, aunts, cousins in Poland who think that the Allies let them down. So, here I am. I couldn't just sit in Canada, I couldn't leave it alone, so I enlisted as soon as I turned eighteen."

"You're only eighteen?" said Ewen, surprised. Stan had a maturity about him that many of the other reinforcements lacked.

"Yeah, I'll be nineteen in May," Stan said.

There may not have been much rest, but there was some recreation. The YMCA showed movies in a large hall every evening. For its part, the regiment issued a syllabus for entertaining their battle-weary soldiers that included expeditions to the Canada Club in Nijmegen and the Beaver Club in Grave, stage shows and an ENSA concert called "Let's Do It." A few lucky men got forty-eight-hour passes to Ghent and Brussels, while the Germans still lobbed some shells at their reserve position, to remind them of why they were there. The mortar platoon practised by firing at German positions across the Maas River, but their training was cancelled when Jerry wouldn't cooperate as passive targets and began firing back. One night, the battalion HQ came under attack with dozens of Moaning Minnie rocket bombs fired at their area, blasting through the roof of one building and setting a barn on fire.

"Listen up, everyone," Sergeant Johnson announced to the platoon, after returning from HQ on the last day of the month. "We're moving to a new position tomorrow, so get prepared. And don't get slack. The Brits lost thirty men yesterday when the Germans ambushed the house they were staying in."

"Is tonight still on, Sergeant?" asked Reiss.

"Sure. The brass aren't going to cancel the first regimental dance since we left England," Reggie said. "Be ready at 1800 for your ride to the party."

"I hope there's some local ladies to dance with because I sure don't want to waltz with Gibbs." Ewen laughed and then had to suppress a memory of Archer, who'd been the platoon's comedian before the arrival of Sandy Reiss. Gibbs was no Woods, however.

"Morrison," Reggie said, "I said goodbye to Rooke for you."

"Who's Rooke and where's he gone?" asked Stan.

"Canada. He's a private, in battalion HQ, and he's served five years with the regiment overseas, so now he gets a month off back home."

"One month for five years of service?"

"Yes, but it has to be five years overseas—time served in Canada doesn't count."

"Bloody hell, I've been here for three weeks. I hope Jerry surrenders before my five years are up," said Gibbs.

Ewen sat at a table on the edge of the dance floor, his left foot tapping to the beat of the music. Sandy had got his wish: he was swinging a stunning brunette to the band's rendition of "Swingin on a Star," while Gibbs and Stan stood next to the bar, laughing. Reggie, a few tables over, was hanging out with some guys from A-Coy. He hadn't broken it off with Rose after all and they were still making plans for their dance in Paris, so he was staying off the dance floor.

The song reached a crescendo and ended with a cheer. The

leader of the band said in Dutch-accented English, "We will be taking a short break. Do not go away!" The dancers jostled for places to sit so Ewen decided to head outside for some fresh air. He took a can of cold American beer and went through a side door to the alleyway.

He'd just lit up when a young Dutchman in his late teens, also carrying a beer, joined him. Ewen recognized him as the band's drummer.

He lit up and said, "Hi, Canadian. I am Walraven."

"Ewen."

They shook hands and toasted. They spoke about the weather—cold—their conversation casual.

Ewen pointed to the young man's shoes. "What type of wood are your shoes made out of?"

"These ones are made from alder, they're called *klompen*."

"*Klompen*," repeated Ewen.

"Yes, in the old days my grandparents had a pair for working days and a pair for Sundays. Since the war started, leather has been difficult to find. When there were no more leather shoes to buy in the shops, we started to wear wooden shoes again. The schoolchildren paint theirs so they can recognize their own."

Ewen thought back to when he had been travelling in the back of the truck from Woensdrecht to Bergen op Zoom. Three young boys, all blond and wearing wooden shoes, had smiled and waved and yelled, "Hello Canadians!"

"It must have been bad, living under the Occupation," Ewen said.

"When this all first started, we did okay out here in the country, but for the people in the cities, it was not good. Food was rationed, everything was rationed. The Germans created some formula and decided how much we needed to eat. It was never enough, and the black market started. The Dutch Nazis, they strutted around in their uniforms, with black shirts and red ties, handing out pamphlets to tell people they would get more food if they joined the party."

Walraven took a swig of his beer.

Ewen thought about the rationing in Canada but knew it was nothing compared to what these people had endured.

"After our Dutch army surrendered, Queen Wilhelmina went to England. We listened to her broadcasts from England until the Germans took over our radio stations. The Germans didn't want us to know what was going on with the war so everyone had to turn in their radios. It was against the law to have one, but many people hid theirs. They searched our house but never found the one we had hidden in the cellar. Then they made it against the law to fly our flag or an orange flag."

"Orange? Why orange?" asked Ewen.

"It is the colour of our royal family. Our bicycles were taken away and sent to Germany to melt down for the war, anything made of brass or copper was taken away. We buried our silver and valuables in the barnyard, and the Germans knew it, but they never found anything."

Ewen tried to picture his family in a similar situation. "You took a big chance, defying them like that."

"We had to attend parades where they showed their power by dragging prisoners—people from the Resistance, anyone who opposed them—behind them. Then, us young Dutchmen were ordered to report for work in Germany, but many went into hiding and joined the Resistance.

"The Germans lived with us, we had to feed them and provide a place to sleep. But my family, we were lucky. The German who stayed with us was a kind man. His eyes always had a look of sadness. I do not think he wanted to be here either. He said he was at university, to be a . . . how do you call a doctor who takes care of animals?"

"A veterinarian," Ewen said.

"Yes, that's it. He helped people with their animals and brought us soap and other things when he could. We never talked too much, I think we were both afraid to be friends. He wasn't much older than me. I was sad too. I think in another time we would have been good friends."

Ewen said, "I met one PW. He was an ordinary farm boy, like me."

Inside the dance hall, the band was tuning up again. Walraven finished his beer. "I have to go. Enjoy the show, Ewen." He held out his hand again. "Thank you, all of you, for liberating our country."

Ewen looked down at feet, at the army boots that had been the first pair of new boots he'd ever had in his life. He had walked a few miles since then and tomorrow they would take him back to Groesbeek and the no-man's-land between him and the Germans in the forest. He hoped he'd still be wearing them for a while yet.

December 2, 1944 – War Diary
NW Groesbeek

1100 — The unit spent the day in cleaning up their coy areas and improving their dugouts and slit trenches. All coys reported their areas in a dirty condition . . . refuse and old equipment was all over the place. The Fus MR had not buried a couple of German soldiers whose bodies had been lying about for days, so "B" coy cleaned up on all this work. Some American dead were found along with some much sought after Garand rifles.

> **Royal Hamilton Light Infantry War Diary**
> **December 3, 1944**
> **Groesbeek**
> 1000 — B and D Coys reported SA and mortar fire
> from in front of their posns. Sniping has been
> going on from a couple of places, one from a
> haystack near the house in front of B Coys posn,
> the other from the gully to the right of D Coy's
> posn.

"We're on patrol again tonight and tomorrow," said Reggie. "And since we were last here in no-man's-land, the brass have come up with a new idea—a bunch of mannequins have been requisitioned from a store in Nijmegen. They're being dressed up like us and they'll be propped up on the line to lure out Jerrys' snipers. Once they start firing, our boys will let them have it."

"That's creative," said Sandy.

"Welcome to the army," said Reggie.

Like Stan Dabrowski, Sandy Reiss had settled in well and the two veterans appreciated the rookies' solid commitment. Reiss, unlike Woods, was oblivious to his good looks, although women were certainly drawn to him. He liked to read poetry and was able to dial into the mood of the others without being intrusive.

"Reiss and Morrison, you're with me tonight. There won't be a moon and it might rain. I need you to be extra alert. I don't want to get shot up like those three guys from the Black Watch last night."

"What happened?" said Ewen. Both he and Sandy tried not to look worried.

"They were on patrol, heading out to a listening post, and in the dark our guys thought they were Jerry."

"Bloody hell."

2030. The three Rileys, each armed with a hand grenade and knife, moved in the darkness. Their objective was to observe and maintain a listening watch on House 100, where there'd been suspected enemy activity. The night's password was "White Christmas."

They inched through a small wood and slithered over the open ground that lay between their positions and the Reischswald Forest. They reached their objective without encountering any tripwires, mines or enemy slit trenches; the house and what remained of its farmyard appeared empty. Ewen listened hard but couldn't hear any enemy movement. Rain began to fall. He pulled his collar up and turned his face away from the wind. The rain and the darkness challenged his senses, but many patrols with Reggie had taught him how to look, listen and learn.

Then he heard something—a radio signal? He signalled to Sandy to remain and keep watch behind a stone wall while he and Reggie probed further.

Moving in unison, silently, they snuck up to the barn and moved to either side of the double doors. They stood tense but patient. Then Reggie raised his hand and pointed at his ear. Ewen heard it too: the faint crackle of a radio and a soft voice. It wasn't English. The rain began to fall harder.

Reggie's head turned towards Ewen. He couldn't see the sergeant's eyes in the dark, but knew that they were focused on the black smudge of his face, sending a message felt but not seen: Ready. Ewen stood straighter and pulled out his knife, reflecting his leader's stance. Someone had oiled the hinges of the door; it made almost no sound as Reggie opened it just enough for the two men to slip inside. The sound of the rain was their friend.

Ewen looked around. A few feet in front, in the middle of the empty barn, a wooden ladder led up to a square hole in the loft, where the faintest of lights shone. Reggie signalled to move behind it. Under the loft, hidden behind the ladder, they listened.

There it is again, thought Ewen. Radio static. A light flickered through the floorboards above their heads. A candle? Two voices. Reggie signalled to Ewen. Ewen nodded—he knew what they had to do: capture the men if they could, kill them if they couldn't.

Without taking a step, Reggie bent down and felt for a pebble on the barn floor. He stood back up and tossed it against the far wall.

Above, footsteps scrambled.

"Wer ist da? Fischer bist du das? Silence.

A pair of silhouetted legs appeared at the top rungs of the ladder. They moved down and the shape of a soldier holding the rungs with one hand, a gun in the other. Two more steps. Ewen's throat tightened as he reached out, grabbed the German, who twisted and rammed his elbow back into Ewen's gut, shouting a warning to his comrade. Terrified of losing his grip on the struggling soldier, and thinking of the gun he held, Ewen ran his knife across the man's throat and dragged him behind the ladder.

The second man pointed his gun through the loft and fired blindly; Reggie threw his knife with deadly accuracy and the German tumbled onto the floor at the sergeant's feet. He gurgled as the life drained from him. Reggie dragged his body next to his comrade behind the ladder.

Ewen went up the ladder. The loft was empty. He smashed the radio then looked around for papers that might provide valuable intelligence to HQ. He found nothing more than a few rations. He went down the ladder to find Reggie examining the badges on the dead soldiers' uniforms. This, at least, would be useful.

They moved out of the barn and made their way back to Sandy who stood with a grenade in his hand; he lowered it when he recognized the shapes walking toward him. No words were spoken. Reggie signalled to move out and Sandy knew he would have to wait to find out what happened.

Time in: 0350. White Christmas.

Ewen leaned against a tree, held his stomach and doubled over. He looked at that night's dinner floating on the mud between his feet. His hands were sticky with blood and pulsed as if they didn't belong to him, but he wiped them on his pants anyway. He moved to one side and bent down, dipping them in a pool of brown water. *How many more? Tomorrow night, is the knife going to be at my throat?*

December 5, 1944
1000 — A patrol reception centre is opened in MOOK. This centre offers baths, food, beds and recreation from men returning from patrols. These men are taken back at night after their patrol as a reward. The men of the unit who have gone there speak highly of it and return the next day to their coy flaunting in the faces of their comrades (a) clean skin (b) clean heavy winter underwear, towels, soap, socks (c) chocolate and things supplied by Auxiliary Services. In spite of (a) (b) and (c) there has been no line up on the coy rosters for patrol work.

Royal Hamilton Light Infantry War Diary Summary, December, 1944

MORALE

There has been a gradual building up of morale during the past few months and at the present time has reached probably its highest point since the landing.

DISCIPLINE

Discipline is good and it has improved from previous months due to the fact that Court Martials for charges of AWL are dealing severely with these cases. Discipline resulting from the men being exhausted through strenuous fighting has disappeared.

The first snowfall in December was lovely at first, but then it melted and made the mud even worse, and even more water leaked through the roofs of the dugouts. "Did you hear about that guy over in A-Coy?" Cowboy asked. "His platoon had a sten gun set up at the end of the trench, cocked and pointing in Jerry's direction, ready for the morning. Well, the whole side of their trench collapsed and the sten gun got knocked down, went off and hit the guy in the foot. Ought to be court-martialled."

Rubber boots and long underwear were issued, and then more snowfall brought a bonus—patrols cancelled two nights running. Fresh reinforcements arrived, and Fred Boucher joined 17 Platoon, marking the first time since the Scheldt that they were up to strength.

"So, what did you do before you joined this merry band?" asked Stan.

"I was a shoemaker. In Moncton. Made 'em, mended 'em."

"Welcome to the front," said Reggie. "See that house and haystack over there? Well, Jerry's right there."

"Guess I'll offer that he gets shod then, not shot," Boucher quipped. Sandy laughed the loudest.

The week before Christmas, the regiment moved back to the

reserve position at Cuijk, where they enjoyed getting cleaned up and receiving some fresh kit, including dry underwear, towels and socks. They had another rigorous training syllabus, preparing for the next offensive, whenever that was to come.

Reggie supervised as they cleaned and maintained their weapons. "The cold weather is tough on our guns. When you're cleaning your weapon, check the firing pins and strikers—they could freeze up in their housings. The lubricating oil they've given us has been tested in the cold, and it works. Use it."

As they cleaned, they talked.

"You new reinforcements seem to have had more training than those who came up in October," said Reggie. "At least you can load a gun."

"I heard from home that it's made front-page news," said Stan. "The fact that the government is sending untrained men here. It's a real screw-up and people back home know about it now."

"It disgusts me," said Ewen. "Because of the lack of trained men, we've had to work harder, be exposed to more danger. So many of us are battle-exhausted or sick, we haven't got the strength to perform as well as we could."

"The graveyards are the evidence of that fact," said Reggie. "A bunch of government guys in Ottawa are resigning over it."

"Can I resign too?" asked Sandy.

When time allowed, passes to Nijmegen were handed out so the soldiers could enjoy YMCA hosted movies, a hamburger at the Blue Diamond or a seat at a Canadian Women's Army Corp show. "Great goils, great show," was Boucher's review.

"Well look at us, all snug in our one-room bungalow," Sandy said. "Ready for Christmas, aren't we? Or Hanukkah, as the case may be. Those evergreen branches complement the brown of the dirt walls, don't you think? The only thing lacking is a big bottle of cognac."

Ewen and Sandy were playing crib, the dampness making the cards stick together. Reggie was reading the Daily Orders and Stan was writing a letter.

"Are you writing your fiancée, Stan?" asked Sandy.

"Fiancée? Aren't you a bit young?" Ewen said.

"Nah. I'm engaged to a lovely Scottish lass. Her name is Betty. It was the last thing I ever thought would happen over here. We're going to get married after this war is over, and you're all invited to the wedding."

"Congratulations," Reggie said. He stood up and shook Stan's hand.

"Enough romance. I beat you again, Morrison," said Sandy. "One more game, three out of five?" He moved the pegs back to the start.

"Sure. I'll be back in a moment. I just need a stretch." said Ewen, moving outside. His back was stiffening up from the cold and his foot ached. That motorcycle accident was going to plague him for the rest of his life, however long that would be. He lit a cigarette and thought about Stan and his Betty, Reggie and his Rose. *Ewen and . . . Stop feeling sorry for yourself, Morrison. You're alive and you're clean and you're dry. And no one's shooting at you. For now.*

To the east, through the beech and linden trees a few hundred yards away, the town's windmill still stood alone like a sentry on a hill. Ewen tightened up his winter battle dress and walked towards it to get a closer look. He would love to get inside to see how the mechanism worked but knew it would be foolish to get too close. Snipers were always out there somewhere. Ewen thought the upper window must have one hell of a view into Germany and wondered how it had withstood all the bombing. The brick tower stuck out like a sore thumb. He had seen a jeep coming and going from the base, probably a forward observation officer. *Crazy bastard, going in there. I guess Jerry thinks no one would actually use it for a lookout, or it wouldn't still be standing.*

Walking back to their dugout, Ewen shivered and then did a double take—in the twilight he thought he saw a donkey. *Nah, couldn't be.* When he stepped inside, Reggie was handing out mail. None for him.

Reggie sat down next to Ewen and opened his own letter, another from Rose. He began to read it aloud, softly:

Dearest Reggie –

I trust you're well and I'm doing fine.

This month we've had a lot of diphtheria cases. Isolation wards have been created and it's forbidden to touch anything in the rooms. It's tough on the men in there. It's a disease that's hard on the heart and we had a death last night.

Some of the patient's eyes, before they're going in for surgery—they look so frightened. So many of them are so young.

A bunch of us from our unit were invited to a party last Saturday. We welcomed the relief. We jumped in the back of a canvas-topped truck and froze all the way there! But it was fun to get out for an evening. You won't believe it, but now we use Calvados for lighter fluid!

We're trying to decorate the wards for Christmas. For some of the boys it's their fourth or fifth Christmas away from home. No one says "the war will be over by next Christmas" anymore, they've heard it too many times.

We have them making paper chains from newspapers and cutting out letters that read "Merry Christmas." The Royal Engineers got us some Christmas trees, one for each ward. We didn't ask where they got them.

We plan to sing carols on Christmas Eve. We know for some of them it may be their last Christmas, even though it's not spoken, I'm sure they're thinking the same thing. We're still looking for someone to be Santa Claus.

The Red Cross has sent a pair of hand-knitted socks from Canada for each patient, so at least we have something to hand out Christmas morning. Plus, they'll get some chocolate and cigarettes. And there will be church services on the wards, and we'll have a Christmas meal at noon with the officers serving.

I hope to get some leave soon and will write as soon as I know. It would be wonderful if we could meet up in Nijmegen before the end of the month. We can have our dance there, and save Paris for when this is all over.

Much love,

Your Rose

He folded up the letter and put it in his left breast pocket.

"Okay. I'd better go to HQ to find out what's up next," he told Ewen, giving him a pat on the shoulder before he left. Gibbs, back from a twenty-four-hour pass to Nijmegen, passed him on his way in.

"Check this out, fellas," he said, pulling a metal cylinder out from his pack. He popped open the cap at the end and pulled out a rolled-up canvas.

"Tah-dah." It was an oil painting, cut from its frame. Ewen saw flowers and fruit on a dark background. He didn't know anything about art, but he thought it looked beautiful.

"Where did you get that?" asked Stan.

"I bought it from the family I was billeted with in Nijmegen. The granddad, he wanted to sell it and I got it for a song." He admired his purchase, and Ewen thought, *Jeez, he's smug.*

"It's probably worth a whole lot. I'm going to bring this home and maybe it's my retirement," said Gibbs.

"Define 'a song,'" said Sandy.

"A few guilders. Some chocolate, some cigarettes. I even threw in some old field rations."

"They've been living under the Nazis for five years and then you come along and take advantage of them?" said Sandy. "That's low, Gibbs."

"It's no big deal, Reiss," said Gibbs. "Where do you get off with that 'holier than thou' attitude?"

"You're an asshole," said Ewen. "We're supposed to be the good guys."

"If you had any sense of decency, you'd make sure they got it back. Maybe it's been in their family for years and years," said Sandy.

"Fuck you guys," said Gibbs. He rolled the painting back up and shoved it in its tube. "You're just jealous that I got such a great bargain. Get your own next time."

Reggie returned from HQ with bad news. "You know that Christmas dinner you guys were looking forward to? It's not happening. We've got orders to move to Driehuizen on the 25th. Jerry has made an advance through the Ardennes and diversionary attacks are expected."

"So Christmas is kaput, then," said Sandy.

"No peace for us. Sorry, fellas."

However, on Christmas Eve a bottle of cognac mysteriously appeared and in their dugout, the men toasted to next year and home for the holidays. Ewen stepped outside and saw the silhouette of a building with a veranda at the edge of the woods. He thought it must have been a hotel before all the fighting started. *I'd like to go there one day and sip a whisky on the terrace. The view might be nice when there isn't a war on.*

Christmas day was bright and cold. The regiment packed up and at 1520 the convoy moved off. They drove over icy roads under a pale blue sky to their next position, on the outskirts of Nijmegen, where the owner of a villa offered his home to the regiment. On Boxing Day, each company took it in turn to eat their Christmas dinner and chocolate, washed down with tinned beer and served up by the officers.

The CO made a speech at each sitting, which ended with, "Next year, home for Christmas, boys."

December 31, 1944

Bokstel

2359 — The ESSEX SCOT R held a parade with their pipe band to celebrate the New Year. There was some indiscriminate firing of weapons but fortunately no one was hurt.

Note: Corporal Kelly produced, directed wrote smashing stage production "Oh What a Lousy War" in Bokstel theatre. It was a great success.

Royal Hamilton Light Infantry War Diary
January 4, 1945
Bokstel
During our stay in this area, the bn although
on short notice to move due to operational
commitments, put into effect a strenuous training
and conditioning programme.

The sound of men moving about the second floor of the large convent, where the whole RHLI was housed, likely exceeded any pre-war level. D-Coy was bunked down in a dormitory with proper beds and sheets, where their dreams were not of the religious variety.

"Oof." Cowboy sat down with a groan. "Could do with one of those cigars right about now. All this PT reminds me of being back at training camp. Anyone find out who had to pay?" The regiment had enjoyed "free" beer and cigars on New Year's Day; the quartermaster was still trying to track down who was going to foot the bill.

"Not yet," said Reggie. "So enjoy all this while you can. Marches and a few lectures on venereal disease beat patrolling at the front any day for me. We'll be back in the mud before you know it, and our evenings won't be spent watching movies and having tea and biscuits."

"Hey, Ewen," called Sandy. "You look a bit like that guy in last night's movie—Van Johnson. Who'd you rather have? June Allyson or Gloria DeHaven?"

"Quit it, Sandy."

Ewen looked round for a distraction. New recruits had been arriving regularly, and Ewen walked over to the young kid who'd arrived last night. He'd noticed him tying fishing flies in the writing room set up by the YMCA. He was sitting on his bed, turning a fly over in his hands, and looking somewhat lost. *Might be eighteen. Just.*

Ewen sat down beside him. "You like fishing?" The boy nodded. Ewen extended his hand. "Me too. I'm Morrison. Ewen Morrison."

The new recruit shook his hand. "I'm Fernand. Fern for short. L'Hirondelle. I just landed in England two weeks ago and got pretty much sent straight here."

Ewen hoped he knew how to fire a rifle. He asked, "Where are you from?"

"Alberta. Saddle Lake Reserve."

"That's a good fly," Ewen said pointing to the nicely crafted buck fly. "Not sure if you'll get much opportunity to fish though." He hoped the kid would still be around when the ice melted.

"Well, there's probably not much you'd want to eat that comes from these waters," said Reggie, who'd joined the pair. "You're Cree, aren't you? Do you speak it?"

"Not much, only a little. I wish I did, but in residential school we weren't allowed to speak our language. Got beaten if we did." The mood shifted as the others listened to the conversation.

"That's brutal," Ewen said.

"I was forced to go. Had to give up my clothes and wear a uniform. They cut off my braids. I ran away once but got caught."

"Kind of sounds like army life," said Stan.

"Too bad you don't speak Cree," said Reggie. "The IO told me to look out for anyone who can. Says there's a special assignment for them." Fern shrugged.

"It may not be as good as fishing, but there's some special entertainment laid on for tonight," Sandy chimed in. "Everyone ready for the big event?"

"What's going on?" Fern asked.

Ewen said, "It's a regimental concert, and Reiss has been practicing his solo act."

"What's that?"

"Oh, just you wait, soldier boy," Sandy teased.

The hall was packed. Catcalls howled towards the stage where A-Coy was setting up their props—a table and four chairs—for a sketch written by the CO. Laughter and heckles showered the officers playing Major Margatroyd T. McClambrain, Captain Lemuel Q. Lardass and Lieutenants Fearless F. Fosdick, I.M. Caput and U.R. Comming,

The audience stomped their boots and whistled their approval as the cast of "The Zigfield Line" took a bow.

"Now," the emcee continued. "The show you've all been waiting for. May I introduce Sunshine Sandy!"

Sandy stepped onto the stage and garnered cheers as he twirled and began his striptease routine.

"Take it all off!"

"No! Please don't!"

"Yeah, baby!"

Sandy, stripped down to his boots and underwear, twirled around and, his back to the crowd, mooned the lot of them to howls of laughter. A chorus line of six "beautiful blondes," singing and high-kicking, rounded out the show.

"So, Fern, back to the convent, eh?" said Ewen. The boy looked a little stunned by the evening's event—a rowdy night out to be followed by sleeping in a nun's bed.

Two days later, 17 Platoon D-Coy were back to the same positions they'd left on Christmas Day, at the edge of the no-man's-land overlooking the Reichswald Forest near Groesbeek. The rain turned to sleet then to snow, and cushy convent life was forgotten.

They were issued with white snowsuits, which were warm, but noisy. The deadly routine of nighttime patrols and recce missions returned, accompanied by the daily grind of intensive training: road runs, forest fighting, wood clearing, platoon lectures on camouflage, weapons inspection, weapons training, lectures on current events, powers of the Dutch police, map reading and compass work and footwear—no one was to wear rubber boots on a march. Who would wear rubber boots on a march? thought Ewen. And finally they were all reminded that going after "souvenirs" was strictly off limits.

"I guess so, especially after last night," Cowboy said. "Did you guys hear what some guys from C-Coy tried?"

"Yeah, I heard the crazy bastards decided to visit some of the downed gliders from Market Garden in hopes of finding some souvenirs. I don't know exactly what happened, but apparently while they were out there a patrol came along and the guys thought it was Jerry, but it wasn't. It was B-Coy, but they didn't know that and to get away they ended up heading straight towards the real Jerrys, who naturally shot at them. Had to hunker down for the night before they could make it back."

Ewen asked Reggie, "Do you think anyone will ever believe what our lives have been like?" Ewen asked Reggie.

"No idea, Morrison, no idea."

On the eighteenth day of January, the platoon celebrated a birthday, undeterred by the fierce weather. "Happy Birthday to you, Happy Birthday to you, Happy Birthday, dear Ewen, Happy Birthday to you!"

"One more time!" Reggie shouted.

"How old are you today, Morrison?" Stan asked when the singing and toasting slowed down.

"Twenty-two."

"Pour the old man another mug of wine!" said Sandy. The bottle, encased in a wicker basket, needed two men to pour.

"Where did you get this?" Ewen asked. "It's the biggest bottle of wine I've ever seen in my life."

"It's a military secret," Reggie said, tapping his nose.

"We have to get rid of the evidence, so drink up," Boucher said.

"Nothing but the best for us, lads. One must have style. But I've got to find the john," Sandy said. "I'm going to use the latest propaganda Jerry shot over to wipe my ass. Did you guys read this?" He waved a sheet of paper in the air.

"No, I didn't see it," Ewen said.

"As I sit on the banks of the Maas, I reflect that it's really a Faas." Reiss sang in a falsetto with a German accent. "At my time of life and miles from my wife, to be stuck in the mud on my Aas."

"I don't get it," Fern said.

"Well, you're not married, so don't worry. Jerry is trying to make us feel homesick for our loved ones, but basically he just wants us to surrender. And that's not happening," Stan said.

"Okay, be right back." Sandy headed out.

"Be careful out there," Stan said. "Make sure you wipe the snow off the seat. The burlap screen whipped up over my head yesterday and a blast of wind nearly froze my ass off. We can't get homesick for Canada in this weather."

Ewen laughed and shook his head. "Reminds me of when we used to push over the girls' outhouse at school. Once we even shoved it over with a couple of girls inside. We got the strap at school and the cane at home, but we sure laughed! We were the rowdy Scots boys."

Sandy and a cold draught blew back into the dugout.

"I think it's time I gave you all some German lessons," he said, "As we're going to be going there—" he waved vaguely in the direction of the Reichswald "—very soon."

"I thought you didn't speak much German, Reiss," Reggie said, smiling.

"Enough, sarge. I speak enough. And besides, the brass have suggested we learn these useful phrases. Okay, I'm going to say it and you're all going to repeat after me."

"Yes, teach!" the men chorused.

Sandy raised his hand above his head: "Hands up! *Hände hoch!*"

17 Platoon played Sandy Says.

"*Ergeben Sie sich!* Surrender, Boche scum!"

"Don't move! *Keine Bewegung!*"

"*Wenn Sie nicht gehorchen, schiesse ich!*"

That last one had them stumped. "'If you'd don't obey, I will shoot you.' Your pronunciation sucks but keep practising—a few more glasses of wine should improve it."

January 20, 1945
Groesbeek

1030 — One German jet propelled plane sneaked in under some of our own bombers and dropped a few eggs in the area of A Ech. No casualties were suffered, but one American in a jeep was dismayed enough to take to the ditch and remove a few posts.

Royal Hamilton Light Infantry War Diary
January 27, 1945
Groesbeek
Cold and frosty.
1000 — D-Coy visited by the unit barber, and with
deep regret many of the boys lost their greatest
asset, the long hair which they claim keeps their
ears warm.

"Hey, did you hear about Gibbs?" Stan said.

"Who's Gibbs?" asked Fern.

"He's a guy who came here with Sandy and me," explained Stan. "Transferred to C-Coy just before Christmas." Ewen thought Reggie had had something to do with that. Gibbs hadn't been missed.

"Hear what?" Cowboy asked.

"He was court-martialled."

"For what?" asked Fred.

"Apparently he stole some stuff, who knows what, from a Dutch local," Stan answered.

"What did he get?" Ewen asked.

"One year in the clink with hard labour," said Reggie, his face impassive.

"What a dumb-ass," Ewen said.

"Extra, extra, read all about it!" Sandy bounced in, waving a mimeographed sheet of paper. "We have a newspaper, gentleman. Shall I be 17 Platoon's war correspondent for the *Bugle Call?*"

"*Bugle Call?*" said Cowboy. "Archer would have thought of a better name, wouldn't he, Reggie?"

"Yeah, he would have." The two men exchanged sad smiles. "And Woods would have said, 'About fucking time.'"

"What does it say about the Western Front?" asked Ewen.

"Apparently the Yanks and the Limeys are up to the River Roer and we pushed Jerry back over the Moder River."

"Where are those places?" asked Fern.

"Not near here," said Sandy. "South of us."

"If our company HQ hadn't gone up in flames the other week, I would have been able to show you on the map," Reggie said.

"Apparently, we're going to have an election back home before the middle of April," Sandy continued. "Do you think a change of politicians will make any difference to us out here?"

"Nah," said Fred.

"Bloody hell, all these politicians giving their opinions about what will happen after the war," said Ewen. "Why the hell don't they just shut up. It's not over—we have to get through the Siegfried Line and win it first."

"The brass behind the lines just need to make up their minds," said Stan. "Not that I'd be happier throwing myself at German bunkers and machine guns, but this hanging around is driving me crazy. It's not rocket science to know the longer we wait, the more the land will thaw and the more it will flood. Conditions are just going to get worse for us on the ground."

"We've been training hard, and we're ready," said Reggie. "But you can bet Jerry is too. And he is fighting for his homeland now, defending it. For most of you, Jerry is just a bomber overhead or a sniper in the distance. The worst you've had to handle is a couple of mortar attacks and not falling into enemy slit trenches out on patrol. Out there," Reggie pointed towards the dark woods of the Reichswald, "Jerry is waiting, in his pillboxes, his trenches and his bunkers. It is his land, not ours, and you can be sure he's going to fight like a fanatic. He's got the Russians knocking on his door at the Eastern Front. It's going to be our turn soon to kick it in on the Western Front."

"When the generals can figure it out, that is," said Stan.

"The old man gave us some hints at O group today," Reggie went on. "From all our recon we know that Jerry has connected his pillboxes and concrete bunkers with trenches, in some places they've dug two or three rows of trenches. They've got MG emplacements and tank ditches. That forest out there is the centre of their resistance. Plus, all houses on the frontier have had their basements strengthened. They can snipe at us from cellar windows as well as from above."

"It says here," said Sandy, reading from the *Bugle Call*, "That in a broadcast, Hitler talked about the distress and suffering of the German people, but that they had to fight on."

"The CO says Hitler has issued a scorched earth policy, that all their own land must be burned as they retreat to prevent us of getting our hands on anything that might help us," added Reggie.

"Bloody hell," Cowboy said. "Imagine doing that to your own home."

Getting ready for patrol, Ewen stopped outside the entrance. He looked down at the mud caked on his boots as memories of Woensdrecht came back. The extra weight would once again slow them down and take away their agility. He said nothing to the others. *No point in creating more fear for the new guys.*

Sandy shrugged on his white snowsuit. "I should have joined the hockey team."

"There's a hockey team?" Fern asked.

"Yeah, they're leaving for Antwerp in a few days. Some tournament."

"I love hockey," Fern said.

"Well, let the Captain know when he gets back. Maybe you can still join," Ewen said.

January 31, 1945
The end of the month sees the bn well up to strength, well trained and ready for any job that might be given to it.

```
Royal Hamilton Light Infantry War Diary
February 8, 1945
Groesbeek
0900 — Description is difficult, for even along
the front that was visible from our observation
point, the whole picture of destruction was too
vast for conception.
```

The world is on fire. From his vantage point, Ewen stared out at the scene. It seemed that every house, barn, haystack was ablaze. In the night, he and the other men stared at the tracers and bombs that were smashing Kleve and Goch in the distance, across the border in Germany. *It reminds me of Caen. Seven months, I've survived seven months and now it's started again.* For the past four hours, the British and Canadian artillery had unleashed hell on the Germans so that the infantry could break through in waves. Ewen tried to push the cotton wool further into his ears, but it didn't make a difference. His head ached. *Me and 500,000 others are probably losing their hearing. I just hope it isn't permanent.*

The night before, just as the sun was going down, the lieutenant had briefed the platoon, his sergeant at his side. "Operation Veritable is going to bring Jerry to his knees. The big show starts tomorrow at 0500 with a barrage, the initial bombardment. It's going to be the biggest one ever, bigger even than El Alamein. The battle plan is in phases, a frontal attack. We're not part of the initial attack. We'll be rotated into the fight. After one phase is completed, artillery and supporting weapons move up and we move into the next phase with heavy fire support.

"We're taking the maximum amount of power to Jerry's front. He has three lines of defence. First, their outposts. Second, the Siegfried Line that runs through the Reichswald. Third, the Hochwald covering our approach to the Rhine near Xanten. Our goal is to clear the Reichswald Forest, break the Siegfried Line and clear the Hochwald Forest to close up the Rhine and onto Berlin."

"That's all?" Ewen asked.

"That's all, Morrison. This might be the last round, men. We've got Jerry where we want him—we're on his doorstep with his back up against his backyard. It's going to be hard and we have to deliver the knock-out blow now. It's going to take guts."

Reggie took over. "It's going to be foot-by-foot through flooded fields and it will be ugly in this mud. The flood plains are poorly drained, there's clay and standing water everywhere. Make sure you pack an extra pair of socks: we could be days or possibly weeks without a change of clothes, but at least you'll be able to keep swap socks and keep your feet dry. The mud is miserable, and this rain is making it worse."

"We should have gone last month when the ground was frozen," Stan said. "This thaw is going to bog every vehicle down in the mud. How are the tanks supposed to get through?"

"I can't answer that," said Reggie. "All I can do is make sure we get through. The Reichswald Forest is mainly pines, but there are some bare leaf trees. That's going to make us more vulnerable. You know the fields that lead up to the woods? The land rises and there are ditches along the fields. This will give us some cover, but remember—the enemy's positions are mostly in the woods and in houses and you can bet there will be sniping from those cellars and bunkers."

The briefing over, the Rileys had a few hours to write letters and pack and unpack, check and double-check their kit.

"Morrison, can I ask you something?" It was Stan. "This is the first action I've seen. What's it like out there?"

"You shoot, you fight, or you die. I've done things that I never dreamed I'd have to do in my life. How many men have I killed? I don't know—I guess as many as I've had to. There's a difference between fighting on the battlefield and deliberate killing when the enemy has surrendered. I've seen some guys so filled with hate that they don't know the difference. We have to live with ourselves when this is over. I can't pretend I haven't done horrible things, but I know I haven't committed murder. That's the difference."

Ewen felt for all the new guys: Dabrowski, Reiss, Boucher, L'Hirondelle. Even though they'd had some good training over the past couple of months, they'd been sent over without full battle training. Not one of the Canadian government's finest moments.

"I'm worried, Reggie," he said later. "Most of the guys in our company are going into battle without having proper training; hell, most of them aren't even infantry. There's you, me, Cowboy . . . "

"We've done what we can, we've shared what we know. When it's our turn to move forward, I guess we'll find out if we've done enough. Cigarette?" The two men shared a smoke in the dark.

The Allied barrage before them shot up the German defences in front and in the Reichswald Forest. It hammered down on Kleve and Goch for two and a half hours. Then, it stopped.

"What's happening?" Ewen asked.

"They're hoping that Jerry thinks the bombardment is over, but it's not. In ten minutes, it will start again and catch him coming out of his trenches getting ready to counterattack. It's a deception tactic," Reggie said.

"Look at their faces Reggie," Ewen said, nodding at the new guys. "This is the first real battle they've seen. They look scared as hell."

Fern, Sandy and Stan stared into the abyss. Ewen couldn't interpret their thoughts, but he recognized the stunned incomprehension on their faces. Ewen wished he had something to say, something to help them, but words felt futile.

A cloud of yellow smoke wafted across no-man's-land to signal the barrage's final minute.

"What's happening?" asked Fern. He'd moved closer to the two veterans.

The tanks started up and moved forward. Ground troops from Canada, Scotland, Wales and England moved forward into the fire.

They had to get the advantage before the Germans surfaced from their trenches.

"Bloody hell," Stan said.

By that evening, the first wave had succeeded in obtaining their objectives. Ewen and Reggie knew better than to celebrate the victory, and their green recruits learned the bloody cost of battle. One Riley was not with them as they dug in that night—Cowboy had been set to check communication trenches at their perimeter, and the man with him, from Tac HQ, stepped on an undiscovered mine and the exploding Bouncing Betty had sent deadly shrapnel in all directions. Sergeant Johnson didn't know if the big man from Alberta was alive or dead.

```
1800 — The reports are excellent. Casualties
have been surprisingly light and mostly from
mines. More surprising still is the fact that
some Germans lived through the barrage and the
prisoners are pouring in. A fair cross-section
would indicate very young men or alternatively
very old, not a sign of first class troops.
```

```
Royal Hamilton Light Infantry War Diary
February 14, 1945
Nijmegen
0930 — A meeting of all officers of the Bde was
held in the Wintergarden Hall to hear Brig FN
CABELDU on our forthcoming operations. Three
plans were discussed, the most important
being the drive to CALCAR and XANTEN. General
information on treatment of civilians and some of
the problems likely to be run into upon entering
Germany were pointed out.
```

"Are you coming to the pool, Morrison?" Fern asked.

"Well, I don't swim, never learned. But I can dog paddle and I sure could use a bath, so I'll go along with you." The two men were sharing a room in their local billet with the Van de Berg family and set off together for Nijmegen's indoor pool. It had been opened up for the troops.

Four days after Operation Veritable was initiated, the Rileys were ordered to Nijmegen. They were behind the lines, but it wasn't a rest; they would be called into battle when required and they knew it would be on short notice. The battalion HQ and two companies were staying in a large school while the rifle companies settled in with billets.

Lounging poolside, an unfamiliar soldier sat down beside Ewen.

"Not a swimmer, either?"

"No. Just here for the fresh water and a bath," Ewen replied. "Morrison." He extended his hand.

"Smithson." He leaned over and shook Ewen's hand.

"Who are you with?"

"I'm with Graves Services," said Smithson.

"Oh."

"Yeah, my job is to take pictures of the crosses in all the cemeteries. One copy stays with us, and one goes to the next of kin. Other guys deal with the registration and paperwork."

I hope you don't end up taking a photo of my cross, thought Ewen.

"I dream of it you know. I dream of crosses and I wonder how their families feel when they see the photo I've taken. Now I understand how those telegram boys must feel. I remember meeting one lad in England, he couldn't have been more than fourteen. It was early in the war and he told me that the woman he handed the telegram to broke out in a big smile and was so excited to get some news about her son. She thought he must be coming home on leave, but it was the War Office informing her he'd been killed in action. She collapsed into sobs and he didn't know what to do."

"A fourteen-year-old kid shouldn't have to cope with that," Ewen said.

"No, he shouldn't. I never thought I'd end up taking photos of crosses. What do you do?" George asked.

"Infantry. I'm trained to kill." It was the truth. He hated it, but there was some relief in saying it out loud. He'd probably never see Smithson again but, when you didn't know if you would be around the next day, why bullshit?

"Well, let's hope this whole shitty mess is over soon and we can go home. Who would believe we're this close to the front and lounging by a pool? It's insane. Well, I gotta go. Hope to see you on the troopship home."

"Wouldn't that be nice. Bye, Smithson."

That evening the YMCA showed *Stormy Weather* starring Lena Horne. The crowd started clapping and the feet were tapping when Cab Calloway and the Nicolas Brothers performed "Jumpin' Jive." Music was a refuge from the war, and Ewen allowed it to distract him.

After the movie, walking back to their billet, Fern said shyly, "Mies sure is nice."

"Who's that?" Ewen asked.

"You know. She's the Van de Bergs' daughter."

"Oh, right, yes." Ewen hadn't really paid much attention to the fair-haired teenager. "Are you sweet on her, Fern?"

"She's teaching me some Dutch. I thought I'd ask her for a walk."

"Why not? I'm sure she'd love some attention from a handsome young soldier like you."

Their days followed an intense training syllabus: forced marches and more lectures on mines and booby traps. As if we need more hardening, thought Ewen. But he knew no training really prepares anyone for the first time you're in the thick of it all. Then news came through—"We're on a twelve-hour notice to move. Now that the Reichswald's been taken, the next operation is on, taking the Hochwald Ridge. The Germans still hold their position around Goch and we've got to secure the start line. We're up, guys. There's a delousing parade and clothing and blanket exchange at 1400. Get yourselves sorted out."

The next morning was spent packing and loading the vehicles, followed by an early lunch before the convoy set off for Germany.

"It seems like the roads might be drying up a bit," Stan said.

"In your dreams, Dabrowski," Ewen said.

"What a godforsaken mess," said Sandy.

"It's only about fifteen miles, supposed to be a twenty-minute drive." Reggie sat at the rear of the transport. "Looks like it's going to take us a hell of a lot longer."

"We'd probably get there faster in a canoe," Fern said, looking at fields flooded by the Germans, one of the legacies of Operation Veritable.

Hundreds of vehicles struggled along a road that was under two feet of water in places, creating a massive traffic jam in one big mud field. Conditions continued to worsen.

Ewen watched the rookies. They were silent as their convoy

inched past bomb craters, makeshift hospitals, unrecognizable war debris, destroyed vehicles and marked graves. Ewen thought of Smithson and knew he wouldn't be out of a job for a while yet.

Two hours later they arrived. Kleve, the gateway to the Rhine, was a pile of rubble.

"Wasn't one of Henry VIII's wives from here?" said Sandy.

February 17, 1945
```
0900 — The CO with coy cmds recced the FUP and SL
but as the woods on our left had not been cleared
as per schedule, the recce party came under heavy
mortar and shell fire with the result that our
operation was cancelled for forty-eight hours.
```

PART FIVE

GERMANY
FEBRUARY—MAY 1945

Royal Hamilton Light Infantry War Diary
February 16, 1945
Kleve
1400— The water point has not yet been
established with the result that water shortage
is becoming acute. All coy cookers were notified
to this effect.

That night, their first night on German soil, was spent in a dank cellar with masses of rubble—stability uncertain—above them.

"The Germans started this mess and look what they've done. It's their turn now," Sandy said. There wasn't an ounce of sympathy in his body.

"Well, I hope the civilians were evacuated, the women and kids and old people. I'm guessing we're liberating some of them from Hitler too," Stan said.

Sandy shot him an angry glance. "You can't tell me the majority of them weren't cheering Hitler on when it all began."

They waited for the call to form up and head to their latest start line, the main road between Calcar and Goch. But the call did not come so they did not head into battle the next day. Instead they waited. And while they waited, the rookies fought to contain their panic, grateful for the sense of surety the veterans provided. The veterans contemplated their own mortality, wondering how the hell they'd made it even this far.

The Major had briefed them all on the plan. "We've been ordered to capture the Goch–Calcar Road and the start line is here." He pointed on the map. "The road runs northeast and almost through the Louisendorf crossroads. Our objective is to seize the high ground southeast of the road. This is it, Operation Blockbuster. We're to go approximately three thousand yards beyond Louisendorf to take the ridge.

"It's a two-battalion front. The attack will be made over open country. Kangaroos will move both battalions. We'll be on the left and the Essex on the right. The Royals are in reserve behind us and we'll get support from the Fort Garrys. Plus, the Toronto Scots are supporting us with machine guns and mortars. We'll follow the two lead companies. We're mopping up. We're facing an upward slope, and we don't know what's on the other side."

Ewen looked at Reggie, who dropped his head. *No, we don't know what's on the other side, do we, my friend?*

"Remember," concluded the Major, "Ground once taken is never given."

Two days later, Ewen and Reggie were leaning against a damp wall, sitting on their groundsheets as the dawn made the overcast sky slightly less gloomy, though hardly bright. "That sky looks like rain, I think," said Reggie. "But I don't know this sky, so maybe I'm wrong."

"Going to make the roads even worse," said Ewen, looking at the mud. "If that's possible. Kangaroos will struggle."

"We'll be on foot anyway. Trust your feet, Ewen. Remember?" Reggie smiled, then stopped, looking up to the sky once again. "I never thought I would come this far. Germany, it's a long way from home." He shook his head. "I wonder if I'm the first from my reserve to be this far from our land.

"This will be my last fight. I won't make it. I'll be heading over that hill and not returning."

Ewen was alarmed. They never spoke about the future. "No, Reggie! Don't talk like that."

"It's how it is. I know," said Reggie.

Ewen had heard of visions and knew some in his own family had them, but it wasn't talked about. He was keenly aware that death was the war's dance, and no one knew when their waltz would be over. "You and me, we've made it this far, and we're not going to end up under a white cross out here."

"You're going to make it. Ewen. You'll be around when it's all over." Reggie put his hand on Ewen's shoulder. "Remember, visit my mother when you get back to Canada."

Ewen stared into his friend's eyes. He nodded, hoping this was a promise he would not have to keep. He didn't ask about Rose.

They stood up and joined the rest of their platoon. No one was talking. Stan pulled out a photo of his fiancée; his hands shook.

"That's your gal?" Ewen asked.

"Yes, this is my Betty." Stan nodded. "Best thing that ever happened to me. She's got the wedding all planned, so I have to stay alive. I'll be in my battledress and she's been stitching a gown. She said we'll get a jeep and tear up an old white sheet into strips to fly off the back. She's got it all worked out . . . "

> *"If you can dream and not make your dreams your master;*
> *If you can think and not make thoughts your aim;*
> *If you can meet with triumph and disaster*
> *And treat those two imposters just the same . . . "*

"What's that, Reiss?" asked Fern.

"It's called 'If' by Rudyard Kipling," Sandy said. "My grandpa gave it to me just before I boarded the troop train for Halifax."

> *If you can force your heart and nerve and sinew*
> *To serve your turn long after they are gone,*
> *And so hold on when there is nothing in you*
> *Except the will which says to them: 'Hold on!'"*

"We're all going to hold on, just like Kipling says," Reggie said. "We'll do what we came here to do. Just do, don't think. Be prepared for close combat. Be prepared for anything."

Reggie checked the rookies' rifles one more time. He said, "Out there, when you have to hunker down, find any hole in the ground. There will be huge explosions all over the place and you can't do much for anyone. You're carrying extra ammunition and the mud will slow you down, but try to keep your wits about you. Don't be a hero and don't do anything stupid."

"Why the hell is this road so important?" Stan asked.

"It covers the approach to the ridge between Calcar and Uedem and will be the start line for the next operation to Xanten," Reggie said. "And when we get there, we've got to hold the position, hold the line, dig in, because Jerry will counterattack as soon as he can."

Ewen saw Fern holding something white against his uniform, next to his heart. Ewen clapped his hand on the younger man's shoulder. "What's that, Fern? Come one now, no secrets."

"Mies, she gave it to me. She embroidered her name on it, and some tulips."

H-hour was moments away. They all looked up at the escarpment.

Ewen looked at Reggie, then he closed his eyes and felt his friend's presence and drew strength from it. They'd been together since England. They'd been through Normandy, Antwerp, Woensdrecht, the Scheldt and so much more. Places he wanted to forget, yet a friendship, and a friend, he wanted to keep alive.

The guns opened fire. The battalion moved forward, first the tanks, then the kangaroos. Several tanks soon got bogged down in the mud, others hit landmines, and the kangaroos couldn't reach their objective. The two leading companies were forced to proceed on foot, under enemy fire from the moment they disembarked. Desperate to keep the momentum going, they returned fire even as rookies fell to the ground in panic. The Fort Garrys and the artillery provided what support they could; flame-throwers inspired the men to get up and keep moving forward.

C-Coy and D-Coy followed, stepping around the dead and injured. They moved over open ground, hiding behind what remained of farmyard walls, sheds and any other possible barricade as they approached their objective, a farmhouse still in German hands.

"Take Jerry head-on, men," Reggie yelled to whoever could hear. "Check your bayonets . . . " He stood and charged the building with Ewen right behind him. Their platoon threw grenades in every window, blasted the kitchen door to splinters and fought hand-to-hand. Once again, it was every man for himself in the chaos.

Finally, the Germans retreated and the farmhouse was theirs—for now. Jerry would be coming back, and they had to dig in.

"Reload, check your weapons," Reggie shouted. "Dig your slits in the farmyard, move, move, move."

Throughout the afternoon and night and the next day, the men endured counterattack after counterattack as squads of Germans infiltrated and retreated, over and over again. One wave swept Reggie away with a blast of machine-gun fire that ripped through his chest. Ewen saw him fall.

February 22, 1945
Telegram from GOC 2 Cdn Div
2nd Cdn Division is proud of the recent achievements of the RHLI. My congratulations to all ranks. You are making history — keep up the good work.

Royal Hamilton Light Infantry War Diary
February 23, 1945
Kleve
2330 — D Coy pushed forward about 500 yards on
a silent unsupported night attack. Success was
achieved and consolidation complete before the
inevitable counterattack was launched. The attack
was beaten off with heavy enemy losses.

They'd advanced through the night, gaining precious yards and
losing no men. Ewen moved on instinct, silently, as Reggie had taught
him. Now they were dug in, surrounded by the night's dead and the
corpses of the last few days. Ewen was numb, and not from cold.
None of the men of 17 Platoon spoke to him—there was nothing to
say. He was the last one now, the only original from the Normandy
landing almost eight months ago. Alive, unwounded. *Why?*

Staring blindly, Ewen looked out across the blasted landscape
under a watery grey sky. Reggie was still out there, somewhere, and
Ewen suppressed the pain in his gut as he thought of his friend's
body in the mud. The Germans had made it impossible to venture
out there to gather up their fallen comrades. The padre and RAP
had not been able to do their duty yet.

At first, he couldn't understand what he was seeing. Emerging
from a wood were two Germans, one holding a white flag. As they
got closer, Ewen could see one was a sergeant, the other a private.
"We want to speak with your commanding officer," the senior
German shouted in accented English.

The Major stood up not far from Ewen. "Well, I supposed we'd
better find out what the bastard wants," he said. "Put down your
rifle, Morrison, and come with me." Together, unarmed, they
began to walk towards their enemy, now standing still, the white
flag hanging limply from a stick.

"You are the Canadian officer in charge?" the Jerry sergeant
asked.

"I am," replied the Major. "Are you surrendering?"

"No. We have our dead here," he waved his hand. "And some wounded men as well. We ask for a truce so that we may recover them. And to bury our soldiers. I think that you too have dead soldiers you would like not to leave here." Both the Major and the German looked at the carnage that surrounded them.

"Will you and your men surrender?" the Major asked again.

"No, we will not. Never. Will you and your men surrender to us?"

A glare was all the answer he received.

"We will allow you a truce. You can collect your wounded and deal with your dead."

"Thank you, Major." He nodded crisply and then the two Jerrys went back to their unit.

The Major radioed the artillery company and ordered them to cease firing until further notice. As the mortars were silenced, German Red Cross men emerged through the grey haze that hung over the area. From their own side, RAP began to move through the wasteland. The grisly task of gathering the dead and tending to the wounded began. The living soldiers, both Canadian and German, eyed each other, memorizing their respective positions even as they went about their grim duty.

Dazed, Ewen forced himself to look for Reggie. He scanned the vicinity of the farm and began to walk towards it. He heard men moaning *Hilfe*, others groaning or wheezing. Buildings smouldered, and charred barns revealed the blackened hulks of dead cows and horses burned alive.

I can't find him. I can't see him. He's not here. Ewen's mind and eyes moved sluggishly as he trudged through the mud, avoiding bodies without looking. Then he saw a shape and he knew. Reggie lay face down in the mud. Ewen's pulse quickened and he ran over, dropped to his knees and rolled his friend over. He felt his neck for a pulse. Nothing. He leaned over his face, hoping to feel a breath. Nothing.

Ewen wiped mud off his friend's face, then whispered, "You went over the hill as a warrior and now you're free of this hell. Go into the sky." He had not felt such pain since his mother died. The stoicism that had sustained him since Normandy vanished and he cried—for his friend, for all the men who'd died, for himself.

He carefully put Reggie's legs together, then bent over and heaved him over his right shoulder. He staggered momentarily under the weight, regained his balance and, with a surge of energy, walked out of the farmyard, carrying his friend back to their platoon.

The Rileys of D-Coy watched their sergeant return on the back of the man who had been his best friend. Stan removed his helmet. One by one, the others did the same, silently honouring the man who had led them.

Then the mortars started up again.

February 25, 1945
1600 — The padre held a burial service for the personnel who had been killed during the action of the previous days.

Royal Hamilton Light Infantry War Diary
March 3, 1945
Uedem
0600 — The R Regt C passed through our coy
positions this morning and gained approx. 800 yds
with slight enemy opposition. This considerably
relieved the pressure on our front and gave us a
chance for some relaxation.

Ewen watched the PWs dig graves in the courtyard in front of the battalion HQ, a grand-looking farmhouse outside Uedem. The padre said his words over the dead, Canadians and Germans both. Two days, two burial parties. And more graves. The distance between their current position and the Goch–Calcar death road was only about ten kilometres, six miles paved with blood. *It all just keeps going on. One man dies, and it all just keeps going on.*

"17 Platoon, with me." The voice was Griff's. Edward Griffith was their new sergeant, who'd been transferred in from A-Coy. Ewen didn't know the man but thought he seemed like a good NCO, someone with experience who seemed to understand this craziness.

One man out, another man in. The war continues day after day, hour after hour, month after month. He remembered the cemetery at Dieppe, visiting it with Reggie, looking for his friend Joseph. *I wish I knew what the right ceremonies are, Reggie. I wish I could have done them for you.*

They fought on to another road, another village, another bit of high ground, attacks and counterattacks, averaging two or three hours of sleep a night. Ewen buried his emotions. Mourning the dead was a luxury that could lead to a grave or a trip to the hospital.

"The press are coming to talk to our company this afternoon," Griff told the men. "They want to get our side of the operation on the Goch–Calcar Road. If you get interviewed, do us proud—this is the chance for the Rileys to make the headlines in the *Maple Leaf*."

No reporter asked Ewen about his memories. That night, he sat in the dark at HQ with the rest of the men and watched *This Is the Life*, drinking tea and eating stale biscuits. "Paymaster's coming tomorrow," Griff told them after the show. "Enjoy this billet while you can. And there's another burial service tomorrow. 1500."

Just before midnight, there was a more interesting show for the men. Somehow, the 4th Field Regiment managed to set fire to their billet, the barn next to the Rileys HQ. Ewen watched the scramble as vehicles and half-dressed soldiers spilled out into the night. Ammunition abandoned in the building exploded, providing a modest fireworks display, and then it began to rain. *Would have thought that bonfire would make a good target for the Germans. Guess Jerry is asleep tonight.* Then he went to bed.

Two days later, "temporary rest" over, the Blue Patch boys moved to their new position, Xanten, on foot. Late that night, a new lieutenant—Ewen had lost track of how many 17 Platoon had had since Normandy—briefed the men on the next phase of their operation.

"This battle is as big as Normandy, men. For Jerry, Xanten is their last town on the western bank of the Rhine. We have to break the northern pivot of the Siegfried Line and reach Xanten and Wesel. The Hochwald is heavily wooded with only one railroad track down the middle. It's going to be dark and mined. We'll go through the forest and the tanks will punch straight onto Xanten. We must break through and we will.

"There's going to be a sixteen-minute artillery barrage from 0530. Then we go in, in two waves. We're going for a feigned frontal assault, just like football, with flankers swinging wide. We're swinging wide to the left. Each objective is vital to the success of the operation. Griffith, make sure the platoon is ready. We form up at 0400."

Griff took over. "First, we have to advance across open country, with Jerry watching. He's here, in the forest, waiting for us." The sergeant pointed out the landmarks on the map. "Jerry is on higher ground and he has a good view. It's a different war for them now, they're on the defensive and they've been ordered to defend their homeland to the last man. While it's all going on, we won't know who's winning, who's losing or what the hell is going on. If one unit doesn't make an objective that's crucial to ours, and we don't know, we're fucked. The whole thing is fucked. We're going out there in a fog of mud, rain and poor communications."

"After the floods we dealt with to get here, why don't they call in the navy?" Sandy asked. Only a few men laughed.

"Watch out for the artillery and mortar fire in the trees. The branches come firing down like spears. Be damn careful." Ewen remembered the Fôret de la Londe—Griff must have been there too.

"Why don't they all surrender and then we can all go home?" asked Stan. "They must know they're done for."

"Maybe they do. But they know what that means—the end of Germany. We're going to march into Berlin, destroy their military and redraw their borders. And their leaders are going to be tried and executed, beginning with the Führer himself. You'd fight, even if you didn't believe in the war anymore, just to stop that from happening. Now, get your kit ready, check your weapons. You've got two hours."

After Griff left them to it, Stan asked Ewen, "Do you think this is it, Morrison? Is this going to be the victory that's going to end the war? I just want to get back to Scotland, to Betty."

"You will, mate, you will," Sandy said. "I'm going to be your best man, aren't I? Not going to miss that."

Ewen knew Sandy's words were bullshit, but that's what these men needed to hear. He himself seemed to have lost the will to be positive.

Ewen looked up at the sky from the start line, watching the barrage. He pulled up his collar and wiped the dew from his rifle as his throat tightened. A few battles ago, he quit asking himself if he'd make it through the day, or the next hour. What was the point?

Griffith led the platoon across open flat country following the edge of the forest for several hundred yards. *So far, so good.* Hope he's sure of which trail to take, thought Ewen. The scouts had told them there were five trails into the forest —along with tripwires, barbed wire entanglements and a trench system covered by machine-gun fire—that would lead them on an angle toward the road in the gap. Griffith looked confident as he signalled the company.

As planned, they passed through the enemy lines from the left flank and reached their objective with almost no opposition. *Could it be so easy?* Then mortars and machine-gun fire blasted them from behind.

"Fire in the hole . . . "

"Move, move . . . "

"Stay down . . . "

"Go, go, go . . . "

He heard screams and through the smoke saw Sandy staring down at the ground, frozen. Ewen ran over and looked at the pit; horrified he saw Stan, bloody, muddy and unconscious. It was seconds before he realized that Dabrowski's right arm was gone and only a stump remained on the left.

"Medic! Medic!" Ewen screamed.

Out of the smoke, a German ran over, his hands in the air. Sandy turned, his face enraged, and raised his rifle.

"No, Sandy, no!" shouted Ewen, grabbing him. He pointed to the white band with the red cross on the man's arm.

"*Nicht schiessen, nicht schiessen* . . . don't shoot, don't shoot." He looked as if he wasn't sure that the crazed Canadian would respect the Geneva Convention.

Sandy shuddered but held his weapon levelled at the soldier. The enemy medic rushed to Stan and tended to him with precision, applying tourniquets and administering morphine.

Sandy shouted, "Stretcher, we need a stretcher!" He was trembling, his face grey, then he gripped his stomach and threw up. The German ignored him and continued to work on Stan until a Riley medic and the regimental padre showed up with a stretcher. The two medics nodded to each other. The Canadian medic looked at Stan and said, "I have to move on. You two," he pointed to the padre and the German medic, "Take him to the clearing station."

Afterwards, when Ewen and Sandy were finally able to get to the schoolhouse commandeered by the Rileys, the MO told them what had happened. The German medic had stayed with Stan until the ambulance left, carrying him and the other severely wounded men back to the Regimental Aid Post for evacuation. Then he had continued to work as casualty after casualty, German and Canadian, arrived.

Everyone had left him to it. "We weren't going to say no to his help. We needed every pair of hands we had. Afterwards, I saw him passed out in a corner. Put a blanket over him, and that woke him up sharpish. Passed him my canteen—rum, medicinal purposes, you know. He took a slug and said *prost*. I wanted to know more about him before they took him to the PW cage. Translator helped. He said they were retreating, but they'd been ordered not to surrender. Almost felt sorry for the chap. He took good care of your friend. And others."

March 10, 1945
Xanten
1500 — A mass burial service in the RAP area was held. The officers in the Bde were lined up in single file facing the graves. On the right all OR in the Bde were formed up facing the graves. The service was most impressive with last post being sounded by a bugler from 4 Cdn Fd Regt, a smartly turned out firing party from RHLI and the ESSEX pipe band playing the lament.

"Strike One!" The umpire, the battalion's MO, hollered.

They'd cleared an area next to the burned-out barn to create enough room for a baseball diamond. The sun was shining brightly, the weather was still mild—perfect weather for a ball game—and the Rileys challenged the Essex Scots to a game before the brigade moved back to Kleve. The Rileys were up for their last bat. Bottom of the ninth, 9–8 in favour of the Essex, two out, the tying run on first. Bets were on, and the spectators cheered.

"Ball One!"

Sitting on the makeshift bench in the afternoon sunshine, Ewen was grateful for clean clothes and dry socks. The pain in his toes was less now that the weather was warmer.

"Strike Two!"

Ewen lit up an English Players cigarette, a treat handed out at today's meal parade. "Here, Reiss. Have a smoke."

"Foul!"

Sandy hadn't been the same since Stan was injured. *Probably never will be. Dabrowski, poor bastard. One moment he's making plans for his wedding, then next he's lying in the dirt with no arms.*

The Canadians had cleared the northern end of the Hochwald and the Germans had withdrawn. D-Coy's major had been captured by the Germans, and Fred Boucher had been found shot-up in a cellar—Jerry had left him to die rather than bothering to take him prisoner. But Fred was going to make it. Ewen didn't think Stan had much of a chance, though. He hadn't said anything to Sandy.

"Ball Two!"

Once they had made it inside Xanten, or what was left of it, Ewen proposed a bet—getting a Nazi flag. The others hadn't known Woods, but they understood the spirit. In the end, they allowed Ewen to be the one to liberate the flag fluttering from a flashy German touring car. They'd had to capture the occupants first, which was a little reckless, but Woods would have liked that, Ewen thought. He didn't know what the hell he was going to do with the flag, but that wasn't the point.

"Strike Three! Batter out!" The MO called out, "The Essex win the game, boys." The teams shook hands over home plate while the crowd clapped, cheered and settled their bets.

With the Germans finally on the other side of the Rhine, the whole front had suddenly gone quiet and, in a couple of hours, they would be in Kleve for a rest, a ten-day recovery period. But rest would give him time to think, and thinking was bad. Ewen had become more comfortable with chaos.

Next month his eleven-day leave was due. He'd had to wait ten months to get it and sure as hell hoped it wouldn't be cancelled because of the manpower shortage. *Goddam Zombies.* Officially they were conscripts, promised a safe ride on home territory only and guaranteed never to have to serve overseas; Ewen and everyone he knew called them cowards.

As they were loading up for the short drive to Kleve, fifty-two reinforcements transferred in, eight assigned to 17 Platoon. Ewen didn't get all their names; some were gangly, others hulky. Their eyes didn't have the weary glaze of experience, and to Ewen it seemed they shone with innocence, fear or intelligence, but not understanding. Griff glared at one new man on the bench opposite. The man glared back. "Zombie," the sergeant whispered to Ewen, nodding at the man in a particularly new-looking private's uniform. Well, well, thought Ewen.

March 12, 1945 – War Diary
Kleve
1830 — Bn vehicles took men to Nijmegen tonight for recreation. The Canada Club and Wintergarden Cinema are the main attractions. There are no definite allotments laid on, first come, first served.

> Royal Hamilton Light Infantry War Diary
> March 16, 1945
> Kleve
> 1500 — The RHLI finally blossomed forth in the
> "Maple Leaf" today by scoring a dash two column
> write up, regarding the Xanten show. At long
> last the strenuous efforts of the battalion are
> being made public in the Canadian Army newspaper.
> This will certainly help to ease the pain that
> previous lack of recognition has caused.

More training, and even more recreation, the CO's priority for his exhausted men. D-Coy and 17 Platoon had done repairs to the house they were living in, making it more habitable than when they first arrived in Kleve. The new men were settling in: Cameron Hutchison, Maurice Glover, Allan Duncan, Roddie Gardner. And Mercer, the Zombie. When he'd introduced himself ("Bruce Mercer. Nice to meet you.") and offered his hand, Ewen had hesitated. He didn't want to be rude, but he wasn't sure he wanted to be friendly.

Sergeant Griffith saw to it that the new additions were brought up to speed, "Things are happening fast. Defeating Jerry is certain, there's no doubt about that, but it's not over. He's not safe behind the Rhine and we'll be crossing the river soon enough. In the meantime, we've got this break. I've got our training schedule—most mornings we've got a ten-mile speed march and in the afternoons there's forest fighting, defence, consolidation and counterattack training. And we've got more bayonet training, especially for you new guys. We can't relax yet."

"Not like your Zombie friends in Canada," Glover said. The whole platoon knew about Mercer now, and the hardened volunteers didn't bother to mask their contempt.

"I'm here, aren't I?" said Mercer, his body rigid as he looked around at the men on whom his life now depended.

"Only because Ottawa finally got the guts to make you," said Sandy. "Shame on you for not showing up earlier. I heard that when they put out a call last year for you Zombies to volunteer to serve like real soldiers, not one of you yellow bastards did."

"Shut it, Reiss," said Griffith. "He's got a blue badge now, not a black one."

"Let's see if you can live up to it," said Glover. "There's too many good guys buried here because we didn't have the men we needed on the ground."

"Back off, Glover, and the rest of you. Mercer's one of us now," Griff said. "Everyone get over it. Fight about it when this damn war is over. Dismissed."

"Look at this, Ewen," Sandy said, holding out a letter he'd just received. "It's from Stan. Can you believe it? Here. Read it. He mentions you."

Sunday, March 11

Dear Sandy,

I guess you're surprised at getting a letter from me—ha ha. I'm at the Number One Canadian General Hospital in Nijmegen and a great gal from the CWAC is writing this for me. Her name's Nan Love and she's from Saltcoats, Saskatchewan, and thinks she's heard of Morrison. Make sure you tell him. The nurses mostly have too much to do here to have time to write letters for guys like me, so she's doing me a great favour. I did meet Rose, the sergeant's sweetheart. She's pretty broken up, but that hasn't stopped her doing her work. She reminds me a bit of Betty.

Nan's also helped me to write a letter to Betty. I'm still alive, but I'm not exactly in one piece. I needed to let her know that I'm not holding her to our engagement. She's so wonderful, she deserves to walk down the aisle with someone who's got more than just half an arm. Sorry you're not going to get to be my best man, Sandy.

I think they're going to be moving me out of here soon. They've got me

so pumped full of morphine I don't know if I'll make it back to Canada or not. If I do, let's get together for a beer.
  Your friend,
  Stan

Still alive, thought Ewen. But does he want to be? He was amazed at the coincidence—Nan Love, the dark-haired girl he'd been too shy to ask to dance at Tupper Hall, was in the CWAC and in Europe.

They headed into Nijmegen that night, in search of entertainment, burgers and maybe old friends. No one asked Mercer to join them.

March 31, 1945
SUMMARY
In the Xanten show, this unit once again showed
their remarkable qualities of leadership and
stamina. Many individual acts of bravery and
gallantry were displayed, some will be mentioned
officially, others won't, but all will have the
supreme satisfaction of knowing they have done
their duty well.

Royal Hamilton Light Infantry War Diary
April 1, 1945
Doetchinchem
1700 — The bn moved off again with all coys
marching and the bn vehicles in convoy in the
normal order of march. Up to now the leading
brigade has not made contact with the enemy with
the result that we are moving ahead rapidly.

As Ewen had watched vehicles inch over the bridge, he stared in awe at the power of the water flowing in the wide river, swollen with spring runoff. He pulled his collar up under his chin—just looking at it made him shiver. He imagined the centuries of ships that must have travelled up and down this strategic waterway, trading and waging wars. At Juno Beach and the Antwerp Harbour, Germany had seemed an eternity away. Now there he was, watching hundreds of Canadians crossing the Rhine while so many weren't.

The Blue Patch boys would have to wait their turn to cross the Rhine. They'd been ordered northeast, back into the Netherlands. They marched and occasionally rode through Netterden, small towns and Doetinchem, and on April 2, the regiment reached the Twente Canal near Zutphen. Small pockets of Jerry resistance didn't slow them down. The next day, the order came to cross the canal.

"Jerry's snipers could be taking aim, so I suggest you paddle your asses as hard as you can," Griff said.

Another canal crossing, Ewen thought. From past experience, bobbing up and down in a raft with Jerry waiting on the other side made him feel particularly vulnerable. He looked at his watch—2130—at least it was dark.

One by one the Rileys crowded into the boats. Each soldier carried their pack, their trenching spade, and pockets filled with ammunition. By 0130 the whole regiment was across, and by early that morning all but one of the companies had managed to reach their objectives.

The following morning, April 4, fair weather with a slight wind promised good visibility, allowing one regiment after another to leapfrog ahead, deepening the Allied bridgehead. Over the next few days, they continued to push north through Lochem, Holten, Lemelerveld and Hoogeveen, severing the Germans from the Netherlands.

The regiment arrived at the small village of Westerbork early in the afternoon of April 12. The men took advantage of the spring sunshine and lounged in a field dotted with yellow daffodils, waiting to find out when the convoy would push off.

Ewen took off his boots and socks to massage his two stubs. He stood up and walked around slowly, enjoying the feel of the earth. Growing up, bare feet were the order of the day all summer, especially when it rained. He'd carry his shoes and slop through the mud and the puddles. By fall, the soles of his feet were as tough as leather.

Spring seemed to have finally arrived in Holland. He wondered where the birds were, or if they'd even show up with the continent blown apart. On the Saskatchewan prairie, he had known spring had arrived when the killdeer and meadowlark woke him up. He had loved watching the oriole, a master weaver, build its nest, and used sneak up to listen to the red-winged blackbird in the bulrushes. The crows had chased the hawks; the blackbirds had gone after the crows.

"Okay men, saddle up," Griffith said to the platoon. "We're off. About seven miles from here is a concentration camp, Westerbork. They were liberated this afternoon by the 8th Reconnaissance Regiment. Their carriers followed a railway track for a couple of miles and found a compound surrounded by barbed wire. There weren't any Jerrys around, so they drove through the gate to the parade ground. Thought the place was empty. Then all the doors opened and people started pouring out, cheering. The 8th have moved on. A-Coy of the South Saskatchewans are guarding the place now;

we're going to take over for a few hours until we're relieved. We head out in fifteen minutes."

"A concentration camp?" Sandy said. Ewen couldn't imagine the thoughts that were running through his mind. The stories of anti-Semitic atrocities had been horrifying. What were they going to find at Westerbork? Could it be worse than the combat casualties he'd witnessed?

April 12, 1945
Beilen
1315 — The convoy arrived at the town of
WESTERBORK. All Coys are concentrated in a field.
A large crowd of Dutch civilians have gathered
around. They seem to take special delight in
putting their names on the vehicles with chalk and
smoking Canadian cigarettes.

Royal Hamilton Light Infantry War Diary
April 12, 1945
Beilin
1330 — D Coy was ordered to take over the
responsibility of guarding a Jewish concentration
camp a few miles from WESTERBORK. The Major
reports that he has never seen anything like it
before.

The truck's tires threw up a trail of dust as they followed a barbed-wire fence along a sandy road. Soldiers with their backs to the fence twisted around to look at the wooden, oblong barracks and watch-towers. Ewen couldn't interpret the look on Sandy's face.

Straight ahead, just outside the gates, was a comfortable house clearly intended for the commandant. Their driver geared down to cross the railway tracks, then parked to the right of the gate. Before he could turn off the engine, a mob ran to greet them, hundreds of people, reaching up, dancing, singing, crying. The veterans, used to cheering crowds and the adulation of a liberated people, had had some sense of what to expect. For the new guys, the intensity was overwhelming; one by one, the Rileys stepped down and were embraced by the crowd.

A major from the South Saskatchewan Regiment pushed through the crowd to talk to his counterpart in D-Coy. Ewen heard him say, "What have you got for me?"

"It's a transit camp."

"What exactly does that mean?"

"Apparently the Nazis had the Jews rounded up and sent here to wait for deportation to Auschwitz or Bergen-Belsen. We believe there are about nine hundred to a thousand here right now. The IO is going through records in the commandant's house with the help of a couple of the detainees."

"Any Jerrys around?" the Major asked.

"No, the SS guards left suddenly last night, but everyone stayed inside to see what would happen. Jerry shot all the animals before they left. One of the Nazi bastards told them, 'If we can't eat them, you're not going to. If we had more time, we'd shoot all of you.'

"Everyone has gone crazy—they got into the Germans' food store and they're preparing a big meal right now. They all look like they could use it. Just make sure no one leaves—they're safer staying put inside the gates until the Red Cross gets here."

"We're here until we get told otherwise," the Major said. The two senior officers saluted one another and the Saskatchewans loaded up and left.

A clamour of German, Dutch and English voices surrounded them—laughter sounded good in every language.

"Reiss—you speak some German, see who you can find to get more information. Then report to the IO," the Major ordered. He looked for the rest of his men, who had melted into the jubilant throng. "Where's everyone else gone? So much for guarding the camp."

A small boy emerged and stood hesitantly near the two Rileys. Sandy crouched down and said, *"Einige schokolade versuchen?"*

Then he looked up at Ewen. "I hope he understands me." Ewen looked at the boy, who was dressed in faded brown overalls and a buttoned-up shirt. He looked to be six or seven years old but his wary grey eyes were older.

"My guess is that he doesn't trust anyone in uniform," Ewen said. "Try giving him some."

Sandy smiled, pulled a chocolate bar out of his pocket and held it out. The boy shook his head. Reiss unwrapped the bar, broke off a piece and offered it. Again, the boy shook his head and pointed his finger at Sandy. His message was clear, you first. Sandy popped the square in his mouth, and chewed, a big smile on his face. Then he broke off another piece. This time the boy took it. As the rich sweetness hit his tongue, his eyes widened and he grinned. Ewen thought that the boy probably hadn't tasted chocolate for a long time, if ever.

"Mein name ist Sandy. Was ist ihr name?"

"Micha."

A man in a worn suit had joined them. He was holding a green glass bottle and said, *"Ich bin Michas Vater. Möchten Sie ein paar Schnaps? Ich habe es aus dem Geschäft der Wachen befreit."*

"Ja, vielen dank," Sandy said. He translated for Ewen. "This is Micha's father. He wants to give us a drink—Schnapps."

"I speak some English. Please, come with me. We have much to celebrate." The man led them inside a wooden building and invited them to sit at a battered table. He produced three old jars and poured a generous couple of fingers of Schnapps into each one. "Westerbork crystal. *Prost.*"

Sandy laughed as their jars clinked. Ewen took a swig and coughed.

Micha's father said, "We cannot believe this day has arrived. For the past couple of days, the Nazis have been burning papers and destroying equipment. When we discovered that the Nazis were gone, our leader said not to run out of the camp, to wait for the Red Cross. Two young men left to see if they could make contact with the Allies. One came back and said that the Canadians were crossing the canal. Then we saw the dust on the road. The tanks."

"You are German, sir?" Sandy asked

"There are German and Austrian and Dutch Jews here. We German Jews came first."

"How did you end up here?"

"We lived in Berlin but after Kristallnacht in 1938 I knew I had to get my family out of Germany. We left for the Netherlands and I tried to get a permit to England. But then the war broke out in September. The Dutch did not know what to do with all us asylum seekers, so we were put in a military compound near Amsterdam. The conditions were not good.

"In early 1940 we were 'asked' if we wanted to go to Westerbork, where they were building a new refugee camp and families could stay together. They built tracks for the railway to come inside and a rail station platform. Every new arrival got a card listing their skills so that work could be assigned. Everyone in the camp had to work. There was a school, a hairdresser, an orchestra, a leather factory. We knew it was all planned to give us a sense of hope and to not alarm the locals.

"I was one of the first to arrive. They needed some of us to serve them, to be the middle people between them and the inmates, and I became the Dutch commandant's waiter. It was a good job; I was able to smuggle some food for my wife and child. At first, when the Dutch controlled the camp, we could receive passes to go to the outside. I tried to get the paperwork done to go to America. But then the country was invaded by the Nazis, and another dream ended. The Dutch left and the SS took over."

Ewen couldn't imagine being so close to getting out, not once, but twice.

"They didn't kill us, but we worked hard making clothing for the German Army. My boy has been here since he was one-and-a-half years old. This is the only life he knows."

Micha was sitting on a nearby bunk, licking his fingers and the wrapper. "He's never had chocolate before," his father said.

"A train went every Tuesday to the east, usually with the sick and elderly and children. We were told they were going to a working camp but no one believed that. Some old people were taken to the train on a cart. After every train left, Micha always asked, 'What happened to them? How come I wasn't allowed to go? Why wasn't I good enough to go?' He thought leaving on the trains was a good thing."

Sandy shook his head and looked sadly at the boy.

"One day, the big boys were playing football and the ball went over the fence. One boy went under the fence to get the ball and a German guard shot him. He was an innocent boy who just wanted to get their ball back. Micha was there."

"How could someone do that?" Ewen asked.

"If you're educated in evil, you act from evil."

"What will you do next?" Sandy asked.

"We will stay here until the Red Cross comes. After that, I don't know. I can't be sad because I'm alive and my family is still here. But we cannot go back to Germany."

Ewen got up and thanked the man for the drink. "I'm going to stay, Ewen," Sandy said, "I've got more to learn." Ewen left the two men to their Schnapps, as Micha napped on the bunk.

Outside, the happy madness continued to reign. People carried armfuls of food and bottles of wine and beer from storerooms to a large building with smoke coming out of the chimney. Ewen could see Canadian uniforms in the crowd.

The inmates who spoke some English tried to communicate. "Hello, Canada!" said a young girl with a big smile on her face and a bigger sack of potatoes in her skinny arms. Her dress was faded and her shoes worn, but the two pigtails that framed her narrow face were neatly braided. She looked about twelve. "My name is Virry. What is your name?"

"Ewen." He bowed. She laughed. "Nice to meet you, Virry."

"It is nice to meet you, Ewen. You must come to help with the feast. Do you like to peel potatoes?"

"Of course."

"This is the best day! We have been for twenty-four hours without guards. After the Nazis left, we were waiting to see what would happen. We didn't know what to do. We didn't know if the Germans were in the bush waiting to shoot us. When we saw the dust coming down the road, we could not wait! All of us ran outside the gates towards the dust, even though it was forbidden. A soldier, he gave me chocolate! Come, the kitchen is this way."

Women, men and soldiers were cooking and celebrating with no sense of order. The aromas of different foods being cooked wafted in the air and the room pulsed with happiness. The future for both survivors and soldiers; everyone just wanted to enjoy the moment and celebrate surviving. Virry handed Ewen a knife. "Now, we work." The pair began to peel.

"Outside the camp there are huge fields where we worked. All the food was for the Germans, but now it is ours."

Cautiously, Ewen asked, "When did you come here?"

"Two and a half years ago, I think. We used to live in Amsterdam. I never really thought about being Jewish. Then we were not allowed to go to the cinema, and I could not go swimming or skating or play in the parks. We had to walk everywhere, as we were not permitted to use the trains or ride in cars. One day, when I came home my mother said, 'You're not going back to that school, you're going to another school.' Why? I asked. She said, 'You have to do that, and you have to wear this yellow star.' I didn't understand the difference between yesterday and today. I had to feel Jewish today and yesterday I did not. I was so confused."

"I'm sure," Ewen said.

Ewen put a peeled potato in a pot and picked up another one.

Virry continued. "My father is a doctor but he couldn't practise anymore. So he worked at Hollandsche Schouwburg. It was a horrible place, where they sent the Jews they arrested to wait to be transported. He installed a hospital on the first floor. Under the noses of the Nazis, he also helped others to escape." Virry looked up at Ewen, fiercely proud. "Across the street there was a kindergarten. From there he worked with the Resistance to hide children."

Ewen didn't know what to say. He peeled potatoes and listened.

"Then we were arrested and sent here. A few months later, in January last year, my father was called back to Amsterdam by the Nazis. In July my mother gave birth to my brother. He is eight months old but my father has seen him only once, when he was allowed to visit in August. Then he was sent back to Amsterdam. I hope he comes back to find us."

"So your brother was born here in the camp?" Ewen asked.

"Yes," Virry said. "Every Monday the train came in the afternoon and was cleaned. We'd sit in the barracks Monday evening, while a list of names was read out over the loudspeaker. Everyone sat in fear of their name getting called out. One thousand people went every week in the cattle cars. The trains went east, to Poland, but we were allowed to stay because my father is a doctor."

Virry stopped when she saw the look on Ewen's face. "I had a German grandmother," she said. "Not all the Germans are bad."

Ewen decided to change the subject. "Do you go to school, Virry?"

"At first there was a school, but then there wasn't. We all just worked. Sometimes I worked on the land, outside the camp, with the guards behind us. There is a telephone line from the farm and the guards used to use it for target practice while we worked, trying to break the line with their pistols. We never felt safe.

"Then we were moved inside. For ten hours every day we sat at a long table and chopped open old batteries. We had to separate the parts and take out the *duppel*, the aluminum. We heard that German pilots dropped the pieces like snowflakes, to try and jam the Allied radar. It was horrible, we all coughed, but at least we could talk. One girl I worked with, her name was Anne, we became friends for a short time. Her family was in the punishment barracks. She had been in hiding so she liked talking to someone new. Then her name was called on Monday."

Ewen was amazed at Virry's matter-of-fact tone.

"A few weeks after Anne left, we were put on the train too. It was our turn to go to Poland. Then, half an hour before leaving, the commandant decided that the whole family should go away together. We got permission to get off and wait for my father. That was the last train that left Westerbork. Three days later a strike broke out at the national railway; there were no trains running anymore at all. That was one of the reasons that last winter was the 'hunger winter' but for us it was a miracle. To think, I could have been on that final train and now I am peeling potatoes with you!"

The heap of potatoes was finished. "Ewen, I will never forget this day, or you," Virry said solemnly.

Ewen smiled at her. "Neither will I, young lady. Neither will I."

April 12, 1945
Assen
2100 — D-Coy, who had taken up former positions at the former concentration camp, were ordered to rejoin the battalion but the D-Coy boys do not like the prospects of leaving the place. In fact, some difficulty was experienced by the Major in rounding up his coy.

Royal Hamilton Light Infantry War Diary
April 13, 1945
Haren
1200 — The convoy is underway again, advancing
slowly. En route the Dutch have thought up a new
one and are now hanging flowers on our vehicles as
well as chalking them up.

The kangaroo rumbled along the road to Groningen, the regiment's final goal in the Netherlands. Ewen dug in his pocket for his cigarettes, oblivious to the noise and the jolts—it beat marching. Back to the wind, he cupped his hands to strike a match. Seven more days, he thought. In seven days, I'm going to Edinburgh, back to the Whites'. I just have to make it through the next week. He'd written the Whites to let them know he was coming. He was going to collect the few things he'd left there and ship them home. Am I tempting fate, planning for a life back home? He felt a momentary flash of anger, remembering how he and Reggie never talked about the future. Reggie had a vision that he wasn't going to come back from that hill and that's exactly what happened. He hoped that somewhere in England a British family had packed up Reggie's things and sent them back to his mother.

"Morrison, can I ask you something?" It was Cameron Hutchison, one of the new reinforcements. He looked anxious, worried that he might ask the wrong question.

"Sure, what is it?"

"How the hell have you survived since Normandy?"

Ewen smiled. If Woods were here, he would have everyone betting to see if I make it to the end.

"I haven't yet, it's not over. But growing up on the Prairies was pretty good training for all this. You're from Toronto, yes? Growing up in the city was probably different, but surviving a Saskatchewan winter and sleeping in a freezing cold slit trench, both are pretty miserable. All we had was straw or hay mattresses and, the minute

215

the weather warmed up, us boys would set up sleeping quarters in one of the bins in the yard. It was great to get out of the house. We had a lot more freedom and a lot less snoring to listen to. I don't know where I was going with that . . . I guess for the past ten months, I've packed a lot of hay in my slit trench and heard a lot of snoring. I don't know, Hutchison. I just know I intend to get through to the end."

"I'm going to fight the Japs when we're done here," the new guy said. "My brother is in a PW camp in Japan and I'm going to do everything I can to get him out."

Mercer shouted over the gears, "Rumours say it's all going to be over soon." The men still didn't like Zombie Bruce much, but they'd learned to tolerate him.

"Yeah, well, don't forget your history. In the last war, rumours of peace just gave those sorry bastards on the frontline false hope," Maurice said.

"It's not over boys, so don't get comfortable. We still have a war to finish off. Jerry is desperate now," shouted Griffith, "and it's not just the Germans we're going to be up against. Groningen is full of Belgian and Dutch SS troops."

"You can bet those collaborators are afraid for their lives," Maurice said. "I don't get how someone could betray their own countrymen and support fascism. Right is right and wrong is wrong. They deserve a good beating and then getting locked away forever."

"Don't go there, Glover. All of you, I know it will be hard, after all we've seen, but if and when collaborators are caught, we're not to interfere. The brass have ordered a strict hands-off policy. It's for the Dutch to sort out their own traitors," Griffith said.

"If it were up to me," Sandy said to Ewen. "I'd have those bastards executed."

The convoy ground to a halt early in the evening. There was no meal break for the troops—the battle for Groningen began without

delay. On orders to do the least amount of damage to Dutch property, they fought to clear the way into Groningen with small arms
and no artillery support. A-Coy got a foothold in the southern
part of the city and from there each company leapfrogged past the
next as they fought their way into the southern neighbourhoods.
After thirty hours of continuous fighting, the Rileys had secured
a bridge, cleared eight city blocks and captured over four hundred
Germans.

In the afternoon, 17 Platoon regrouped in a small side street
while flame-throwers drove snipers out from the last remaining
buildings. Ewen took off his helmet and wiped his brow. He looked
up to see an elderly woman was hobbling towards a square, her
head covered by a black scarf neatly tied under her chin. In one
hand was a furled umbrella she was using as a cane; the other
clutched a small woven basket that looked empty. She looked to the
right, as if checking for oncoming traffic.

Has she got dementia? Ewen thought. Then he grabbed at Cameron, who'd started to move to the entrance of the alley. Before he
had taken two steps, a sniper took aim and the old woman went
down. "She's an old lady, what the fuck!" Cameron yelled.

By nightfall the southern part of the city, south of the canal, was
in Allied hands. Ewen stared at the prisoners walking past in the
dark. Most were very young or very old and looked surprisingly
happy.

Out of a smouldering building, two Red Cross men emerged
carrying a stretcher, stumbling toward the weary platoon. Ewen
looked down at the blood-stained German uniform of the soldier
they were carrying. "Bloody hell," Sandy said.

"He's in rough shape," one of the medics said. "He took a bullet
in the thigh, but he'll make it. A couple of local women helped him
out—lucky for him one of them was a nurse. Can you carry him
back to the aid post? We're taking Jerry's medics and getting the
rest of the wounded."

"Sure," Ewen said. "Sandy, give me a hand." *I hope the Japs are treating Cameron's brother as well as we are this Jerry.*

The soldier was conscious and Ewen could see the fear as well as the pain on his face. He looked young enough to still be in middle school.

"*Mein name ist Herbert,*" he said, his eyes focused on Ewen's.

"*Mein name ist Ewen.*" He took the front of the stretcher, Sandy the back, and they carried the wounded lad as carefully as they could.

Sandy and Ewen reached the aid post and put Herbert's stretcher down on the ground. Sandy wobbled and sat down, chest heaving as he caught his breath. Ewen put his hands on his hips and stretched out his back.

"You guys are Rileys, right?" one of the medics asked.

"Yeah," Ewen said.

"Word just came in. You're going to be relieved in the morning—forty-eight-hour rest and reorganization in Haren for you guys. Well done. You might as well wait here for your company to catch up."

The two soldiers sat down on either side of the stretcher, while the medical personnel dealt with the more serious cases. Herbert would have to wait for his turn.

Ewen tried to speak German, "*Du bist ja noch kinder.*"

Herbert looked confused.

"Good try, Ewen. But the accent is terrible and the grammar worse." Sandy said to the boy. "*Er meinte, Sie sind noch ein Kind.*" Then, for Ewen's benefit, "I told him that you meant he's just a kid."

"*Wasser, ich brauche Wasser . . .*"

Ewen passed him his water bottle. Sandy held up his head while Herbert gulped down the whole bottle and then nodded his thanks.

Ewen said to Sandy, "Ask Herbert how old he is."

Sandy complied and translated. "He said he's sixteen."

The boy was looking a bit brighter, and Ewen was curious. This was his first, and might be his only, opportunity to learn about the ordinary men he'd been fighting for months and months. For the next hour, Ewen asked questions, Sandy translated and Herbert talked.

"Are you in the Hitler Youth?"

"Yes. I was in the fourth grade when I joined. Everybody joins the Hitler Youth when they are ten years old. We met once a week and went scouting, played sports and games like learning to hide. We got a uniform and used to parade. It was fun.

"The girls were told to have as many children as possible. Mothers get a gold medal if they had eight or more children. A silver for six or seven. And a bronze for four or five. They were told to prepare for motherhood, that it's their duty to breed a new generation of sons and daughters."

"How long have you been a soldier?"

"About two months, since I turned sixteen."

"What regiment?"

"The panzer division." Herbert tried to laugh. "But we don't have any tanks."

Ewen and Sandy smiled at each other. That was good news if they were heading back into Germany.

"Most of the railroads are destroyed. There is no gas and the roads are filled with people running from the Russians. In my unit, we cannot communicate with our leaders, no one knows what is going on. It is all so hopeless. We are told every day we cannot surrender. That you will kill us and mistreat our civilians. We want it over."

Herbert closed his eyes, exhausted. He roused suddenly and lifted his head. "Friedrich! Did you find Friedrich?"

"Who?"

"Did you find Friedrich?"

"Who's Friedrich?"

"My friend. He is a senior soldier. He had been on the Eastern

Front. He told me to run towards the woods beyond the streets. He said he would cover me."

"I don't know. He may be a PW now, but in this chaos, you probably won't know for a while what happened to him," Sandy said.

"I hope he is okay. He was wounded nine times in Russia. He told me that in winter he put straw in his boots and newspapers under his clothes to try to stay warm.

"This morning I said to him, 'We've lost the war, why don't we surrender?' He said, 'If we surrender, or turn around, we'll be hung. Haven't you seen those who tried to desert swinging on trees?' So, I sat thinking either we get shot by the enemy or hung by our own men. Friedrich, I know he wants to go home to his wife and children. He said our oath of allegiance, obedience and loyalty could be a trap, forcing us to do criminal things."

Ewen did not want to think of the terrible things he'd done.

"Tell us about growing up in Germany," Sandy asked. "My grandparents immigrated to Canada from Russia before the last war but we always stayed in touch with our relatives in Germany. Then we lost touch." Then he added: "I'm Jewish."

No one spoke for a moment. Herbert continued.

"We lived close to the Polish border. My father worked for the railway, then he lost his job. He started working for a liquor factory making schnapps from potatoes. At that time, we had five cows, twenty pigs, chickens, geese, ducks and even doves and rabbits. We had to sell a cow or some pigs in order to pay our debts. Horses were rare, so our cows pulled the plough."

Ewen remembered milking fifteen cows twice a day, separating the milk, storing the cream and taking it to the train to be shipped to Yorkton. "Tell him we had cows and pigs as well. Tell him I came to the conclusion that the best place for a cow is in the roaster! Seems like all farmers were in the same boat."

They shared a laugh.

Sandy asked, "What about the Nazis?"

"My father was against the war. But then two men came. They were from the party. They said my father could join the railway again if he would join too. What to do? He had a family to feed and a big mortgage to pay, so he joined. It took only four weeks and he was back with the railways."

That's what we heard in Canada," Sandy told Ewen. "Our German relatives wrote to tell us how at first, after Hitler became chancellor, life did seem better for a while. Then they stopped writing."

Herbert continued his story. "My mother always went to the church, there was this famous priest who held meetings for people who opposed the Nazis. She went in the evenings, but then she was warned by my teacher and she stopped going.

"One day we were sent home from school early. On the way home, we heard soldiers coming. My friends and I jumped in the ditch to watch. The soldiers marched in perfect time, looking straight ahead. They sang military songs about going to war. We were laughing."

Ewen could easily imagine how exciting it would all seem to a ten-year-old farm boy.

"That evening, on the radio, we heard we were at war with Poland. We were told it was revenge for the last war."

Ewen offered Herbert a biscuit. "It's army rations and tastes like dust, but it's something."

"I like to bake cakes. My favourite is apple cake . . . My mother liked my help, she was so busy. But then I was called up to serve the Fatherland and I couldn't help her anymore. When I turned fourteen, the Reich said I was grown up and had to work, before I would join the army. So I lived in a camp and we learned about agriculture and practised military drills. I was there for one year. I got to go home for a couple of weeks at Easter. Then, I had to go to a camp in Poland, close to the border of Germany, where they were settling Germans from Romania. Those people, they had wanted to come to Germany, but the Nazis made them settle in Poland instead.

"There were about thirty of us boys there. We had a house-keeper and she had an assistant housekeeper. Those two women washed and mended our clothes and looked after us. They made us breakfast and dinner. Before each meal, we said grace, 'Fold your hands, bow your head, and thank the Führer for your bread.'"

At last, Herbert stopped talking and closed his eyes.

The medic finally came to take his vitals and assess the German boy's injuries. "It's a wonder how the bullet went through his thigh and out his ass. It's a miracle it didn't hit the bone or his family jewels. He'll ship out in about twenty minutes. He's lost a lot of blood. Tell him he'll most likely end up in a PW convalescing hospital here in the Netherlands."

Sandy translated for Herbert, who nodded drowsily. Then he said, *"Das letzte Hemd hat keine Taschen."*

Sandy translated for the final time. "'The last shirt doesn't have pockets.' So very true, Ewen."

April 15, 1945
Groningen
1130 — The coys are waiting to be relieved and anxious to move on. The morning has been quiet for our own troops. A few PWs are coming back. The Dutch Orange organization is busy rounding up collaborators and bringing them to a collecting post near Tac HQ. No love is shown by the patriots to these collaborators.

Royal Hamilton Light Infantry War Diary
April 15, 1945
Haren
1300 — There is quite a rush throughout the bn this
morning as an early breakfast has been laid on
and we are to be ready to move in approx one hour.
There is a long move ahead and most of the men are
not very keen on the idea of leaving Holland. The
distance to be covered is about 125 miles.

Haren had been a two-day haven of peace: clear skies, warm spring weather and no snipers, no mortars, no machine guns—no fear. Some men hitchhiked into Assen, others preferred just to sleep, luxuriating in real beds, surrounded by real walls. Haircuts were arranged with the local barber, and the YMCA put on a show.

The nearby lake, with its cottages and boats, reminded many of summer resorts at home. "Bet you'd like to try some fishing there," Ewen had said to Fern. Instead, they went to a dance and social evening at a local café. Mercer had asked to join them, and they were all feeling so good about life, even the Zombie was welcome to come along. Maurice stayed back at their billet. "All I want is a quiet evening with a book. Can I borrow that western of yours, Morrison?"

The men danced and drank and enjoyed themselves, with Fern, whose Dutch was passable, thanks to his relationship with Mies, providing translation. The following morning everyone, except Maurice, was heavily hungover, but they dragged themselves out of bed for a breakfast of cheese and bread, and a bath parade. As they were leaving the local sanatorium, they were approached by two middle-aged Dutchmen. The taller one said, "Canadians, in that house over there, in the cellar, there are Germans. They have been hiding there for some time."

"Thanks for the tip," said Griff. "Come on guys, let's go. We'll show the brass what 17-Platoon is made of. It'll be a bonus for the Lieutenant if we can make him look good with the Major."

"We're not exactly ready for combat, Sarge," said Ewen. The Canadians were clean but unarmed.

"Those Jerrys aren't going to know that we've just come from the showers and that you're hungover, Morrison," said Griff.

They entered the house, calling confidently to one another and stomping through the front rooms, slamming doors until they found the entrance to the cellar.

"Reiss, tell them to surrender," the sergeant whispered to Sandy. "Tell them we won't kill them if they come out with their hands up, and they'll be treated as prisoners of war. Better us than some angry Dutchmen looking for payback."

Sandy shouted at the door in German. Seconds of silence. Then they heard footsteps on the stairs and the door began to open. "*Nicht schiessen! Wir geben auf.*"

As the first soldier, his hands behind his head, came through the doorway, Maurice grabbed him and pulled him to one side. Six more pale, grizzled, fearful Jerrys followed. They looked too exhausted to care that they'd just surrendered to a bunch of unarmed Canadians. 17 Platoon were congratulated on returning from the bath parade with seven fresh Jerry PWs.

Back at their billet, there was a surprise for Ewen. Two surprises.

"Morrison, mail for you," said Griff, handing him two letters.

Ewen was stunned—who would be writing him? He never got letters, not one since he'd landed at Juno.

The first had a Canadian stamp and was addressed to Sgt R. Johnson and Pte E. Morrison. Ewen's hand shook slightly as he ripped open the envelope.

> *Dear Reggie and Ewen —*
>
> *Well, you won't believe it but I'm back in Canada. I told the medical officer that you two couldn't manage without me, but they sent me back home anyway.*

At Groesbeek I took a lot of shrapnel in the guts. I won't bore you with the details, but they shipped me to a hospital in England. I showed up back here in Alberta aboard a CPR hospital train with seventy other wounded vets.

I'm on the mend, but think about you guys a lot. Don't think I'm getting sappy here, but I'm sure glad to count you guys as friends at times like this. I hope those rookies can help you get to Berlin. Have you got a Nazi flag yet? Woods, that sorry bastard, wherever he is, will come back to haunt you if you don't get one.

Well, you two keep your heads down and your socks dry. Let me know how you're doing when you get a chance.

Kick Jerry in the ass and get back home!

Cowboy

He had to sit down before he could bring himself to open his second letter. This one had a Belgian stamp and was addressed simply to Pte E. Morrison.

It was from Rose. Reggie had talked so much about her and shared the letters that she'd written, that Ewen felt as if he knew her without ever meeting.

Dear Ewen,

I am sorry that it has taken me so long to write you. I wanted to, after I heard about Reggie but, to be honest, it was too difficult. Just thinking about him hurts so much. Every day I see pain and mutilation and death, but nothing prepares one for the death of someone we love.

We only knew each other for a year and, although the days we actually got to spend together were few, they were so very special and wonderful. I miss him every moment.

He told me all about you and talked about you in his letters to me. I know you were his friend, and that in your soldier's way, you may have loved him too.

We've been moving around a lot, from hospital to the front and back again—wherever we're needed the most. I haven't been to Paris yet. I don't think I want to go now.

Please, Ewen, take care of yourself and stay safe and strong. Back in Canada, there will be a girl who will love you as much as I loved Reggie.

You are in my prayers,

Rose

No one wanted to leave the Netherlands, but now they were on the road back into Germany and the convoy, the troops travelling in carrier vehicles, followed the routes laid out by the battalion: code-named Diamond, Iron and Pearl.

They crossed the frontier in mid-afternoon, and the men were silent, absorbing what this journey into the land of their enemies meant. Ewen thought of Woods and his rage, Sandy of his family and relatives. Lots of guys must be thinking of payback, Ewen thought. He thought of Reggie but knew that his friend would have felt dishonoured by vengeance.

Ewen saw three children standing in a barnyard door, one wearing a coat several sizes too big for her. Three sets of hands held a rake with a limp piece of white cloth hanging from the end—we surrender. Their sullen faces broke his heart. *They're just kids. Where are their parents?* Ewen waved. They waved back. *How many years is it going to take for them to recover? For how many generations would the world grieve?* Ewen didn't want to be a pessimist—as Cowboy had said, any old jackass could be a pessimist—but the fact was that things were going to get a lot more desperate for those kids before it got better.

The convoy drove through destroyed towns, shelled countryside, past tons and tons of rubble, dead animals and dead soldiers and human misery. An elderly woman, dressed in black, sat knitting on the bumper of a shelled-out automobile. As the vehicles drove past, she seemed more concerned about dropping a stitch than a bunch of Canadians roaring in to occupy her country. Ewen figured she'd just come to terms with the fact that there wasn't much she could do about anything anymore. Perhaps, he thought, she's making something for tomorrow, so it can't be a bad thing.

After twelve grim hours on the road, they arrived at their next position near Hamm, in the heart of western Germany.

When they'd settled in, Griffith and the Lieutenant came back from a meeting with the CO. "The IO is going to come by tonight at 2300 to brief us on what our next moves are going to be. Now that we're back in Germany, the old man has said this booklet here has to be read by you all, tonight—top priority. It's the 21st Army Group's policy on non-fraternization. We're going to be here for who knows how long, and the brass want you to be clear on what's expected of you. Read it and sign it. Before 2300. Reiss, hand them out."

Ewen took his copy, sat down and read.

No-fraternization means having nothing whatever to do with the German people except the minimum contact required for the execution of military duty.

All acts of fraternization are absolutely forbidden.

The following are examples of fraternization:

- shaking hands with Germans;

- permitting children to climb on motor vehicles or to congregate in areas around military premises;

- associating on familiar terms especially with women;

- visiting German houses;

- drinking with Germans;

- playing games or sports with them;

- making or accepting gifts of any sort (even from children);

- attending German dances, entertainment of other social events;

- accompanying Germans on the streets, in theatres, taverns, hotels, or elsewhere, except on official business;

- communicating with Germans on any subject except official business.

The above examples are not exhaustive.

*Disciplinary action will be taken in all cases of fraternization.
Sexual intercourse with German women is a flagrant breach of the
non-fraternization directive and will be dealt with by CM. Due to
propaganda German women may be in fear of Allied soldiers and may
consent to intercourse through fear of the consequences of refusal. Where
consent to intercourse results from fear, the crime of rape is committed.
In cases of sexual intercourse with German women, where the circumstances indicate the woman's consent was induced either by force or fear,
a charge of rape should be considered.*

Ewen turned to the back page and signed his name. Then he passed
his pen to Sandy, who was sitting beside him.

The non-frat order made Ewen think of Herbert. He wasn't sure
if their conversation constituted a violation of the non-frat order
or not; regardless, he'd do it again. Even though he was the enemy,
Ewen didn't feel any animosity towards him—he was just an ordinary farm boy who'd been drafted into this war.

"I'm not planning on fraternizing with anyone," said Sandy. "My
family, we've got a score to settle with those Nazi bastards. I don't
care what anyone says—every civilian is as guilty as the soldiers."

Ewen could understand his anger. He was the only one in the
company with relatives in Germany and he had no idea if they
were still alive. Ewen felt that Germany's soldiers and civilians
would have to deal with their own humanity soon enough.

That night in his slit trench, at about 0320, Ewen woke up from
a horrible dream: someone was holding a gun to his head. He
wasn't sure what was worse, a snake in his slit trench or dreaming
about someone trying to kill him. He looked at his watch, they'd be
forming up soon. He lit a cigarette and stared at the stars.

By early afternoon the next day, the battalion arrived at their
new location on the outskirts of Oldenburg. Each company was
taken to their assigned area by guides assigned by the battalion
they were relieving.

They had barely organized themselves before Griff announced, "Okay, Morrison and Glover, we're up for recce patrol tonight."

Fucking hell, Ewen thought, the war could end at any time now. It's two days until my leave to Edinburgh and I'm on patrol tonight? Ten months on the frontline scouting behind the line, I don't want to end up under a mound of dirt with my helmet hanging on a wooden cross.

April 20, 1945
Grobenkneten
0220 — The scout patrol report that at the road and rail crossing, there is a large crater that would make traffic impossible. The enemy were heard chopping trees, sounds of voices and dogs barking. We presume the enemy are withdrawing and forming road blocks. There is no evidence of mines being laid and the town of DOHLEN was given a bit of harassing artillery fire.

```
Royal Hamilton Light Infantry War Diary
April 20, 1945
Grossenkneten
0745 — Our recce patrol has still not been heard
from. The Intelligence Officer suggested that
another patrol much stronger be sent out to find
out what happened.
1150 — The Coy "Lost Patrol" of last night was
finally located.
```

"Where the hell have you been?" the Major asked. "We thought we'd lost you men."

"We weren't lost," Griffith explained. "We were behind Jerry's position and had to work our way back, very slowly, through the woods." Ewen remained silent.

"Okay, what do you have for us?" the Major asked.

"The road here looks good. Jerry felled a couple of trees at this point, and there are signs of mines further along and a few craters. The biggest challenge is to clear the roads of mines so support weapons can be brought up. The road's pretty sandy, but passable."

Outside HQ, Ewen, anxious to get going, extended his hand to Griffith. "That's me done until May 2. The war had better be over when I get back."

"Lucky bastard," Maurice said.

"Where are you going?" Griffith asked,

"Edinburgh."

"Got a sweetheart there, Morrison?"

"Nope, there's a family I'm going to stay with, the Whites. I spent a couple of furloughs in their home before we came over."

Now that his long-awaited leave back to the UK was finally here, every moment that he was not on the road back to Scotland was an irritation. Ewen saw the paymaster, turned in his weapons, went to the bath parade and double-checked his identity documents and leave pass. He hopped into the back of the troop truck dressed in his clean battledress and web belt, his haversack filled with allotted rations. His journey would take him overland to Calais, by boat to Dover and then north on the train to Scotland.

Riding in the back of the truck with a handful of other soldiers heading for Paris, Brussels and other liberated cities on the continent, Ewen suddenly realized he was travelling back, in just a few hours, across land that had taken weeks and months to liberate.

The number of refugees on the roads astounded him. Thousands were heading west to escape the Russians, choosing to take their chances with Allied occupiers. Others, former forced labourers, were trying to get back to their homes, what remained of them. All looked hungry and broken, many with their possessions loaded on wagons hitched to malnourished horses.

Ewen had witnessed families migrating from the southern part of Saskatchewan to the north and eastern sections during the Depression, travelling hundreds of miles with a team of horses, maybe a couple of cows and all their remaining possessions on a wagon box. They had relied on the farms they passed for water, vegetables and milk. But that paled in comparison to the scale and desperation of this migration. There's precious little charity to spare here, thought Ewen. How many millions of people were displaced? The elderly, the children, the crippled. How many children had lost their fathers?

Their transport passed temporary relief camps set up in old military barracks, castles, and even bombed-out structures deemed usable because they still had four walls. They've endured six years of war, thought Ewen. It will take years and years to rebuild. So much for the Great War and "never again."

Hours later the troop truck stopped near the waterfront in Calais. Those bound for Dover walked to the harbour where, on the wharf, they handed over their documents for inspection one by one. Once cleared, they walked up the plank and sailed into the English Channel, four long horn blasts signalling their departure from France. Ewen remembered the last time he'd been at sea, bound for Scotland. It had been 1943, on a troopship from that steamed past the Isle of Islay and the Mull of Kintyre before entering the Firth of Clyde and docking at Greenock.

Then he remembered the last time he had crossed the English Channel. Ewen held his gut—he had to sit down. A wave of nausea overcame him that he knew wasn't seasickness. The faces of the men he'd travelled with last July appeared before him. Opening his notebook, he wrote down the names of all the men in his platoon since Normandy—he put an "X" beside the names of those who died, pausing when he came to Reggie's name. He prayed he would not have to add any more crosses.

He was alive when so many weren't. He told himself he had no right to feel sorry for himself: he had his limbs; he was alive. Quiet moments like this were what terrified him, when his mind was not focused on what needed to be done. Here, with nothing to buffer the pain, Ewen didn't believe his efforts mattered—did any of it matter? What was the point? He'd worn the uniform and accepted the role that came with it. Military politics aside, Ewen was proud to be a Blue Patch boy, because of the men he fought with. If nothing else, fighting to stay alive with his friends mattered.

Finally, Dover's white cliffs came into view. Around him, men began to sing: "They'll be bluebirds over . . . the white cliffs of Dover . . . ". Morrison looked back across the channel, hoping all the boys would still be there when he got back.

April 21, 1945
Grossenkneten
1000 — There is very little to record this morning as all coys report all fronts quiet.

May 2, 1945
Oldenburg
Surrender Leaflets Fired into the City

The Second Great World War draws rapidly to a close. The Allied Armies occupy more than one half of the Greater German Reich.

Through these five years of world suffering caused by the lust of the German peoples your city has escaped the weight of destruction from the air. Now your hour has struck.

Powerful armies stand at the city gates while the air forces wait the signal to attack. Within a short period the victorious forces of the United Nations will be in your town.

Will they find the town untouched by war or a mass of rubble crushing on the twisted bodies of soldier and citizen alike? IT ALL DEPENDS ON YOU! If Oldenburg resists our forces, the houses will be tumbled into their cellars and streets. All the weapons of modern war are ranged against the town to ensure that resistance is crushed by fire and steel and not by the blood of our soldiers.

Take your choice. If you want to live and have your city live with you, get the misguided soldiers and sailors to lay down their arms and surrender the town before it is flattened.

If there is resistance think twice before you join in. There is no mercy for the civilian in arms or for his property.

Ewen had been travelling for two days when he crossed the Dutch–German frontier to get back to his regiment, now stationed just south of Oldenburg.

The medieval city, with its narrow and windy streets, was miraculously still intact. After six years of war, it hadn't suffered an aerial or artillery attack—yet. One of the guys returning with him told Ewen that Oldenburg had become a zone for convalescent centres and that there were red crosses painted on several rooftops to deter aerial bombing.

So much had happened during the eleven days of his leave. The

233

entire Western Front had collapsed and the Russians had taken Berlin. Hitler had committed suicide three days ago.

Ewen checked in at HQ, retrieved his weapons and found his company and platoon stationed in houses they had cleared looking out over the Kusten Canal. As he walked up to the door, he heard familiar voices. He hoped everyone remained safe. He called out and reached for the door handle.

"Morrison, you're back," Maurice said. He turned down the flame on the cooker.

"Yes, I am," Ewen said. The platoon had positioned themselves at the back of the house, windows and entrances blacked out, to keep enemy snipers at bay.

"You're just in time for this week's compo rations best feature—treacle pudding, soaking in molasses as is the tradition," said Sandy, shaking his hand. "As you can see, it's one big mess in one big pot. That's what happens when you leave a cooking job to a damned amateur." Ewen thought of MacLeod.

"Quit your whining, you'll never have tasted anything like it," Maurice said.

"Of that I have no doubt," Sandy said.

Ewen pulled a bottle out of his kit. "Add some rum for flavour. I happened to come across our daily rum ration at HQ and brought you lads a bottle."

"Good man," Maurice said. He took the bottle, opened it and poured rum over the pudding. He passed the bottle to Cameron. The relaxed men ate and talked and drank.

"That's quite a bruiser, Morrison," Bruce pointed at Ewen's left eye. "What happened? Did you get into a fight?"

"No, not really a fight. There's quite a number of British servicemen home on leave who found out the girl they had left behind hasn't been as lonesome as they imagined. We Canadians are a real smash hit with the local ladies, so they aren't very endeared to anyone wearing this uniform."

"Did you steal someone's heart, Morrison?" Glover asked.

"No, nothing like that. I just I walked into The Standing Stones on Princes Street . . . "

"I know The Standing Stones," Griffith said. "Is Gordy still pulling pints? He's a vet from the Great War. Damn hard to understand the man with his Highland accent, but he's got a great sense of humour."

"He's still there. And still hard to understand. Anyway, what I didn't know was that there was a very unhappy Scottish sailor who'd been drinking all afternoon, venting his anger that a Canadian corporal had stolen his girl. He shouted to the whole pub that the next Canadian to walk through the door would get his fist right between the eyes." Ewen pointed to his head.

Everyone burst out laughing.

"I didn't know what hit me. The sailor was tossed out on his ear by Gordy's ex-boxer bouncers and I didn't pay for a drink all night."

"What else did you do, other than getting slugged?" Maurice asked.

"I stayed with the Whites—that family I knew from before. It was great," Ewen said, remembering. Mrs. White had been looking out the kitchen window as he pushed open the wrought iron gate to her path. Maggie, their Scotty dog crossed with a lab, raced down to greet him, her body wiggling back and forth with joy. Mrs. White's short, stout frame stood there like a welcoming grandmother, arms out ready to hug her boy. "Ewen laddie, so good to have you back with us. Come inside, tea is on. Malcolm is in the kitchen with the other laddies, they're two brothers."

Seated at the table, with Malcolm at the head, were two other Canadian servicemen. Malcolm struggled to his feet; he'd been at Passchendaele twenty-eight years before but, unlike Ewen's uncle, he'd survived. He hugged Ewen like he was his own son.

"Good you're back laddie, sit yourself down," Malcolm said.

Mrs. White introduced him to the two soldiers, clearly brothers, Thomas and Barton MacPherson. Ewen only needed to know the names of their regiments to know which battles they'd fought.

After supper, Mrs. White played the piano, and they sang "Danny Boy." Ewen thought of Archer, and Woods with his harmonica.

"That it? Come on. What else did you get up to?" asked Sandy.

"I wandered up to see the Edinburgh Castle. There's a graveyard there for soldiers' dogs." He put on his best Scottish accent: "Berkin dugs here lie at rest, The yappin worst, obedient at best, Sodgers pets and mascots tae, Still guard the castle to this day."

Everyone laughed.

"I went to a few dances at the Legion Hostel—the Lambeth Walk, the conga. Ate fish 'n'chips and then I decided to come back. Figured you could use a little help to wrap it up."

"Well, yesterday the boys of A-Coy found a store of brand-new Jerry underwear. I saved you a pair. It's your welcome back gift," Sandy said. He walked over to his kit, pulled out a pair and tossed them over. "Here you go."

"You've got to be kidding me," Ewen said. They were well made and, well, who couldn't use a new pair?

"So, fill me in. What's been happening?" Ewen asked.

"The old man has been talking with the mayor, by telephone if you can believe it. It's still working. The Commandant refuses to surrender, and the CO's told them they'd better convince him to be on the move by midnight or the town is going to be blown to smithereens. We've got seventy-two guns aimed at the city. We're just waiting," Griffith said.

Ewen looked at his watch: 2350. "That's what we do best."

"Brigade's ordered us to push forward right into Oldenburg tomorrow, so we're not done yet. We don't know if Jerry will be gone or not, but we're going in regardless. No one slack off. I don't want to lose anyone this close to the end." Griff looked round at his platoon, who appeared less than alert at this late hour.

They lit up cigarettes and contemplated what might be their last operation of the war.

Ewen looked at his watch again: 0020. "Listen, guys. No artillery. Guess Jerry's leaving the city after all."

After a long night of waiting and wondering if they'd have to engage the enemy, they woke up to clear, windy, cool weather and orders to form up beside the canal. Maurice divided up the platoon's compo rations and everyone stuffed them in their kits. No one dared to think that the war must be just hours away from being over. Griffith, determined to keep the men focused, emphasized their orders.

"Time to go. The CO has met with Oldenburg's mayor and we're crossing the canal. I've got the ferry site location," said Griffith.

When 17 Platoon arrived at the shoreline, they were greeted by an enthusiastic group of civilians—refugees from the look of them—unloading the assault boats from the Royal Canadian Engineers' trucks. After they crossed to the other side, only fifty yards away, they were greeted by German harbour police, then the CO gave them their orders, to surround the Gestapo Headquarters that had been identified by the town officials. All the Riley companies prayed for no opposition from Jerry, soldier or civilian.

As they walked through the main square, they were passed by men from the scout platoon, riding in a commandeered German vehicle, broadcasting to the German civilians, police and displaced people. "They're saying that they will be safe, but to get off the streets," Sandy said. They probably can't believe their eyes, thought Ewen. A few Canadians in a German army car, shouting orders at them in their own city.

The Gestapo HQ was abandoned, with the exception of a handful of Hungarian soldiers who immediately and happily surrendered. Cameron and Fern escorted them to the PW cage. One who spoke English told Griffith that more of their regiment wanted to surrender, but they were ten miles out of town.

For the rest of the afternoon, they patrolled the streets to stop looting and any civilian violence. Two men from B-Coy passed by on their way back from the battalion HQ to their post. "Seriously pissed off, guys," one called out. "HQ is next to a brewery, but the old man has put a guard on the place. Doesn't want us celebrating too much!"

Royal Hamilton Light Infantry War Diary
May 3, 1945
2130 — The rest of the night seemed quiet. There was little celebrating as champagne and beer were unavailable but most of the troops were tired and eager to rest.

Royal Hamilton Light Infantry War Diary
May 4, 1945
Oldenburg
1300 — ENGLISH and CANADIAN press including
photographers arrived to take pictures and get
a write up of the surrendered HUNGARIAN bn. Up
to this time we had taken at least 400 PWs.
The IO made a quick last minute tour of the
coys checking that they had all the necessary
information.

"We're certainly out in the sticks now," said Ewen, surveying their new position several miles northeast of Oldenburg. "What's this place again, Griffith?"

"It's called Barghorn, according to the map."

"How long are we going to be here?" asked Sandy.

"No idea. The IO has gone to brigade HQ to find out, but we're probably going to be all night. Don't know about tomorrow."

Woods would have said, 'Fucking typical,' thought Ewen as he pulled up his jacket collar. Trying to stay warm in the damp cold was always tougher than in dry cold. *Never thought I'd prefer a prairie winter. This rain sure is cold.*

They were sheltering in an old stone building that might have been a storeroom. Through the open doorway, they could see a small pond and a lot of flat, grey fields. Cameron shuffled a deck of cards and Maurice, Sandy and Bruce joined him for some poker. Griffith was propped up against the wall, writing a letter.

"Do you think it would be okay if I did a little fishing, Sarge?" asked Fern.

"Where on earth did you find a fishing pole, L'Hirondelle?" he asked.

"That corner over there." He pointed then reached into his pocket and held his palm out to Griffith. "Brought my own flies, though."

"Go ahead, kid. Catch anything and it's fish dinner for all of us."

After a dinner of compo rations—Fern had not been successful—the men were smoking and chatting quietly. Maurice had borrowed Griffith's flashlight and was finishing Ewen's western novel. It had stopped raining and there was little light left in the grey sky. At the sound of a scrabbling noise, each man reached for his rifle. They relaxed when they saw that the shape in the doorway belonged to one of their own.

The runner from A-Coy leaned against the door frame, breathing hard.

"What's up?" asked Griffith. "What's the rush? Are we moving out?"

The soldier lifted his head and laughed. "It's over! The bloody war is over."

The card game stopped. The writing stopped. The reading stopped.

"News just came over the wireless . . . Jerry's surrendered. The German general in charge of Holland and this part of Germany is making it official tomorrow morning."

17 Platoon stared at the man in stunned silence. This was the moment that they knew, believed, trusted, would come. Now that it had, they had no idea what to do or say.

Ewen stared at his rifle on the ground. *He would never have to use it again. He'd never have to kill another man. It was over. No more hunkering down in a miserable slit trench waiting for orders, for water, for food . . . for the next shell to land. No more patrols. No more rivers to cross. No more long, miserable foot marches. And no more wondering if he'd make it through.* He looked out through the doorway. All was quiet. It was over, yet everything carried on.

He ran his hand through his ginger hair and got down on one knee. He rested his arms on his thigh and hung his head. *Thanks, Reggie. Thanks, lads.* It was the only prayer that mattered.

May 4, 1945

Message from the Commander, First Canadian Army

From Sicily to the river Senio, from the beaches of Dieppe to those of Normandy and from thence through northern France, Belgium, Holland and northwest Germany, the Canadians and their Allied comrades in this army have carried out their responsibilities in the high traditions which they inherited. The official order that offensive operations of all troops of First Cdn Army will cease forthwith and that all fire will cease from 0800 hrs tomorrow Saturday 5 May has been issued. Crushing and complete victory over the German enemy has been secured. In rejoicing at this supreme accomplishment we shall remember the friends who have paid the full price for the belief they also held, that NO sacrifice in the interests of the principles for which we fought could be too great.

PART SIX

CANADA
NOVEMBER 1945

Ewen pulled up his collar and leaned over the railing. He couldn't stop shivering. The waves of the Atlantic Ocean had taken his ancestors from the old world to the new; today the waves were taking him home. He stood with his feet wide and his knees slightly bent, swaying in rhythm with the roll and pitch of the ship. He was one of twelve thousand army, navy and civilian men and women on board the *Queen Elizabeth*. They'd been at sea for five days and in a short while they would dock in Halifax.

On July 29, 1943, he'd sailed to England on the same converted liner with the Argyll and Sutherland Highlanders. That first voyage, they'd had to worry about U-boats and access to the decks was limited because of blackout hours. Now, after twenty-eight months, he was sailing back and would soon be walking on Canadian land again. Ewen wondered how his older brother Finlay was doing; as far as Ewen knew, he was still in the navy. Looking at the rolling waves, Ewen thought of the sailors and merchant seaman whose graves were below.

Just like the trip over, every non-operational space was filled with bunk beds. Passengers only had two meals a day, due to the sheer numbers on board, and they ate in relays, standing in long lines waiting for their turn. Ewen had peeled potatoes, mountains of them, on the way back, so he got a little more to eat. Strangely, he'd grown a little taller since he left Canada and was now almost six foot, but still only weighed in at around 140 pounds.

For two months after VE Day, the Rileys had served as an occupational force in Germany, enjoying CWAC shows and Dominion Day celebrations in Aurich, and attending numerous educational and civvy-street lectures. One afternoon, he watched an educational film at the YMCA Hall with what remained of D-Coy. It warned them about fake schools that were being set up to scam soldiers when they first arrived back in Canada. Unbelievable! After what we've been through, there's guys who never left the country trying to cheat us? How low can some people sink?

They moved to Amersfoort, back in the Netherlands, at the beginning of July, and all the men were happy to be back in a country they'd liberated. Fern had visited Nijmegen as often as possible to see Mies.

On July 16, Ewen had turned in his weapons. That was the moment that the war really ended for him, in his heart. The killing was over. Weaponless, he and the Rileys spent the weeks that followed playing sports, everything from horseshoes to basketball, going to movies and enjoying leave in other European cities. Ewen learned to play bridge, loving the challenge of the game's strategy. He even helped a local farmer with his harvest, what harvest there was in the Netherlands. Ewen knew that throughout Europe, and probably the world, there were going to be food shortages this winter. The war might be over, but it would likely be years before homes and infrastructures would be rebuilt.

Helping the farmer made Ewen realize one thing—what he didn't want to do when he got back to Saskatchewan. Although part of him just wanted to get home, he figured these months of transition from war to peace probably weren't such a bad thing. They had given him time to recover from the mental and physical exhaustion and to think about the future.

On August 28, the people of Amersfoort started to decorate the medieval streets along their canals with cedar and spruce arches as, for the first time in years, the country prepared to celebrate Queen Wilhelmina's birthday on August 31. That was the same day they heard the news—"We're heading home boys. We'll be leaving Holland sometime between Oct 20 and 30. There'll be a stay in England but we should sail home no later than December 7. We're finally heading home."

Eighty other Rileys stayed behind, drafted to go back to Germany for a stretch of occupational duty. Fern was happy to be among them. "This keeps me close to Mies. We'll have time to sort out our plans," he explained to Ewen. "I want to marry her and for us to start a life together in Canada, but I don't know what I'd do back there. For sure we'll get married, but she's torn about leaving her family, which I understand. What kind of a life would she have with me in Canada?"

"There are a lot of programs to help us integrate back into life back home," Ewen said. "Vocational training, land grants for farming, loans to start up businesses—heck, we can even get bursaries to go to university."

"I heard all that. But a hundred bucks to buy civilian clothing and a war service gratuity of $7.50 for each thirty days of service isn't going to last very long."

"You could apply to have a farm through the Veteran's Land Act."

"What exactly is that? Do you get free land?" Fern asked.

"No, no, you get a loan, if you can put some money down. They give you a deal on the interest rate. Then you have to spend a few years showing the progress you've made."

"That's not going to work for me, Ewen." Fern shook his head. "First, I don't have any money to put down. And second, well, they've treated me the same as you while I've been over here, but back in Canada I'm not the same as far as the government's concerned. I heard Status Indians aren't eligible for the Veterans' Land Act loans if they lived on reserve lands. It's so damn complicated."

"How come?" Ewen asked.

"I'm a 'ward of the state.' Still can't even vote. I heard we have to deal with Indian agents instead of Veteran Affairs. Apparently, some of those bastards have made it really difficult for us guys. Some Indian agents are like little dictators, they're power hungry. Going through Indian Affairs to get to Veteran Affairs, it's a nightmare. One guy tried to find out about his benefits and all he got was the runaround. Some guys have been told they have to renounce their status to apply for veterans' benefits and some Indian agents have even taken names off bands' lists while they've been over here. They were happy to give us the right to fight but seems like they don't respect our rights when they're finished with us."

"Jeez. Maybe you'd be better off here in the Netherlands."

"I don't know. I just don't know."

Ewen paused before asking Fern a question that had been worrying him for some time. "Fern, I promised Reggie that I would visit his mom if anything happened to him. I want to do it, for him, but . . . well, I just don't know what I'm going to say. Is there something traditional I should do, something I can do to show my respect?"

"She's not going to expect you to know things. I'm Cree, so I can't really help. They probably have their own traditions—you could take some tobacco or tea? But I think the real gift she's going to want from you is to hear about her son. You're her last connection to him."

Ewen nodded. That sounded about right to him.

On deck, Ewen cupped his hand and lit a cigarette and thought about the future. *I'm twenty-two and the only thing I'm sure of is that I don't want to go back to farming. What options do I really have now?* Perhaps he could get a truck driving job or maybe set up a transport business—he and his friend Mike had talked about that before they'd both signed up. Ewen knew that would mean getting additional mechanical training. Still, it was a possibility.

As the Halifax skyline came into view, the cheers that rose from the deck and the dock merged in a roar. The local reception committee met every ship bringing their boys home. A band played as they disembarked.

Some of the men stepping down onto Canadian soil bore terrible injuries. Ewen thought of the hospital troopships and the men who'd lost legs and arms and who'd never even be able to feed themselves, like Stan, if he were still alive. Many would be in an institution for the rest of their lives. He hoped Cowboy had recovered and wondered how he was doing. Maybe he'd head to Alberta to see him.

Ewen was missing a couple of toes, but the only visible scar he had was a small one over his right eyebrow that would fade with time. But even those who appeared unscarred were damaged souls. Some guys had taken their own lives. Others were finding relief in the bottle; Ewen was determined not to be one of those. He decided if anyone asked about the war, he'd take Tristan's advice— bury it and tell people the subject wasn't up for discussion.

There was barely time to enjoy the welcome in Halifax before they were hurried onto the overnight train to Ontario, to Hamilton. The five hundred Rileys had been told what to do when the train pulled in. At the depot, they were to disembark, line up and wait to be dismissed before they could be greeted by family and friends.

Ewen looked out the window when he heard the cheering. The hometown crowd must have been waiting for hours, hoping to see someone they knew. It looked as if the whole town was there to greet them—the Red Cross, the Legion, the local press—people were everywhere. Soldiers and civilians were both were in tears, as this day so long awaited had finally arrived. There was no one on the platform for Ewen, but the crowd wouldn't let any soldier stand alone. Several women and girls hugged and kissed him until his cheeks looked as if they'd been tattooed red.

The brass allowed them five minutes of joy, then orders came over the loudspeaker to fall in and line up. The Rileys marched together, for the last time, down King Street to Victoria Park, while the band played their regimental song, "Mountain Rose." Mayor Sam Lawrence formally welcomed them back and, after his speech, the Royal Hamilton Light Infantry proceeded to the armoury for coffee and sandwiches provided by the Red Cross and Legion. The men got their pay, furlough pass, ration book and were given thirty days to fill out their discharge certificate.

As Ewen left the armoury, an older man approached and shook his hand. "Is there anything I can do for you son? Anything you need?" If the Hamilton locals saw a soldier standing alone, they'd immediately ask if he needed a bed for the night, wanted to make a phone call, send a telegram, needed a meal—nothing was too much for their brave boys.

"Yes, sir, there is. Could you get me to the Six Nations Reserve? There's someone there I need to see."

Ewen spent the night with the man and his wife, Locky and Mary Mackintosh.

"We lost our boy at Normandy," Mr. Mackintosh said. "So, we meet every train that comes in and do what we can for you lads coming home."

Ewen nodded. He understood. The Mackintoshes were just one of hundreds of couples, fathers and mothers, whose sons were buried in Normandy, in Belgium, in the Netherlands.

"I served in the last war. I know what you've been through son. And I know the fears you face now. When I came back, I decided to be a teacher and I've been teaching for over twenty years now. If there's one thing I believe, that's don't teach the next generation to hate. That's not a legacy to honour those who didn't come back. Yes, never teach hate."

Ewen woke up the following morning, still instinctively reaching for his weapons before realizing where he was. It was an automatic response he hoped to lose sooner rather than later.

His head rested on a real pillow. *Soon I'll just be plain Ewen Morrison, not Private Morrison. I'm completely on my own now. I'll be walking in shoes again, not boots. And if I put on a pair of running shoes, it won't be to scout for the enemy, a sniper's rifle pointed at my chest.*

For more than three years, he'd lived in a uniform, surrounded by men in the same uniform. Now, despite all the lectures and pamphlets, he knew it was up to him alone. He imagined how tough it would be for some guys—years apart from their family, their wife a stranger, not knowing their kids. There were a few officers he could think of who would probably resent losing the power of their command. And what about work? There were hordes of demobbed men all applying for the same jobs, the competition between them fierce. How were they all going to survive the peace?

Mrs. Mackintosh cooked him a huge breakfast of eggs and ham and toast. Mr. Mackintosh insisted he borrow their 1940 Saratoga Chrysler. The Six Nations of the Grand River Reserve was only about twenty miles away, but he was going to need a car. "Proud to help you get there, son," he said. "A mother needs to hear about her child. You're honouring your promise to your friend. I respect that."

Driving southwest along Highway 6, he crossed the Grand River and kept going. Ewen had trouble keeping his eyes on the road. After the devastation of Europe, he wanted to drink in the pristine woods and countryside, the clear blue sky. He figured the temperature was around five degrees below freezing. There had been an early snowfall. The clouds moving in suggest more might be on its way.

Ewen wasn't sure where the reserve land started. All he knew was that Reggie's mom lived in a community near the centre. When he got to Hagersville, he figured he'd gone too far. He turned around and then took the next road to the left hoping he could find someone who knew her and could give him some directions. Maybe a store or a gas station? He could always ask for the school. Reggie had said his mother was a teacher.

He came to a crossroad and pulled over to the shoulder. An old Model T truck coming from the north slowed down as it approached. Ewen put the Saratoga in park, opened the door and got out, waving.

"Excuse me, do you know where Mrs. Emily Johnson lives?"

The driver nodded. "Head down that way," he pointed west. "Go for two miles and you'll see a cluster of houses on the north side. She lives there."

"Thank you."

As he drove, his stomach churned. She didn't know him and didn't even know he was coming. What if she wasn't at home? He remembered Reggie talking about his mother when they first met at the base at Strood Park. What was he going to say?

He saw four houses about three hundred yards in from the road. With snow on the ground and more on the way, he decided not to chance driving into the yard and parked on the shoulder. He got out and started walking up the drive. As he got closer to the houses, he noticed a woman bundled up on the porch of the second from the right. He started walking toward her.

She had a woollen hat pulled down and a big scarf wrapped around the lower part of her face. Her eyes, though: they were dark and bright and focused—Reggie's eyes. Ewen knew he was at the right place.

He walked up the three steps to the porch and removed his beret.

In a quiet voice, she asked, "Which one of my boys were you with?"

Ewen's gut twisted as her question sunk in. *Reggie's brother, he must have died too. How does anyone survive this kind of grief?* He still felt the pain of losing his mother—this woman had lost two sons.

"Reggie, ma'am. I was with Reggie," Ewen said.

Mrs. Johnson pulled her hands out of her heavy coat pockets and stood up. She took two steps forward and put her arms around him.

She looked up into his blue eyes. "Tell me about my son, Ewen."

Ewen looked down.

"He was a warrior."

She nodded.

"He was my friend."

Together they went into Reggie's home.

252

POSTSCRIPT

Pte. Ewen Morrison, L104559, was officially discharged from the Canadian Army on January 15, 1946, three days before his twenty-third birthday. He made it from Juno Beach to Oldenburg, ten months on the front line, unwounded.

He did not return to farming; after growing up "as poor as church mice" in the Depression he had no desire to return to life as it had been.

He married Janet Agnes "Nan" Love on August 16, 1947, at the Saltcoats United Church. He worked for an engineering company for forty years, raised four children and had eight grandchildren. Today there are fifteen great-grandchildren. Ewen died at the age of seventy-three on August 24, 1996; Nan passed on March 2, 2015, aged ninety-two. They rest in the Port Coquitlam Municipal Cemetery in British Columbia.

AUTHOR'S NOTE

In 2017, I left my job in downtown Vancouver and moved to Saskatchewan to begin teaching at Chief Gabriel Cote Education Complex, a First Nation reserve school near Kamsack, a small community eighty kilometres from Saltcoats, where both my parents were born. My first assignment was to teach Grades 8 and 9, and I had no idea what I was in for.

After one year, I discovered a remarkable coincidence. I'd returned to BC for the summer break and, while going through a trunk of my mother's things, found a little black notebook I had never seen before. Going through its pages I realized that it was my father's, from the war. In it he had written the names of some of the men he fought with, and on the second page there it was— F.J. Cote L36956, Kamsack, Sask.

I was stunned and texted my principal, Jonas Cote, right away. Had I actually ended up teaching the descendants of soldiers my father fought with? I had been researching and trying to write the story of Ewen Morrison and the Rileys, but this discovery seemed like destiny. Who needs fiction? I had to believe that what I was doing was some form of karmic payback.

My father never talked about the war to me or my three siblings. Five years after the only occasion he mentioned his wartime First Nations' friend, I travelled with my parents to Scotland. One afternoon in Edinburgh, he set out on his own to find a certain pub and the White family, but both were gone. Again, he didn't explain. A trip to Europe in 1985, during which I shared a few days on a tour bus with a group of Canadian veterans who'd been invited back to the Netherlands to celebrate the 40th anniversary of their liberation, made my curiosity about what had happened to my father grow.

My mother had shared a couple of stories about my father's war, particularly his scouting and reconnaissance experiences with a First Nations soldier from a reserve in Ontario. It was a miracle that he made it from Normandy to northern Germany—ten months—without a wound. My mother implied that my father believed, as do I, that the skills this friend taught him are what helped to keep him alive. She had forgotten the name of the reserve and could not recall the soldier's name. Even after extensive research, I have been unable to confirm who he was, so in this story I named him Reggie Johnson. I know he died sometime after October 1944 and that he had a brother, another volunteer, who also died in the war. My father told my mother about his friend's premonition, his vision of his death, and that he had visited his friend's mother after the war; these incidents are true.

When his time came, my father died from a heart attack. He was a man of love and I believe how he died symbolized his heart broken by the enormous pain of war that he could never release, because he knew it could destroy him as it had so many veterans. My father had to do terrible things as an infantryman and scout on the front line; he killed many men. After he passed in 1996, I was overcome with an intense desire to comprehend his wartime experiences, but I began my research only after my mother died in 2015.

Stan Overy, the Royal Hamilton Light Infantry's regimental archivist, was my first contact. Two weeks after my call, a USB of the Rileys' complete War Diaries landed on my doorstep.

In five years, I have made five trips to Europe: I travelled overland from London to Oldenburg, Germany; I walked on the stones at Dieppe and the sands of Juno; I toured battlefields from Normandy to the Rhineland and visited the museums of Westerbork Concentration Camp and Bergen-Belsen; I went to Caen, L'Abbaye d'Ardenne, Falaise, Y'pres, Arras, Antwerp, Groesbeek, Bergen op Zoom, Woensdrecht, Groningen. In each place, I met people who offered advice and suggested other places to visit and other leads to pursue. It was pure magic.

At Dieppe, after a rainy, stormy walk on the shoreline, I was sitting in a small restaurant. While I waited for the server, I pulled out a black-and-white photo of my father in his uniform from the pages of my journal. The server must have noticed it, because at the end of the meal he brought me an unordered cognac in a crystal glass—on the house, he insisted. I tried to decline—this seemed like I was profiting from my father's war. (Months later, a Swedish friend suggested that I get over it and allow people to give because perhaps it was a part of their healing.)

I met many wonderful people, who generously shared their stories with me, and they have been the inspiration for a number of characters. After spending time in Europe and learning how civilians survived under Nazi occupation for so many years, I wanted to honour them and those who fought for the Resistance; thus their stories are woven in.

Virry de Vries Robles' and Micha Schliesser's accounts of Westerbork Concentration Camp are true. My father's company, D-Coy, was sent to guard the camp the day Westerbork was liberated. Ewen Morrison, Virry and Micha were all there on that day, but did they actually meet? Probably not and we'll never know; however, I chose for them to meet. The first time I met Virry and her caregiver Karen at Café Blek in Amsterdam, Virry brought her yellow star. I touched the fabric and questioned if what I was creating was bringing back too much pain to those I needed to speak with. Virry told me I must write; the "Anne" in her story is Anne Frank. Micha has since passed.

I searched for a German soldier who fought against my father's regiment. A conversation between friends in Sweden led me to meet Heike, Herbert Gatzsmaga's daughter. His story of growing up as a child in the Nazi era is true, as are his wartime injuries and becoming a PW. However, he was taken prisoner by the Americans in the Battle of Craigshelm, five hundred kilometres from Groningen. I have taken the liberty of transferring him to the Rileys, so that the two ordinary farm boys could meet. Herbert and Heike brought a wholeness to the story.

Rose was inspired by Rosemary Wilkinson, whom I met in Calgary at the Military Museum in Calgary after my mother passed. She was my last connection with that generation of women who volunteered to do their bit so the boys could get back home. She passed in 2018.

My mother served in the CWAC in the Netherlands and Germany, part of the Occupation Force. Before she died, Nan told me about a letter she had written for a young Canadian serviceman who had lost both his arms. For all her life, she said, she wondered what choice his Scottish fiancée had made.

Fern L'Hirondelle was inspired by Fernand Morais, a Métis Mi'Kmaq and Acadian from New Brunswick, who loved to fish.

I'd read about the battle of Verrières Ridge in Normandy and wanted to feel the land; there at the Troteval farm, I met Guy Frimout, who was four years old when the Canadians liberated the area.

In Belgium, I met Roland Demuth, who organizes the annual liberation commemoration events in Antwerp. He presented to me, posthumously on behalf of my father, a medal marking the 60th Anniversary of the Liberation of Belgium. For the past 15 years he had one extra medal to give out and after we met and he heard about Ewen and what I was researching, he chose to give it to me.

I owe so much gratitude to everyone who trusted me with their stories. You have been my teachers. And you provided me with a glimpse into the young lives of a generation of men and women who lived through the tumultuous period of the Second World War.

ACKNOWLEDGEMENTS

Dhyan Vimal patiently sat with me in Kuala Lumpur creating the outline and brainstorming themes back in 2015. He inspired me to live the creation from start to finish. Sandra Bijl, a friend from the Netherlands whom I met in Kuala Lumpur, drove me here and there, including Normandy and Verrières, generously helping me with my research. Through Karin Groothedde, another old friend from the Netherlands, I met Ben Wijnhoven, the owner of the Hotel de Wolfsberg in Groesbeek, where I would stay on three more trips. Ben introduced me to Jeanne Melchers, a Second World War historian from Groesbeek, who arranged for us to tour battlefields in her car with the hugely knowledgeable Marco Cillessen, also a historian.

I spent Christmas 2018 in Groesbeek at the hotel, and learned (from Marco) that the de Wolfsberg was in the same area that my father and D-Coy had spent Christmas 1944.

On the morning before I left, Ben and I sat down for a coffee. "Janet, you have made so many trips here and you have paid so much money," he said. "What do you need? What can I do?"

I got teary-eyed. Then Ben said, "I'll host a big party for the book!"

On that same trip, I had travelled to Bergen op Zoom and stayed at the Grand Hotel de Draak, where my father had spent Halloween in 1944. The hotel receptionist suggested I contact Paul Versijp, the city's Head of Cabinet, who invited me to return the following year for their 75th anniversary celebrations to mark their liberation. In turn, Paul introduced me to Robert Catsburg, a local historian who took me through the Rileys' contribution in the Battle of the Scheldt.

To stay at the Stad en Wal B&B on a street called *Canada Lane* and participate in the festivities was one of the great experiences of my life. I spent Halloween at the de Draak, seventy-five years after my father. Paul introduced me to Lisa Helfand, the Canadian Ambassador to the Netherlands, and Colonel Timothy R. Young, Canadian Defence Military Attaché to the Netherlands, Belgium and Luxemborg.

In Bergen op Zoom I also met Her Royal Highness Princess Margriet, who was attending one of the ceremonies. In 1940 the Dutch royal family moved to Canada after the Nazi occupation of the Netherlands and Princess Margriet was born there. She is very interested in what women did during the war and it was such an unexpected delight to chat with her.

Colonel Young connected me with Joel Pedersen, a former soldier and Saskatoon police officer who holds the rank of Chief Warrant Officer in the Canadian Army Reserves, one of only two First Nations CWOs in the country. Joel generously took the time to critique the manuscript from both a military and First Nation perspective. Candace Lee Lickers, Communications Officer for the Six Nations of the Grand River was sent the manuscript to critique out of respect for choosing the Six Nations Reserve.

Teaching at Chief Gabriel Cote Education Complex has been a gift. Some days it's been extremely tough to work here as a non-Native, but Jonas always has my back and I've learned a great deal about the horror of residential schools from those who endured them, and about the generational trauma that continues today. In writing this book, my intent was to celebrate the friendship between a Native and non-Native soldier. If every non-Native teacher worked in a First Nation school, perhaps it would aid the healing between cultures, because the divide of racism—on both sides—remains deep.

In 2008, Cree elder Phil Mechuskosis L'Hirondelle gave me the spirit name, Standing Tidal Horse Woman. It was a humbling experience and I'm still learning and growing and hoping I can live up to the name.

To my nephew Robert Gillespie and his wife D'arcy for their generous contribution to the book launch in the Netherlands— thank you for getting me there, financing the plaque and more.

Don Turner, now passed, was our dear family friend. "Uncle

Don" was taken prisoner in Dieppe. He fought with the Queen's Own Cameron Highlanders of Canada. His son Doug kindly shared his father's personal memoir.

To Lynn Duncan and Kilmeny Jane Denny of Tidewater Press I owe a massive thank you. I wrote this in the truest voice I could; they are making it heard. As a storyteller I have done my best to weave my father's journey and those he met within the historical record of the Second World War. They were ordinary people of diverse backgrounds and nationalities, forced to do their best in extraordinary times.

So many people who helped in researching and the creation of this book. To old friends and new friends and to my family far and wide—thank you.

This is everyone's book . . . it took an army to create.

Belgium – Lucas Catteeaw, Roland Demuth.

Canada – Trisha Carleton, Bud Code, Rory Cory, Jonas Cote, Ralf Gasteiger, Gordon Harder, Greg 'Cowboy' Hisey, Jean Kavanagh, Phil and Gisele L'Hirondelle, Alandra Napali Kai, Stan and Pam Overy, Joel Pedersen, Lynn Punnett, Madleine Rab, Hamid Seshadri, Rose Wilkinson, Colonel Timothy Young, Barbara Zatyko.

France – Leslie Nechville Schmitt, Guy Frimout.

Germany – Claus Ahrens, Lars and Ulrike Dedekind, Herbert and Heike Gatzmaga, Bridgett Peters, Fritz Rohricht.

Malaysia – Master Dhyan Vimal.

The Netherlands – Guido Abuys, Sandra Bijl, Anita Bruijns, Robert Catsburg, Marco Cillessen, Patrick de Jager, Virry de Vries Robles, Karin Groothedde, Jeanne Melchers, Micha Schliesser, Karen Schloszer, Harry and Janske Temminck, Alice van Bekkum, Paul and Ingeborg Versijp, Ben Wijnhoven.

United Kingdom – Philip Baldock, Johnna Doyle, Rob and D'arcy Gillespie.

United States – Doug Turner.